late summer

Unremembering Me
There Were Many Horses

late
summer

luiz ruffato

*Translated from the
Portuguese by Julia Sanches*

OTHER PRESS
NEW YORK

Production editor: Yvonne E. Cárdenas
Text designer: Jennifer Daddio
This book was set in Gotham and Goudy Old Style by
Alpha Design & Composition of Pittsfield, NH

10 9 8 7 6 5 4 3 2 1

Library of Congress Cataloging-in-Publication Data
Names: Ruffato, Luiz, 1961- author. | Sanches, Julia, translator.
Title: Late summer : a novel / Luiz Ruffato ; translated from the
Portuguese by Julia Sanches.
Other titles: Verão tardio. English
Description: New York, NY : Other Press, [2021] |
Originally published in Portuguese as O verão tardio in
2019 by Companhia das Letras, São Paulo, Brazil.
Identifiers: LCCN 2020054794 (print) | LCCN 2020054795 (ebook) |
ISBN 9781635420203 (paperback) | ISBN 9781635420210 (ebook)
Classification: LCC PQ9698.428.U44 V4713 2021 (print) |
LCC PQ9698.428.U44 (ebook) | DDC 869.3/5—dc23
LC record available at https://lccn.loc.gov/2020054794
LC ebook record available at https://lccn.loc.gov/2020054795

Finisce la tarda estate

—BATTIATO/SGALAMBRO

And ever in my forever that same absence

—CARLOS DRUMMOND DE ANDRADE

tuesday,
march 3

my feet heave me through a vast desert. Yellow sand and yellow sun, eyes bleary, throat parched; in the horizon, dunes upon dunes, a cloudless sky. Then, at the bottom of a dip, something resembling a blue pool. Spent, I let myself roll downslope. I slump over the water, and as I bring my wet hand to my lips, the pool turns to quicksand and swallows up my thin, withered body. I try to scream, but my voice catches. I grab at the edge to no avail. Little by little, I sink. I lift my arms in a last-ditch effort, and hear sounds in the distance. I struggle to keep my head above sand and, closer now, make out the words "Mister! Mister!" as I feel someone shake me. Sweating, I open my eyes wide and behind my glasses see the startled face of a young man in uniform who reeks of cigarette smoke. "How's he doing?" Then, to someone behind him, "Coming to, at least." I'm seated on a bus. Outside is the tiny Cataguases coach terminal, still the same as when I was a child. People hug on the platform, birds trill in the trees, news trickles from

the television, and the scent of diesel mixes with the
mustiness of the air conditioner. I look at the uniformed
man, "It's nothing. I'm fine. Thank you," and try to get up.
"Need a hand?" he asks. "That's all right," I say, "I'm fine."
With a shove, I am on my feet. I bolster myself as I study
the redcap and spy my backpack in his hands. He makes
way for me. My legs teeter down the narrow aisle. I reach
the steps and lurch down them, coming face-to-face with a
small cluster of people who eye me quizzically. The young
man hands me my backpack, and the bus driver, harried
but wanting to appear cordial, exclaims, "Quite the scare,
huh?" He gets back on the bus, shuts the door, reverses.
The crowd gradually scatters. I enter a small hall with
ticket booths and bystanders awaiting their arrival and
departure times, then collapse onto a wood bench. Beside
me, a toothless old woman who looks like a defeathered
chick turns to face me, flustered. My forehead, feet, and
pits are drenched in sweat. A woman in a headscarf scrubs
the red-tile floor with a wet rag. I wipe my glasses with the
edge of my shirt. The wall clock reads 8:30. My lungs fill
with the hot morning air, and suddenly I feel better. I get
up, take a long sip of chilled water from the drinking
fountain, walk through the turnstile to the bathroom, and
relieve myself with a sigh in the recently disinfected urinal.
I wash my hands and face. Outside, on the cruddy
sidewalk, I pass a shop selling cookies and sweets, another
selling trinkets, and yet another that sells smoothies and
snack food, then finally make my way into a boteco, a dark

and narrow café bar that runs the length of the building. The radio is turned to a local station with the volume on high, drowning out the sound of running water in the sink, where a hulking figure stands with his back to me. "Good morning," I say, and the figure grunts. "Coffee with milk, and a buttered roll, please." The man turns off the faucet, wipes his hands on his dirty apron, and places a plastic semitransparent sugar bowl and a stainless-steel saucer on the grimy bar. He shoves his hairy arm into a brown paper bag and pulls out a roll of bread, slicing it in half and smearing both halves with a thin layer of margarine. He arranges them in a plastic, faux-straw basket, and asks: "Black or white?" Something about this man, with his long, soiled strands of greasy hair, face studded with barbs of grayish whiskers, his belly bulging against the buttons of his shirt, and pants slipping down his legs, rings a bell. "Black or white?" he repeats. Confused, I ask, "Excuse me?" And he says, impatiently, "The coffee: black or white?" "Oh, white." He dumps out some of the coffee and fills the rest with milk, dunks a long metal spoon in the steaming liquid, and sets the glass on the saucer. I've got it! We went to school together...Alcides... Alcides...The Beast. That's what we called him. Because, besides being really strong—he was already fat back then—Alcides turned out to be shockingly cruel toward anything that moved: he killed birds with a slingshot, drowned kittens, and once even doused a mare in gasoline and set her on fire. Even the teachers were scared of him.

He's the devil, they'd say, crossing themselves. He lumbers back to the sink. "Pardon me, but aren't you Alcides? I think I remember you from . . ." The man turns to face me, bilious and red-eyed. Leaning over the bar and spooking away the mosquitoes, he cuts me off and yells: "What are you on about? Keep your small talk to yourself. You think you know me? Fuck you! I don't know you! And I don't want to know you. Got it? Now sit there nice and quiet and drink your coffee, then get the fuck out." His breath, vinegary, mists up my face. My legs wobble, my lips pale, and I become light-headed. He turns up the volume on the radio, which is playing sertanejo, and angrily pretends to count and recount his profits from the day before, a couple of ratty bills and a fistful of gummy coins. I try to quiet my hands, which tremble either from shock at the verbal assault, my recent nightmare, or the medication I've been taking. I chew the bread with difficulty and wash it down with small sips of milk coffee. Cowed, I ask what I owe. He grunts something or other, and I leave the money on the bar. I stagger back to the hall. The old woman is gone. I sit back on the wood bench next to a woman reading the Bible—black curls in a bun, light-gray long-sleeved shirt, dark-gray skirt below the knee, chunky masculine shoes. According to the wall clock it's just before nine. On the bench opposite, a very young mother watches her two small children as they prance this way and that, a grocery bag on the floor beside her. A teenager stands in his backward cap, XXL Los Angeles Lakers tee, shorts, and oversized headphones, swaying to the beat of the music sounding from his cell phone. Gibberish trickles from the television. Outside, the woman, with her headscarf, dustpan and broom, sweeps up piles of trash on the curb. A dusty bus pulls up to a stall. The backward-capped teen and the young mother with two kids begin to move. Others follow, and soon an assembly is formed. My neighbor is still absorbed in her reading. When I first moved to São Paulo, I used to like wandering the coach terminal on weekends and guessing the destinations of the countless, glassy-eyed faces that filed past me. Judging from the way they walked, the clothes they wore, their accessories, and even the food they ate, I tried to imagine whether things were going well for them, or poorly. I did this to quell the loneliness that drove me out of my room in a modest boardinghouse in Pari every Saturday and Sunday. Or maybe I did it to confirm that I—who often felt invisible as I wandered anonymously through the crowd—was real. There, in that purgatory-like space, I saw myself reflected in those men and women—haunted but resolute, vulnerable yet sturdy—and this somehow attested to the fact that I existed, even if it was a notch above nothing. These forays were short-lived. As soon as I found a job, I rented an apartment in Vila Prudente, met Marília, and lost interest in other people's fates, busy tending to what I mistook for my own happiness. Though I visited Cataguases on occasion, the city and everything it represented had already begun to lose focus in my memories, like a photograph that fades little by little until suddenly it's only a series of whitish smudges without meaning. And so thirty-five years passed, and in the last nineteen of them, my sister Isinha's faint voice over the phone was the only thing that could assure me there had once been a place called Cataguases, where a man by the name of Oséias used to live. Isinha would tell me stories about relatives and acquaintances that felt as real as the stories in the books I read as I lay in the narrow, uncomfortable beds of cheap hotels in the rural towns where I stopped to rest from my day-to-day as a traveling salesman. And here I am again, the threads that tie beginning to end in a tangle. I cross the street, dazed by the light brightening the morning. The cabbie, who'd been chatting with his colleague under the shade of a fig tree, climbs into the car. I place my backpack in the back seat and sit down next to him. He asks me where I'm going and tries to strike up a conversation: "Where you visiting from?" "São Paulo," I answer. "Oh, that bus arrived hours ago," he remarks indiscreetly. "I was killing time," I say, feeling embarrassed as I feign interest in the string of low, roughed-up houses that sweep past the window. He goes on: "São Paulo! I used to live there. Taboão da Serra. Heard of it? I quit school at seventeen, to the dismay of my late mother—God rest her soul," he crosses himself. "And my father, who was scared I was headed down the wrong path—his words," he smiles, complacent, "sent me to live with Uncle Lenildo. I worked at a law firm in Morumbi, as an office boy. I got my driver's license and soon I was driving around Mr. Garibaldi, Esquire, himself. Garibaldi José Mendes da Costa. He was fond of me and always encouraging...I did that for five years. Then one Christmas I met Gi, Gisele, that's my wife. We went out, fell in love, and suddenly I was back here every month. I tried to convince her to move to São Paulo, I painted a picture of Paradise, but Gi said she wouldn't leave her family. No way, no how. It went on like that for months. Me sweet-talking her and her stringing me along. Then she got pregnant, and you know what that's like. Mr. Garibaldi promised me the moon, said he'd help me out the first few months and all that. But Gi dug her heels in. There was no way around it. I had to let it all go. With the money I'd saved I bought a piece of land in Santa Clara, built a small house, got this taxi license, and here I am. I've been at it for over...a decade now! I don't regret it, not one bit. Ninfa's a gem. I've got a photo of her right here. Have a gander." The cabbie pulls his cell phone from his pant pocket and shows me his screen saver, a picture of a little girl with mischievous black eyes. "Her name's Ninfa?" I ask. "Yeah, Ninfa," he says, proud. "Gi's the one who chose it. Isn't it something?" "Yeah, it's beautiful," I answer. In Granjaria, the cabbie pulls up beside a tall rough-concrete wall, in front of an enormous iron-plated gate. I pay for the ride, and he hands me a card. "If you ever need anything. Sizenando Robledo Neto's the name, but everybody calls me Nonô." I nearly say, Sizenando?! I used to know your pops, Sizim. He was a little bit older than me and we lived in the same neighborhood, Beira-Rio, he even went out with my sister Isabela for a while. I think of asking him how he's doing but decide against it. I thank him, slip his card into my shirt pocket, grab my backpack from the back seat, and step onto the sidewalk, where I press the intercom buzzer and watch the car disappear around a corner. The sun beats down on my head. I'm exhausted. I wait a second, then press the intercom buzzer again. A woman's voice echoes back. "Who is it?" I ask if Rosana is in. "No, Dona Rosana is out." Disappointed, I'm about to give up when the voice crackles again. "Who is it?" "Oséias, Rosana's brother." "Oséias?! Uncle Oséias?! From São Paulo?! Uncle Oséias, it's me, Tamires!" Tamires...Oh, yes, Rosana's daughter... "Morning Tamires, how's it going?" I hear a clicking sound, and the side door pops open. "C'mon in! Did the door open?" I push it, "Yeah, it opened!" A house with an old-style facade comes into view. I cut across a small, overgrown garden that looks as though it was once much larger and had been sacrificed to make room for the garage, which clashes with the rest of the building. From the kitchen door, a young overweight woman about the same height as me—long, straight brown hair and a baggy dress that makes her look even chubbier—waves at me cheerfully. I walk around the silver Honda Fit. She welcomes me with enthusiasm and pulls me into a firm hug, "You don't remember me, do you?" I try not to look shocked—she was a little girl when I last saw her, eight or nine years old, dumpy and shy... "You were only knee-high," I explain, awkwardly. She shows me in and says, "I filled out, didn't I? Mom's always saying it's a shame I took after Dad's family. If I'd taken after Grandpa Nivaldo, I'd be skinny like her... Or like you..." She lets out a sorrowful laugh and I sigh. "When did you get in?" "Not long ago." "From São Paulo?" "Yeah, São Paulo." "Huh, where's your luggage?" "I haven't got any," I say. "Everything I need is right here." I point at my backpack. She calls for the housekeeper, who seems to be running the vacuum somewhere. "Kelly! Hey, Kelly!" A woman in her thirties emerges in shorts, a red tank top that reveals white bra straps, and straightened black hair up in a ponytail. Tamires has me give Kelly my backpack. "Put it in the guest room," she orders. Kelly studies my clothes and asks, with a touch of disdain, "Will he be sleeping here?" Tamires senses my embarrassment, and brusquely replies, "Maybe, Kelly, maybe." The housekeeper retreats, annoyed. Tamires pulls up a chair and gestures for me to sit at the table, which is set for breakfast. On the checkered oilcloth sit a ceramic teapot, a Moka coffeepot, napkin holders, a plastic container with fresh white cheese, another with turkey ham, a pack of whole-grain bread, a jug half-full of fresh orange juice, a used mug, a chipped plate with melon peels, and a knife and fork. "Coffee's probably cold, but Kelly can make more." "That's all right, Tamires, I had some at the bus station." "Won't you even have some juice?" "No, don't worry about it." "Go on, have a glass of

juice..." she insists. "All right then," I say, wanting to be
polite. Kelly goes back to vacuuming. Tamires walks to the
cupboard and asks, "Are you on vacation?" "Sort of." She
fills a glass with juice, sets it in front of me, and stands
against the white-tile wall. "Does Mom know you're here?"
"No," I say. I adjust my glasses, "It's a surprise." "A surprise?
Mom hates surprises," she jokes. "You'd better call...Have
you got her cell phone number?" "I don't have a cell phone,"
I say. "You haven't got a cell phone?! How is that even
possible in the twenty-first century?" she asks, shocked. I
hang my head, embarrassed. "And how's Rosana doing?"
"She's fine," says Tamires. "She's a difficult person, you
know," she adds with a touch of irony, trusting I am on her
side. "Sure you don't want anything to eat?" she insists.
"No, thanks, I'm not hungry. Won't you sit down?" I ask.
"I'm on a diet," she says, thirstily, then apologizes, "I was
on my way out when you arrived. I run a delicatessen. We
sell cold cuts, fine spices, imported drinks," she explains.
"I'd love if you could come see it, it's on the street that
runs between Rui Barbosa and Santa Rita Square. You
know the one I mean?" "Yeah, and of course I'll come," I
say. As I drain my glass of orange juice, Tamires tells me
about how Rosana and Ricardo had wanted her to go to
Juiz de Fora to study medicine or law. "But I rebelled.
Instead, I signed up for a regular degree right here, in
business administration. I never finished it. Halfway
through, I started seeing this guy. He wanted to open a
deli, and I thought it was a great idea, but neither Mom

nor Dad would lend me the money for it. As far as they were concerned, being a shopkeeper was beneath them. They think they're important. They of all people...Mom, you know her story, and Dad..." She trails off. "Anyway... Of all people," she repeats with sarcasm. "In the end I got a loan from the bank. My relationship had gone downhill in the meantime. But the business worked out, and I make about as much as Mom does as a school principal, to everyone's surprise." "Ah, so she's finally the principal?" Tamires turns to face me, snidely. "It's all about contacts, contacts, contacts, Uncle Oséias..." "Yeah, Rosana was always excellent at those," I say, and my remark sounds malicious, though I hadn't meant it that way. Back in the kitchen, Kelly asks if she should fix up the guest room. "You'll stay with us, won't you, Uncle Oséias?" "Maybe, Tamires." "Mom's going to lose it," she quips, and with perverse delight, says, "Yes, Kelly, do fix up the guest room." "Does Rosana ever talk about me?" I ask. She hesitates and blushes, then says, "Sometimes." I change the subject: "And are you...Are you still in touch with Isabela? João Lúcio?" "No, very occasionally. Aunt Isinha is too poor for us and Uncle Jôjo is too rich..." she jests. "Mom says," and she apes Rosana's mannerisms, "Isinha's never been able to stomach how well we've done for ourselves! The woman is green with envy. But it's not my fault things haven't worked out for her." Her impersonation is perfect, and makes us both laugh. "I'm sorry but I really have to get going. I'm already late as it is." Tamires disappears down the hallway, says something or other to Kelly, and returns with a purse and a set of keys. I get up, and she gives me a hug, says she's happy to see me. "I'll call Mom on my way there and let her know you're here." She then suggests, "Why don't you try and rest a little?" I hear the sounds of a car being unlocked by the electronic key, of the engine humming, of the metal gate opening and then closing. I don't know what to do, so I wait, exhausted. The monotonous ticking of the grandfather clock lulls my eyelids. I grab a napkin and slowly wipe my glasses. I open the cupboard, take a glass, and fill it with tap water. I drink the warm liquid, which tastes of chlorine. I study the fridge magnets one by one. Nearly all of them are from New York—a yellow cab, an apple, the Statue of Liberty, NY, I Love New York—while some are ads—gas, mineral water, mini-mart, butcher's, burger joint, pizzeria, dial-beer. I wash my glass and set it bottom up on the dish rack. I'm starting to regret having come. Tamires was right, Rosana is going to—"Oh, you're still here?" Kelly is back in the kitchen. "I thought you'd gone out with Tamires." I ask awkwardly for the guest room, and she leads me to a bedroom with a twin bed, a nightstand, a two-door wardrobe, and a coatrack that holds a dusty felt hat. I ask Kelly to draw the curtains, and she says she'll switch on the AC. I insist there's no need. "In this swelter?" she questions, dismayed. I say I'm allergic. She shrugs, points to a folded towel on the bedspread, and leaves. I throw open the windows, which look out onto a small concrete patio at the back of the house. Light pours into the room, bathing it in yellow. A soft gust rustles the branches of a lone rose-apple tree. I lock the door, and, wearied, remove my glasses, slip off my shoes and socks, lie down in my clothes and everything

i awake with a start, heart surging, and grope around for my glasses. Where am I? My body is numb, drenched in sweat. Oh, I'm at Rosana's…Cataguases…The sun is already high in the sky. I wonder how long I was out for. I feel nauseated. I jump to my feet, unbolt the door, look for the bathroom, find it, go in, kneel beside the toilet bowl, and let out a stream of liquid that is hot, sour, and viscous—a mix of orange juice, milky coffee, and a buttered roll. My temples throb. Tears roll down my face. I'm no longer queasy. I unroll some toilet paper, clean the rim of the toilet bowl, flush. I rinse my mouth and wash my face at the sink. Back in the guest room, I slide on my glasses, pick up my towel and backpack, and return to the bathroom. I brush my teeth. The mirror shows pallid skin and deep-set eyes. I undress, step into the shower and turn it on. Warm water runs over my emaciated body. I turn off the water, towel myself off, pull on a clean pair of underwear and a shirt, step into the same jeans, leave the bathroom, and walk back to the guest room. I shove the dirty clothes into my backpack, which I toss in the wardrobe. I slip on a pair of clean socks and sneakers. Wet towel in hand, I set out in search of Kelly and find her sitting in the kitchen, at the ready, broom, squeegee, and a bucket full of cleaning products in hand. "Can I get in there now?" "Sure," I say, embarrassed, and add, "Sorry, I'm not feeling well." She says nothing. "Where should I hang the towel?" I ask. "Outside, on the clothesline," she says, gesturing with her chin at the concrete patio at the back of the house. The grandfather clock reads 11:40. How strange . . . I walk back, stop at the bathroom door and ask, "That clock . . . does it show the right time?" Kelly spritzes the air with aerosol. "It's never really worked. Though I don't reckon they ever sent it to get fixed." "Do you know what time it is?" "Just shy of two." I must look awful, because Kelly, hostile moments earlier, suddenly seems more gracious, like she might even feel sorry for me. "Dona Rosana called. Said I was to let you know I'm not a cook. If you want something to eat, there's sliced bread, cheese, and turkey ham in the fridge." "I'm not hungry," I say. "But if you like, I could make you a grilled ham-and-cheese sandwich," she says, kindly. "I really appreciate it, but you don't have to do that." "It's no trouble." "No, thank you. Really." I head back to my room, I need to go out, keep myself distracted. Sizim . . . I wonder what became of him. On the wall opposite the headboard is a print of a crying boy in rags. Marília liked strolling through the Praça da República market on Sundays. We would arrive early and linger at every stall as she guessed the prices of the objects on sale and haggled with merchants. She hardly ever bought anything. She just liked to practice her negotiation skills. I put on my baseball hat and leave the room. I bump into Kelly in the hallway as she hefts the broom, squeegee, and bucket of cleaning products into the storage closet. I spy a thermos in a corner of the kitchen near the sink, and laugh with a sense of childish vengeance—some things just never leave you. Though the design is modern, the white-and-blue thermos by the sink calls to mind another thermos—red, with a white lid, base, and handle—that had once held watered-down, fermented coffee and had been an important presence in our childhood. Kelly interrupts my daydreaming to ask, "You sure you don't want me to fix you up a ham-and-cheese sandwich?" "No, thanks," I answer. "How about some coffee? It's freshly made." "Sure, that'll go down nicely. Don't worry, I'll serve myself." I clumsily open the thermos and pour a splash of coffee into a glass, turning down Kelly's offer for a cup and saucer—an unpremeditated gesture that wins her over once and for all. I ask if I can have some sweetener and she says, with a twinkle of amusement, "There's no sugar allowed in the house." Kelly pours herself a glass of coffee and walks to the doorway. Pulling a cigarette from her packet, she asks, "Do you mind?" Though I've become increasingly sensitive to smells, I tell her to go ahead, adding, "I used to be a smoker myself." "Well, that's unusual. Ex-smokers are usually a pain in the neck." She has a funny way of saying *neck*, drawing out the e. She lights her cigarette with a small green lighter and blows out the smoke with satisfaction. She asks, "Was it hard?" "Quitting? It's been...let me think...eight years,

give or take. Doctor's orders." "Oh…" She sighs, and under
her breath, as though embarrassed, says, "I've tried…I
mean, I try…I just can't…" I finish my coffee, turn on the
faucet, rinse the glass, and place it bottom up on the dish
rack. "Have you worked here long?" I ask. "Every Tuesday
and Friday for about six years." "Do you like it?" Kelly
practically chokes on her cigarette smoke. "Show me
somebody who likes working! I work because I've got to. I
have two kids. Leandro, sixteen, and Larissa, fourteen…
They count on me…" "What does your husband do?"
"Husband? I sent that man packing! Bastard slapped me
upside the face. I took a knife, tore up his clothes, and said
to him, You get out of here right now, or I'll slash up more
than just your clothes next time!" She says this without
rage and with a touch of humor. "What did he do?"
"Coward shat himself, excuse the French," she scoffs. "Ran
away to Rio so he wouldn't have to pay alimony. I hear he
works as a street vendor now…Anyway…Thank God I
make enough to raise my kids. They're my pride and joy."
She tosses the cigarette butt in the trash can. "Men! What
do I need them for? Honest. They're all the same, I have yet
to meet a decent one." She glances at me and adds, "With
all due respect. I'm generalizing." "Don't worry, most of the
men I know aren't any good either." And we laugh. "Right.
Gotta get back to work. If Dona Rosana comes home and
finds that everything isn't just the way she likes it, she'll
throw a fit." "I'm going to head out. When does everyone
usually get home?" "I'm not sure. There's never anyone in by

the time I leave. Dona Rosana goes straight from work to the gym. I don't know about Dr. Ricardo, though." I say goodbye to Kelly and close the gate. I make my slow way to the center. The sun burns my skin, even as I shelter in the shade of the trees along the sidewalk. The air around me dances, as though spellbound by the heat rising off the cobblestones. The roar of cars and motorcycles choking the streets has replaced the hum of the hundreds of bicycles that once swarmed the city at the sound of the steam whistles at the textile mills. My childhood smells of cotton carted down from the Northeast in canvas-covered truck trailers unloaded by men with muscles that gleamed as they formed the bales into white, snowy peaks. Whole families lived off the paltry wages they earned as millhands and lived in row houses on the banks of the Rio Pomba, whose waters brimmed over every year, wrecking the families' few pieces of furniture, dampening the walls, and getting the children sick. There's hardly a textile mill left, and though the money has changed hands, floods remain a constant. The city is ugly, dirty, and reeks of piss. Trash is strewn on the sidewalk. Beggars and street vendors compete for the attention of passersby. In botecos, bars, and restaurants, people lounge about in the thrall of television screens. The pedestrian way of Rua Comércio is a window display of stories. A deformed poster from the last electoral campaign catches my eye. Though in pieces, I recognize the face. I buy a bottle of water from the ice cream parlor and ask the teenager behind the cash register who the current mayor is.

She gives a tense smile, as if I'd caught her red-handed. A
man dressed in shorts, a polo shirt, and casual shoes
interjects as he resignedly wipes his son's sticky face. "The
mayor's that crook Marcim Fonseca!" I turn around.
Defiantly, he continues, "The man's a white-bellied rat! Do
you know him?" "I'm not from here," I say, intimidated, as I
shake my head and cross the street. Marcim Fonseca...
Who would've thought... I sit on a bench beneath a
sibipiruna tree on Rui Barbosa Square. I sweat, unmoving. I
take small sips from the water bottle. The digital display on
the publicity stand reads 31°C. Márcio Luís Fonseca... We
were at the same high school for a couple of years. Colégio
Cataguases. In my freshman year, the papers I wrote earned
the praise of Mr. Haroldo Flávio de Carvalho Sá, a steely
teacher whose name formed a perfect Sapphic verse, with
stresses on the fourth, eighth, and tenth syllables, as he
liked to pompously remind us. Authoritarian, dark-suited,
and somber-tied, he had a habit of humiliating the poor
students—calling them dumb, ignorant, and dim-witted—
and showing leniency toward the sons and daughters of the
city's wealthier families, no matter how stupid they were.
What's more, he kept a close eye on anyone with the nerve
to espouse *independent ideas* on any given subject,
categorizing them as *rockers*, *potheads*, and *perverts*, whether
they were longhairs in colorful shirts, tight jeans, thick
belts, and bags with shoulder straps who reeked of
patchouli; or else took part in youth groups that on
weekends helped out at mass, visited shelters, orphanages,

and needy families, or planned trips to abandoned places where they could drink, smoke, and make out in secret. In the grips of a nationalist fervor, Mr. Carvalho Sá not only went after students but also spied on his fellow teachers, whom he accused of *subversion*. He informed on students and teachers alike to the chief of police, Aníbal Resende, a well-known browbeater who tortured prisoners by whipping them with wet towels so as not to leave marks on their bodies, as he himself bragged in conversation at Bar Elite. (Though both were dead, the two remained close: there were streets named after them in a middle-class gated community in the suburbs.) Mr. Carvalho Sá had little affection for me, seeing as I was *working class*, but he admired what he called my *dedication* and *perseverance*— though not my intelligence, an attribute reserved for people with *pedigree*. The papers I wrote completely lacked originality; I had simply learned to walk the steady tracks of a winding road, and wrote just the way he wanted me to, which is to say correctly. The sentence, he used to lecture, is feminine. And like all women, it is vain and enjoys dressing up. The adjective is the accessory of the sentence. Too many, and the sentence turns vulgar. None, and its beauty is dulled. I learned this lesson early, and became a virtuoso of his preferred style: the Brazilianness of Alencar modernized by the restraint of the neo-Parnassians, he used to say, even though we couldn't make head or tail of all that mumbo jumbo. After putting me on display in front of the classroom and making me read off the lined paper covered in cursive

letters—highly legible, at his insistence—I'd transcribe the
text on the chalkboard for the class to copy. All the while,
Mr. Carvalho Sá would sit at his desk pretending to quietly
read some hefty tome that he used as a cover to better
surveil his students through thick, heavy glasses, cracking
down on the *troublemakers* and *jokers* by whacking them on
the head with a yardstick he'd commissioned for the
purpose. Mr. Carvalho Sá's name struck fear in the hearts
of the teaching staff. So, while toadying up to him may
have inspired the hostility of my fellow students, it also
spared me some bother in other classes. And I strove to
please Mr. Carvalho Sá not out of a sense of admiration or
pride, like the others, but out of sheer indifference.
Wanting them to stop harassing me, I became suggestible—
satisfied, the people around me drew away, leaving me
alone, broken inside, detached from the world. With time,
this lassitude turned me into a character in my own
life—always prone to agree and guarded with my feelings
and opinions—and I grew more and more isolated. I wipe
my glasses with the edge of my shirt. The digital clock reads
16:42, and my stomach growls. I need some food to appease
it. I'm a bit unsteady on my feet as I get up and walk down
Rua do Comércio, the sun beating down on the naked
heads of passersby. I enter the first decent-looking diner I
come across, on Rua da Estação. In a corner, two women,
perhaps a mother and a daughter, are eating coxinhas and
drinking Coke. Opposite, by the door, a man with a
half-full tulip glass of beer is entranced by the movement

on the street. I go up to the counter and ask the server if they still have the set menu. He shakes his head. "Just sandwiches," he says, gesturing at the pastry display, "And savory snacks." Everything makes my stomach turn. I order a meat sfiha. He sets it on a paper plate and then places the plate on the counter. "To drink?" I study the drink dispenser and point to the cube filled with a gurgling light-red liquid. The server fills a very thin plastic cup, which warps between his fingers, and puts it down beside the sfiha. He quotes the price. I pull my worn leather wallet from my back pocket and take out a bill. He goes to the cash register and hands me some change. I head to a table behind the man drinking beer. I eat slowly, helping the doughy glob down my throat with sips from the sugary drink, which I assume is strawberry. Mosquitoes buzz round and round, then land on the thick and greasy sheet of semitransparent plastic that sits over the checkered tablecloth. Sweat dribbles down my forehead, face, belly. Marcim Fonseca... Though we grew closer in our second year, we never became friends. The trainee history teacher, Malu, helped dispel the animosity I inspired in my classmates. Malu and her pixie-short black hair. Malu and her thigh-revealing dress. Malu and her *advanced behavior*. The daughter of Principal Guaraciaba dos Reis, she was attending university in Belo Horizonte. In the very first couple of weeks, *bursting with ideas*, as Mr. Carvalho Sá liked to spitefully say, she'd drawn lots and divided the class into three groups, then explained that we were going to work on a *project* about the Early Modern Period, which we would then present in *seminars* throughout the second semester. My partners were Marcim Fonseca and Graciano Barbosa, our subject the French Revolution. Graciano was one of the *troublemakers*, defying teachers from the back of the classroom and taunting his enemies during recess. We all coveted his blond curls, set atop his sculpted chest and arms. Scrappy and vain, he suffered from intellectual poverty. Were it not for his singular gift at cheating on tests—achieved through either charm or menace—he may not have finished high school. Years later I came across signs with his name on them all through the city— Graciano Barbosa, Responsible Engineer. The deafening fans in the four corners of the diner circulate the muggy air. I take my hat off and run my right hand over my sopping head, then wipe the sweat on my pants. I collect the paper plate, plastic cup, and dirty napkins, then throw them in the trash. In the bathroom, I try to keep my sneakers from touching the yellow puddle that oozes along the rutted floor. I hold my breath and empty my bladder. Not a single drop of water trickles from the faucet in the small, grimy sink. I leave the diner. My body is still feeling the effects of the long journey, almost eleven hours of no sleep. I amble, plodding over rocks on the sidewalk, which unfurls in a long ember carpet. At the Tietê coach terminal, I had tried to recognize the faces of the passengers traveling with me, to no success. I'm from another time...At first I visited my family two or three times a year. Only Mom and Rosana

were still living together; Isinha had gotten married, João
Lúcio had relocated to Rodeiro a long time ago, and Dad
had withdrawn to a rental shack in Paraíso, where he sank
into booze the rest of his diminished disability pension—on
account of emphysema, which he refused treatment for.
Even though they were separated, Mom always stopped by
to pick up the countless shards of glass on the floor, air out
the bedrooms, thick with the stench of cachaça and
cigarettes, do the dishes, make food, leave him clean
clothes, and collect the dirty laundry. I wander down
Avenida Astolfo Dutra in the shade of oiti trees. The
Lava-Pés creek stinks of sewage. Whenever rain comes
down hard on the headwaters, the creek overflows and
pushes back up its banks the piss and shit dumped into it by
the colonial mansions. The digital clock reads 17:58 and
29°C. Rows of cars honk frantically, their racket muffled by
the trilling of thousands of sparrows swooping back into
the trees, where they perch on branches to wait out the
long night. During my fourth year in São Paulo, I bought a
Volkswagen Beetle 1600, which I paid for in installments.
As a sales representative for a farm supply company, I used
it to reach small rural towns in the interior of the state,
where I sold manure, chemical fertilizer, pesticide, and seed.
A natural segue for me, since as a kid I loved visiting our
family in the countryside, outside Rodeiro, with my
mother. Eventually, I started visiting only once a year, on
Independence Day. I was married to Marília by then, and
we spent Christmas and New Year in Paraná with the

Kempczynski family. Marília never stepped foot here in Cataguases. Nicolau, named after his maternal grandfather, never met my mother. When Nicolau was very young, Marília would say she didn't approve of us traveling alone together. By the time he was a bit older, Nicolau himself resisted, at her instigation. My mother's back problems made it impossible for her to come to São Paulo. Nicolau, a face in a photo album, a voice over the phone, was never a body for my mother to hold in her round arms and study with her nearsighted eyes. When she died—terminal pancreatic cancer—I grew disillusioned and never went back. I'm exhausted. My legs ache, my back aches. I sit on a bench. Lamps glow in the windows. A black-tufted marmoset climbs down an oiti tree, fishes something from between the sidewalk's hexagonal pavers, bounds back up the trunk, and watches me with interest through the branches as he chews. One morning, I'd pulled up to the curb out of the blue while my mother swept the footpath in her headscarf. I climbed out of the car and said, Ô, Dona Stella, good morning! Slipping on her glasses, which she always wore on a cord around her neck, she propped her broom against the wall and hugged me with feeling, Sweetheart! What's all this about? You just about gave me a heart attack!, she said, in feigned reproach. C'mon, let's head in, Go on, get inside. She covetously nudged me through, wanting for herself all the time we would've wasted had the neighbors come out to greet me. The house smelled clean; the furniture of linseed oil, the parquets of Polwax, the towels of indigo. Though Rosana still lived with her, they hardly saw one another. Rosana taught at various private schools during the day, studied school administration in the evenings, and spent weekends cooped up with Ricardo. Mom still took in sewing work, doubled over the electric sewing machine João Lúcio had given her, which, as she liked to remind us, had saved her skin. I wouldn't have been able to pedal another day, she would say, showing us her legs webbed with varicose veins. You should get surgery, Ma, we would urge her. To which she always replied, Now you write this down, the day I step foot in a hospital will be the day I die. And that's what happened. A decade later, illness laid waste to her in under six months. Streetlamps and headlights turn on. I get up and my feet heave me sluggishly to Rosana's address. That Saturday, after some coffee and cornbread, tenderly stored away in a square Duchen biscuit tin—We need something to spoil our guests with, somebody's always showing up out of the blue, she reasoned—I took her with me to the center. She stifled her glee—someone might mistake it for smugness—as we made our slow way down the street, ready to offer a ride to any acquaintance we saw on foot or at the bus stop. After stopping at two or three notions stores—she always needed thread, buttons, needles, ribbons, collars, clasps—we had lunch at Azulão. Between each forkful, she carefully filled me in on every important development since my last visit—weddings, baptisms, the deaths of relatives and acquaintances, though never any intrigue, scuttlebutt, or slander. At my request, she broached the evergreen subject of her children: João Lúcio's financial rise, Isinha's domestic sorrows, Rosana's efforts. Dad's name hardly came up, and Lígia's never. In the evening, as she fit fresh sheets on the bed so I could sleep, tears drew furrows in her wizened face. These empty rooms...Everything is so quiet, she lamented. It won't be long before Rosana leaves too. And then there won't be anyone left...She stood, patted down her dress, and said, See if you can rest a little, hon. On an embroidered white cloth over the nightstand stood a photograph of Dad, João Lúcio, me, and Sino, a black mutt, in front of the house. Dad had been explaining that the dog got his name because, when they brought him home as a puppy, he wouldn't stop wagging his tail. He's like a *sino*, Mom had said, a clapper, and Dad had jokingly exclaimed, Sino it is then! I dozed. That night, under the dim light of the kitchen, as Mom stood guard over the minestrone, we sorrowfully reminisced about the past, and each reflected alone on our mistakes. Early that Sunday, we went to see Isinha—she was living in Thomé at the time—and convinced her to come out with us and bring the kids: Deliane, around four, and Diego, still in diapers. On the road to Leopoldina, the cool air mussed their light-brown hair—the two of them were so alike, they'd even got themselves into a similar mess. When we got back, in high spirits, Wellington stormed out of the house, drunk. He greeted us with insults, made a scene, picked a fight with me, and threatened Isinha, who held Diego bawling and spluttering in her arms, as Mom fled with Deliane onto the sidewalk, causing a ruckus that, to our dismay and embarrassment, the neighbors watched from their window. Isinha still puts up with her husband to this day—an alcoholic, unemployed, aggressive, two-timing nuisance. But he's a good dad, she argues, And he's never laid a finger on me. In the distance, near the source of Rio Pomba, lightning torpedoes the lowery sky. A zephyr eases the heat. I stop by the tall rough-concrete wall, catch my breath, press the intercom buzzer. Rosana's gravelly voice rings out almost instantly, "Who is it?" "It's me, Rosana—" I don't have time to get my name out before I hear the side door unlock. "Did it open?" "Yeah, it opened!" The silhouette of the house appears before me. I cut across the concrete strip and enter the garage, inside it a red Renault Duster. The kitchen light falls on Rosana's slender but athletic body as she waits by the door, radiating a halo of hostility. Reaching out her hand, she hurriedly ushers me in as she asks, "Have you been smoking in here?" "I quit smoking eight years ago, Rosana." "Then it must have been that idiot Kelly! I should fire her lazy ass today!" The sharp smell of Bom Ar air freshener sends me into a coughing fit. Rosana throws open the window and flaps her hands and arms to dispel the odor. "I hate the smell of cigarettes!" She turns on the vent. Little by little, my belly stops spasming and my breath returns to normal. I dab my tears with a couple of paper napkins. I wipe my glasses with the edge of my shirt. Stuffed in rosy patterned leggings and a black shirt, in colorful sneakers and a bandana holding up her hair, Rosana shows off the perfect curvature of her muscles. She turns off the vent and asks, "Have you had dinner?" "No, but I grabbed a bite in town." "There's some cheese, turkey ham, and sliced bread in the fridge if you want. You could have a ham-and-cheese sandwich." "No, I'm all right, thanks." She pours a slimy green liquid into a cup. "Could I have some water?" I ask. She opens the fridge, takes out a glass bottle, pours some water into a cup, and sets it down on the table. "Is it me, or have you lost weight?" "We're cut from the same cloth," I say. She shrugs, satisfied. We took after Dad, Rosana and me, lean and slender, with dark-brown hair and eyes. João Lúcio and Isinha took after the Morettos, Mom's side of the family; a little shorter, obesity-prone, their eyes and hair light brown. As Rosana chats with me, she glances sidelong at her cell phone, which vibrates in her left hand. She drains the gooey green liquid, places the glasses in the sink, tosses out collard stems, a green apple core, and lime peel, and asks, "How come you're visiting Cataguases now, after all these years? How long has it been, anyway?" She rounds the table where I sit and runs her index finger along the surfaces of the furniture and the appliances, pretending to inspect Kelly's work. "Since Mom's funeral. Almost twenty years," I answer. I try to change the subject. "I noticed you collect New York magnets..." Disarmed, Rosana stops what she's doing and says, with childlike glee, "Oh, New York...I've been going once a year, around mid-November...Are you on Facebook?

You aren't, are you? You should be, though. I got back in touch with two friends from college. We chat every day now. Bia lives in Juiz de Fora and teaches at a state college, she's a real whiz. Divorced, and her kids are independent. She's just making the most of life. Lurdinha—she despises her name so we call her Lu now—lives in Brasília. She's married to a civil servant who works at some ministry. He passed the public service exams and everything, so they're living it up. We got back in touch about six years ago, and it's like we were never apart. You haven't been to New York, have you? Oh, New York…" Rosana rolls her eyes up in delight. "We fly over with only a small carry-on and come back with a ton of suitcases. I only ever fill two bags, but Lu sometimes brings home three. She outdid herself last time—came back with four! I think her husband's got some deal on with the airport officials. She's never been stopped. We always stay in this wonderful hotel on Forty-Fifth Street, right next to Times Square. We go shopping in Jersey Gardens, in Elizabeth." When Rosana says Times Square, Jersey Gardens, and Elizabeth, her pronunciation is meticulous. "We take a train from Penn Station to Elizabeth, then a cab. We usually take the bus back to Port Authority, in Manhattan, on account of all the shopping bags." She takes a breath and looks at her cell phone out of the corner of her eye. In the meantime, I praise her, "Your English is fantastic!" Rosana blushes. "I don't have an accent, do I?" "Not even a little bit," I insist. "I've been studying, twice a week. For years now," she says with pride, adding, "We don't just go shopping either! We visit museums, go to the theater, concerts…" Her cell phone rings to the sound of an old telephone. She wraps up, "We have a lot of fun, but we do the cultural stuff too." And then apologizes, "Gimme a minute, I should take this." She disappears down the hallway. I get up. My legs ache and I feel faint. I rinse the glass and place it bottom up on the dish rack. At night, the rooms appear to deflate and shrink in size. Crickets chirr in the overgrown garden. I walk to the open kitchen door. The air is still. Snippets of telenovela dialogue seep from neighboring houses. Figures appear at the windows of the low building across the street. Rosana has changed. She's almost certainly Botoxed her lips, cheeks, and forehead. Her eyes are peculiar, and they hardly blink. She probably has implants too; her breasts look perter. She had her nose done a long time ago. She couldn't stand the shape, which she'd inherited from Mom. She's been dyeing her hair ever since she spotted the first white strand, before she'd even turned thirty. But the skin on her neck betrays her age…She's back. Before she gets a word in, I say, "It's crazy how amazing you look." Without thinking, she says, "I know. I don't look any older than you, do I? I could pass for your younger sister, don't you think?" She continues, "Did you know no one's ever guessed I'm over fifty years old?!" "You really don't look it," I concur, prepared to keep her fantasy alive. Rosana is older than me, probably approaching sixty. "You know I'm a principal now, right? So many responsibilities," she says, pleased. "Tamires mentioned it."

"A mountain of problems... But you get used to it." She removes the bandana and lets her hair down, fixes it and puts it up again. "You separated, didn't you? Isinha hinted at something." "Yeah." "What was your wife's name again?" "Marília." "Marília! She never visited, did she? At least, not that I remember." "No, she never did." "What about your son..." "Nicolau." "How old is he now? Twenty-nine?" "Twenty-seven, he'll be twenty-eight this year... In August." "Oh... Tamires is older than him... I had her pretty young though." Keeping up the lie about her age requires certain temporal acrobatics from Rosana. "Tamires works in retail now, you know," she notes with a touch of scorn. "She could've been anything! A doctor, a lawyer... But no, she went into retail. Runs in the blood, doesn't it?" Lord, what a phony! Does she really believe I've forgotten Dr. Normando, who ran an underground poker ring? And what about Ricardo and Roberto, and their rackets—I've known the two since they were kids. I am sitting on a white-painted metal bench while Rosana stands against the dividing wall between the backyards. "And Nicolau, what does he do?" If we'd been anything more than voices in the dark, she might have noticed how uncomfortable I looked. "He... I mean... We don't talk much..." But Rosana isn't interested, and she isn't listening. "C'mon, let's head in," she says. I take the opportunity to steer her monologue in another direction. "Have you spoken with Isinha lately?" We sit. She at the head of the table, and me in the same seat as before. Rosana's hands are neat and thin, with long fingers and red nail polish. She's always been enormously proud of them, ever since a teacher in primary school sang their praises—the hands of a pianist, she'd said—and is always finding ways to show them off in conversation, flaunting them to relatives, neighbors, acquaintances, and strangers, The hands of a pianist... "No... Isinha's difficult, you know. She's never been able to stomach how well we've done! The woman's green with envy. But it's not my fault she married a drunk!" I think of Tamires's impersonation— she'd used almost the exact same phrasing—and for a second I can't help laughing. "What about João Lúcio?" "I never really got on with Jôjo. We haven't spoken in years. Did you know he's filthy rich?" She catches her breath, asks, "Anyway, what are you doing here, Oséias? You'd never even seen this house, had you?" "No... It's beautiful. Well done! I had the address from the time I sent you the paperwork and power of attorney so you could sort out the mess with the inheritance. Remember?" "Will you be staying long?" "No, don't worry. A day or two and I'll be out of your hair." "Oséias, why'd you turn up like this, without warning?" Rosana is like Dad: she'd pretend to let go of something, creating a diversion that allowed her to close in on her opponent. "I don't know, Rosana." "What do you mean you don't know?" She gets up and paces around the kitchen, performing her frustration. "Don't even try to fool me! Twenty years and you're nowhere to be found. I only ever hear about you when Isinha calls. Now, all of a sudden... What do you want?" "I don't want anything from you,

Rosana. Calm down." "Are you broke?" she asks. "No, Rosana, I'm not broke." "Well, then, I don't get it…" "Can you imagine if Mom heard you talking like this? You sound like you're about to turn me out. What would she think?" "That you're being cynical, Oséias. That's what she'd think! Now quit beating around the bush: What do you want?" "You may not believe it, Rosana, but I honestly don't know…Maybe all I want is some peace and quiet…" "Peace and quiet?! Here? Hahahahaha. You're putting me on—" "No, it's true! You don't have to believe me if you don't want to, but it's the truth." "Gone and become a Buddhist, have you? Do you want to make peace with Ricardo too?" she asks, sarcastically. "Of course not! I'll never—" "Careful, that's my husband you're talking about!" She plants herself in front of me, finger wagging. "Rosana, now you're the one being cynical. Ricardo's no saint. You know it, I know it, Tamires knows it—" "Don't you dare bring up my daughter!" she yells, slamming her open hand on the oilcloth. "You're right," I retreat. "What do you want, Oséias? Aside from causing everyone distress?" she presses, beside herself. We hear the metal gate open. "It's Tamires. I don't want her to see us arguing. I'm going to shower, collect myself, sleep. I have to go to work early. Think about what I asked. Sleep on it. I'll expect an answer from you tomorrow!" "Goodnight, Rosana!" She strides down the hall in a fury, without saying goodbye. I hear the sound of the car being locked, the whir of the metal gate closing. Tamires steps into the kitchen. "Hey, Uncle Oséias!

Have you had dinner yet?" she asks, pleasantly surprised. "I had a bite earlier." "Oh, you won't join me then? I don't often eat at night, but I fancied a nibble..." She's no good at pretending. Feeling sorry for her, I decide to tag along, "All right then." She smiles and says, "Gimme a minute." She sets her purse on the table and disappears into the house with her cell phone. It can't be easy being Rosana's daughter. My sister needs to feel that she is adored, courted, and praised. I don't think she's cheating on Ricardo. Cheating requires dedication, and Rosana is impatient, her faithfulness shaped by an enormous moral inertia, though at the same time she needs constant reminding that she is pretty, smart, and interesting. She needs to be able to measure herself against other women, including her own daughter, and to come out on top, infinitely superior. Tamires returns to the kitchen, grabs the keys to the Honda Fit, unlocks the car, opens the door, and squeezes in. I sit in the passenger seat. She turns on the engine. The metal gate clicks open and she reverses. "There's nothing to eat at home. Mom's always on some diet, and she makes everyone do it with her," she remarks, pitching the car toward the center. "Dad's got the right idea. He has dinner every night before coming home." "Where are we headed?" I ask. "Cachorrão do Leo. You know it? It's super trashy!" She laughs. Lightning no longer flickers in the dimly starred sky. A full moon steals through sparse clouds. Tamires drives in silence for just over five minutes, then parks. We climb out of the car, still silent. Tamires's body strains under its weight, and her legs lumber. From a bar in the distance comes the hubbub of voices and the din of sertanejo music. Cachorrão do Leo is a trailer parked under a spray of oiti trees and six tables arranged on the sidewalk. Four of the tables are taken, two of them by cooing young couples, another by three blathering teenagers, and another, at a remove, by a man sitting alone. We set up next to the teenagers, and the server soon comes over to take our order, hard-plastic sheet menu in hand. Without looking, Tamires orders a burger with everything, "The works." The server smiles—he knows her—and runs through it all, "Lots of cheese, lots of bacon, mayo on the side." "That's right! And a Coca-Cola Zero." Though I'm hungry, my stomach is sensitive to everything. In the end, I order a grilled ham-and-cheese sandwich and a regular Coke. Tamires stares at the individual sitting alone behind me, and finally excuses herself, "He's a friend, I'm going to say hi." I turn around to get a better look: roughly forty, black clothes, hair falling down his shoulders, tattooed arms. The air is thick with the smell of grilled meat, which attracts a gentle and wary black-and-white stray dog. The teens' chatter is riddled with slang I can just barely make sense of. Tamires scuffs back. "Uncle Oséias, so . . . what's your son's name again?" "Nicolau." "That's right, Nicolau. I remember him being super cute . . . Grandma Stella was always showing us photos of him, black hair, big blue eyes . . ." "Yeah, our little Pole . . . Not a drop of Moretto in him. He takes after his Mom." "What does he do?" I blush, take a deep breath. I can't hide my unease. A train whistles somewhere nearby, startling us. The train treks across the city, its dozens of freight cars once laden with iron ore now carrying bauxite. "Train's still running, then?" I ask. Tamires says, "Two or three times a day." "The worst part is that none of the wealth stays here," I sociologize. "Just muddied rivers and hollowed hills," she adds. The ground shakes and the wheels squeal, drowning out our words. As a kid, on my way home from school, I used to sprinkle gravel just to see it turn to dust. Once, I put down a coin instead, and it vanished like a soap bubble. The server carries back a tray with the cans of soda, glasses filled with ice, a napkin dispenser, straws, and bottles of ketchup and mustard. Tamires cracks open the Coca-Cola Zero, tips it into a glass and takes a sip. Little by little, the dun-dun-dun dun-dun-dun dun-dun-dun of the train fades into the distance. "Are you still in touch with your cousins?" I ask. She thinks for a second, then says, "I don't know if you're aware, but Deliane, Aunt Isinha's girl, has joined an evangelical church." "I know...Universal Church of the Kingdom of God. She's already got two kids, hasn't she?" "Yeah, though I haven't met them. I see Diego sometimes. He works with cars, buying and selling them, that sort of thing. He's just a bit lost, you know." The server brings over the sandwiches. Tamires snaps up the burger, slops it with mustard, ketchup, and mayo, and takes an enormous bite. I open the can of Coke, tip some in the glass, take a sip, and bite into the ham-and-cheese sandwich, chewing slowly to convince my stomach to keep it down. "Daniel's in college, taking evening classes," she says. After a short pause, I ask, "What about João Lúcio's kids?" "Ah, those girls!" She chases the burger with a glug of soda and wipes her mouth and fingers on a napkin. "Can't say I know them. We saw each other a couple of times at Grandma's, when we were really young. I wouldn't recognize them if I saw them now." One of the young couples leaves. Tamires takes another large bite of the burger. Mouth full, she says, "I feel sorry for Mom..." I wait, saying nothing. "She's a miserable person..." Tamires chews anxiously. She takes a sip of Coke, wipes her mouth, sips again. "Have you seen her Facebook page? She posts a new photo every day. She's always posing, trying to look sexy. All so her friends will say things like, You look so pretty! Oh my God, you don't age! What a hottie! And emojis posted by machos who think they're heartthrobs... Deep down, she's terrified of getting old. She needs it, the constant fawning. She says she's got a thousand-something friends. Hahahahaha! Poor thing...I feel sorry for her. And she's totally obsessed with having a perfect body. She works out every night! And she's had God knows how much work done. Dad even says, half-joking, I married one woman, but I'm living with another..." Tamires takes another spiteful bite of her cheeseburger. We sit in silence. I finish my ham-and-cheese sandwich and polish off my already tepid Coke. I wipe my mouth and hands, collect the dirty napkins, and set them on my plate. "We're like three rogue planets living under the same roof. Now and then our paths cross and we'll be on the verge of destruction. But even though we resent each other, we also depend on one another to survive. Magnetic forces…Orbits…" She takes another sip of soda and has the last bite of cheeseburger. "What about your dad?" I ask. She chews more slowly now, relishing the final morsel as though clinging to a fleeting pleasure. "He lets me do my thing," she says. She wipes her lips and fingers. On her plate is a mountain of napkins soiled yellow, red, and white. "He minds his business, I mind mine. We put up with each other, and that's enough." She takes a final sip of Coke. "He knows I don't approve of his choices… There's no going back though, is there? Once you lose respect for someone…" Tamires calls the server over and asks for the check. He wonders if we've enjoyed our meal. The man in black is gone. Only the young couple's cooing and the teenagers' animated shrieking remain. The clouds in the sky have also faded away. Though the hubbub from the bar has died down, there is still the jangle of sertanejo music. The server approaches us and hands me a piece of paper with numbers scribbled on it. But Tamires grabs it and says, "My invitation, my treat." An astute observation; she must have noticed that morning how destitute I am. Tamires's hand carefully feels around her purse, and after a few moments her fingers clasp a designer leather wallet and pull out a credit card. "Shall we?" The server hands her the receipt with a grateful "Thank you! Goodnight!" We get up. He collects the plates covered in used napkins, the empty cans, the ketchup and mustard bottles, and the unused straws. We stroll down the footpath below the dense foliage of oiti trees obscuring the streetlights. Tamires unlocks the car with a click and squeezes through the door. I sit in the passenger seat. She connects her cell phone to the stereo, and Neil Young begins to sing "Like a Hurricane." How odd, I think, and say, "Your Mom used to listen to this sort of music!" Tamires smiles and points out, "I'm an old soul, Uncle Oséias. Old-school...Or maybe just plain old." She grabs a packet of rolling papers and a baggie. "Mind if I smoke?" "Weed?" I ask, both surprised and alarmed. "Weed!" she says, tickled by my incredulity. "Huh, so you smoke?" "It helps," she explains. "Manages my anxiety, relaxes me." "I don't mind...Can I open the window?" "Of course," she says. Tamires carefully sprinkles weed on the paper, rolls and seals it with saliva, twists one end, pulls out a matchbox from the glove compartment, lights the joint, takes a long drag, and holds her breath. The funk hits my nostrils, and I try to hide the ensuing waves of nausea. "Lighters kill the essence of the weed," she philosophizes as she blows the rest of the smoke out the half-open window. "When are you gonna visit me at the store, Uncle Oséias? Or do you think it's undignified to work in retail too?" "Who am I to say whether anything's undignified?" "Dad doesn't think it's dignified to run a deli." "He of all people," I remark and regret it the moment the words leave my mouth. "Yeah, he of all people..." she echoes. "You know how he makes a living, don't you?" I don't, though everyone in Cataguases has a theory. "Of course you do, Uncle Oséias. Though I appreciate your not saying anything." For a moment I consider insisting that I don't, but there's no point. She takes another drag. "I need some time away, in a spa." She confesses this meditatively, staring up at the ceiling of the car. "Aren't you scared the cops will see you?" I ask. "C'mon. Do you really think anyone's got the guts to mess with the daughter of Ricardo Alves, aka True-Blue Ricardo?" Her sardonic retort conceals a hint of immodesty. Tamires wets her index finger and thumb with the tip of her tongue, puts out the ember, stashes the joint in the matchbox, and tucks it in the glove compartment. She turns on the engine and drives in silence while Robert Plant sings "Stairway to Heaven." I wipe my glasses with the edge of my shirt. Five minutes later she stops diagonally on the street and opens the metal gate with the remote. I ask her if Ricardo parks his car in there, wanting to know if my brother-in-law is home. Tamires says, "Dad hasn't been driving since he got sick." "Sick with what?" I ask, trying not to sound sadistic. "A load of stuff. Diabetes, high blood pressure, high cholesterol, angina... A load of stuff." She locks the car with a click. "Dad's got a Ranger, but Jiló keeps it after he drops him off." "Jiló?! He's still alive?" "Very much alive, and at Dad's beck and call twenty-four hours a day." She shoves open the kitchen door. "All right. Thanks for the company, Uncle Oséias. Goodnight!" "Night, Tamires." "I'll see you at the shop tomorrow!" "You bet," I say, entering the guest room. I switch on the lamp.

Outside, the towel I hung to dry on the clothesline lolls motionless. Though I need the bathroom, I don't want to bump into Ricardo. I remove my glasses, put them on the nightstand. I take off my shirt and pants, hang them on the coatrack. I slip off my shoes and socks, nudge them under the bed. I switch off the lamp. I lie on the mattress in only my underwear. Moonlight spills through the window, bathing the laminate wood floor. My body aches...I'm exhausted...Jiló...Strange guy... A contemporary of Dr. Normando... Ricardo inherited him from his dad... Driver...Security guard...He does it all...They say he's burdened by death...Where there's smoke there's Jiló, people used to say, with dread...Smoke...deliane's evangelical marcim fonseca's mayor sizim dad forbade isinha joão lúcio jôjo rosana calls him jôjo to this day rodeiro family plot monkeys eating popcorn nicolau nicolau nico lau lau nico big blue eyes wonder if dona eva's still alive i've had so much rotten luck evil eye what is evil eye feast your eyes on gale of the wind there's no wind still air hot i've got to pee lígia the ground the coffin what have you come here for window open rose-app

wednesday,
march 4

i wake up guts in a knot, bladder ready to burst. I put on
my glasses, get out of bed, and unlock the door, the house
sunken in silence. I walk to the bathroom, switch on the
light, sit on the toilet, and sigh as I pee and relieve my
aching stomach. I should flush, but the flushing mechanism
is loud and might startle Rosana, Tamires, Ricardo... I
press the button, wash my hands, switch off the light, rush
across the hall, enter my room, lock the door, and listen
carefully. I hear nothing. The moon is probably high in
the sky. I lean out the window. The towel hanging on the
clothesline and the rose-apple tree seem to float in the
half dark. I strip the bedspread and lie over the top sheet.
The coatrack recalls a gangly man with a hat in his hand.
I used to sleep well, even though I spent most nights on
uncomfortable beds in rural hotels. I would turn in at nine,
nine thirty, exhausted after dinner and several hours of
selling manure, fertilizer, pesticides, seeds, run through the
itinerary for the following day, and then grab a book—I

always packed one—*The Maltese Falcon, The Lady in the Lake, The Long Goodbye, The Pillars of the Earth, The Godfather, The Postman Always Rings Twice,* Dorothy L. Sayers, Agatha Christie, Sherlock Holmes, John le Carré, Sidney Sheldon, a history of the First World War, a history of the Second World War, *For Whom the Bell Tolls, All Quiet on the Western Front, Ben-Hur, Quo Vadis,* Luis Fernando Verissimo… I would wake up at six, in high spirits, have breakfast, skim the newspaper for things to discuss with the clients, and by eight I was ready—either to work the square or head on to the next town. On Friday evenings, I would make my way back to São Paulo, after a week on the road, sometimes more. I didn't mind my job, but Marília was always upset, complaining that I was away too long. She used to say I enjoyed it—time away from the family—and in a way she wasn't wrong. Marília was bossy; furniture, food, clothes, travel, it all had to be her way. On the road, I had certain freedoms. Before Marília, I used to spend my time off cooped up in the cinema. I'd watch a movie on Saturday and another on Sunday. That was how I met Marília, at Cine Arouche. I walked in and happened to glance over at her. She smiled a little awkwardly, and I smiled back. Without much thought, having overcome my crippling shyness, I asked if the seat was free. She said yes and gestured to the chair beside hers. I went to the bar, ordered a coffee, paid, placed my coffee cup on the table and sat down, embarrassed and already regretting my nerve. But Marília took control of the situation. Eight months later, she had moved into the small apartment I rented in Vila Prudente, and I began to spend weekends grudgingly watching romantic comedies that she borrowed from video rental stores, sitting comfortably on the living room sofa, eating pizza and drinking guaraná soda. Mom never forgave Marília for not condescending to visit Cataguases, and she never let me off the hook for being so submissive to my wife that I never took Nicolau to receive his grandmother's blessing, not even by force. She took this enormous sorrow with her to her grave, though she seemed happy to see her children gathered around her at the hospital, keeping her company in her final moments. That was the last time we were all together. I didn't even come home for Dad's funeral two years later. We had traveled by car to Araucária to visit Marília's relatives. Though I promised to visit the family plot in Rodeiro at the earliest opportunity, I'd put it off and off and then off again until finally it had slipped my mind altogether. Rosana looked after Dad at the end of his life, forgiving him his animosity. Rosana had studied at Colégio das Irmãs thanks to a scholarship she was able to get through her godmother, Dona Magnólia Prata, who had a great deal of clout, despite being descended from the city's more modest founders, and even though many had turned their noses up at her marriage to Dr. Normando, a notorious bookie several years her senior. Dona Magnólia was an old customer of Mom's, and when Rosana was born, Mom had decided, *with a mind to the future* and without consulting Dad, that Dona Magnólia should be

the godmother at her daughter's baptism. In addition
to the occasional visit to put in an order for clothes,
Dona Magnólia called on us religiously on Children's
Day, Rosana's birthday, and Christmas—and spoiled her
goddaughter *rotten* with presents—always in the company
of her two boys, Ricardo and Roberto. Dad couldn't
mask his deep aversion to the presence of those two self-
important and intrusive boys, the fruit of a marriage too
inappropriate to be permitted under our roof. Dad liked to
call attention to more than just Dr. Normando's reputation
as a hardened crook; there was also his philandering side,
or Naná, the lover he kept in Casa Branca. But what
angered Dad most of all was Dona Magnólia's subservience:
every Friday she sent her maid, in uniform and everything,
to tidy and perfume the room of the brothel where her
husband would spend the weekend frolicking with his lover
on a fresh set of silk sheets. So Rosana grew up feeling
like she was different, a swan among ducks. When she
was small, Dona Magnólia started taking her to Carnival
shows at Clube do Remo, to fancy weddings at Santa
Rita de Cássia Church, and to dances at the Social Club.
Rosana became the linchpin of contention between our
mother and father. Dad couldn't reconcile the money spent
on *trifles* for a daughter who in return treated them with
growing disdain, and went so far as to tell people she was
an orphan being raised by *Auntie* Magnólia, who was in
charge of *managing her fortune*. While Mom laughed off
these *innocent fantasies*, Dad despaired: he could see Rosana

drifting further and further away from them. The conflict
came to a head just before Rosana turned fifteen. At her
daughter's request, and with Dona Magnólia's money, Mom
had agreed to let Rosana make her debut at Clube Meca.
Dona Magnólia said she would pay for the dress and shoes,
for classes in etiquette, ballroom dance, and posture, and
for the hairdresser and portraitist, while Mom would be
responsible for the jewelry, *at least the jewelry*, and went
into debt on account of a prohibitive pearl necklace. She
wanted desperately to participate in the ceremony itself, but
knew Dad would never have permitted such *extravagance*.
One day, during one of her countless arguments with
João Lúcio, wanting to humiliate him, Rosana announced
that the party was underway. Outraged, he asked Mom to
explain. All hell broke loose in the house. Rosana spent
days hiding at her godmother's, afraid of her father, who,
to our surprise, neither argued nor fought nor reprimanded
anyone. But he stopped talking to Mom for about two years
and never addressed another word to Rosana. A photo of
rosana's first waltz with dr. normando was published in the
jornal cataguases but mom hid the newspaper the neighbors
gossiped joão lúcio grew even more distant

i wake up to the sound of the metal gate—is it opening or
closing? Closing. I'd dozed off. It's probably Rosana leaving
for work. The birds are in a commotion. Outside, the cars
roar. I put on my glasses. Get out of bed. My head already

aches. I go to the coatrack, collect my shirt and pants, get dressed. I sit on the bed, pull on my socks and slip on my shoes. I grab my toothbrush from my backpack. Press my ear against the door, no sign of movement. I cross the hall, enter the bathroom, and lock the door. I urinate. Wash my face, brush my teeth. Flush. I leave the bathroom and steal into my room, slip my toothbrush back into my backpack. I put on my hat. I catch my breath, tiptoe into the kitchen and check the grandfather clock even though it shows the wrong time, head into the garage, round the Honda Fit, open the side door, and make my way outside. I breathe in the hot and sunny morning air. I amble. A woman, rather elderly, sweeps the footpath. I say good morning. She stops, says good morning, and watches me for a few moments, leaning on the shaft of the broom. Marcim Fonseca... I'll go find Marcim Fonseca! I wonder if he'll remember me. I'd never have pictured him in politics. One time, we went to his house to work on Malu's project about the French Revolution. Marcim lived in Vila Minalda. His dad was a textile worker, his older brother was a textile worker, his sister was a textile worker. His mom—short, shy, milk-bottle glasses, and the saddest eyes—offered us a jug of raspberry-flavored juice with ice exactly like the one on the Q-Suco juice packets and a bamboo basket filled with zeppole covered in a dishcloth embroidered with two chickens. Marcim was visibly uncomfortable. About the smallness of the living room, the tears in the sofa's pleather, the plastic sheet over the television screen, the nerve of the two cats rubbing against our legs and mewing, the music sounding loudly from the neighbor's house, about his youngest sister, who kept showing off her legs to our lustful eyes, and about the voraciousness with which Graciano and I threw ourselves at the zeppole and the Q-Suco juice. Marcim sulked for more than two hours. He was anxious for us to wrap things up and regretted having agreed to host us at all. The row house where he lived was so close to the river that from the armchair where I sat I could see the water flowing calmly beyond the small backyard and the skeletal guava trees, one of which had a yellow mutt tied to a rope, dolefully wagging his tail and ears to shoo away the flies. We never stepped foot in there again. Instead, we met at the school library or at my house, though never at Graciano's, who must have been embarrassed of us—his dad owned a gas station. Mom was fond of Marcim, but she liked everyone. Dad, on the other hand, mulishly insisted that Marcim had *shifty eyes*—and maybe he was more perceptive than all of us. If there was one person I thought might be drawn to politics, it was Cesinha. A friend of Lígia's, Cesinha was one year ahead of me. During his junior year of high school, he and Aladim, the chemistry teacher, decided to start a small newspaper. Aladim was a nickname. Everyone called him that because he taught us chemistry with magic tricks. Friendly, with black curly hair that fell down his shoulders, he had a great sense of humor, played guitar in a Beatles cover band called the Revolution Band, and had women sighing over him, despite rumors that he was a queer. Mr. Aladim, Cesinha, and a couple other students stuck colorful posters up around the school announcing the arrival of O Intrépido. One morning in August, shortly after the holidays, they stood at the entrance to hand out their student newspaper, which had been composed with a typewriter on legal paper and then mimeographed. They'd hardly begun distribution when Zé Leal and Zé Adão, two monitors who were chummy with Carvalho Sá, showed up and brutally confiscated the papers. They set fire to them right then and there, causing a disturbance that was quickly dispelled. They claimed the newspaper preached naturism, vegetarianism, the legalization of weed, and free love, all of which was enough to make Carvalho Sá livid. But the straw that broke the camel's back was a caricature Cesinha had drawn depicting the teacher with an enormous head and tiny body, sitting on the edge of his bed in his underwear with a look of fear on his face above the caption: My God, what's gotten into my head? Mr. Aladim didn't teach that day. The following week, Mr. Arruda, the substitute teacher, informed us he had moved to Rio de Janeiro, in search of new professional challenges. I never heard about Mr. Aladim again. Cesinha was suspended for a week, and his mother, Dona Alice, was seen leaving the office of Principal Guaraciaba dos Reis in tears. She was always crying. Crying, crying, crying, because she just couldn't understand why people were always going after her Vevé, as she called her husband, A good man, a hard worker, who only wants what's best for people, like Jesus

Christ...Dona Alice couldn't understand why people were always attacking her Venâncio for being a communist, when being a communist was no different in her view than being a Catholic, except without mass or pastors. Her husband was in prison at the time, at the Penitenciária de Linhares in Juiz de Fora. When he came home a few years later, people gathered at their house, which was three blocks from ours, because despite everything the neighbors were still fond of Dona Alice and Seu Vevé. He arrived home in a shocking state: emaciated and blind in one eye, with teeth missing and a tremor in his hands. Seu Venâncio never worked again. He spent what little time he had left afraid to leave his room, unable to sleep, wary of everyone, pissing blood and refusing treatment, as Dona Alice would explain whenever she came across my mother sweeping the sidewalk. It's heartbreaking, Dona Stella, just heartbreaking. Principal Guaraciaba dos Reis reminded Dona Alice that, *next time, if there is a next time,* he'd have to expel Cesinha from school, It would be devastating, Dona Stella! Alice continued, despairing, as though it wasn't enough for her Vevé to be away, locked up like an animal, Now Júlio César, Lord Almighty, what'll become of the kid? I stop at a bakery at the entrance to the old bridge. Walk in, say hello, order a buttered roll and coffee with milk. After the scare, Cesinha cleaned up his act, applied for a job at the Caixa Econômica, and moved abroad. He never came back. I wonder if Dona Alice is still alive. And what Carla, her daughter, is up to. The wall clock reads ten to eight. The server, a teenager, places a glass of milky coffee and a Colorex glass plate with an open-face buttered roll on the brushed metal bar. I ask for sweetener and she scans the room for it with her eyes, finds the bottle, grabs it, and places it in my hand. It's hot out. The glass of coffee burns my fingers and lips. I chew slowly. Peninha, my nickname, Peninha...Even after I shot up and reached a height of 1.74 meters, I remained weedy. I used to spend hours exercising—pull-ups, jumping jacks, crunches—so I could bulk up and become stronger. I'd eat raw eggs, a dozen bananas, enormous bowls of pasta...Someone once told me that jerking off strengthened your biceps and chest muscles, so I did it three or four times a day. None of it was any use. I was still Peninha. Peninha, a small feather. Fethry was a character from a comic book, Donald's clumsy cousin. Peninha, a small sorrow. Peninha, a shame... Peninha...There was a house between Vila Teresa and Beira-Rio whose owner, Zé do Bem, raised all sorts of fowl. Peacocks, swans, guinea fowls, geese, pheasants, teals, ducks, chickens...It's gone now. According to Isinha, it's been replaced by a supermarket. Seu Zé do Bem was already old back then...I wonder if anyone remembers him. I need to stop by Tamires's shop...Wellington won't die...How could a person who drank like a fish still be alive? So many people I used to know are gone now...I wipe my hands and mouth with a couple of paper napkins, crumple them and place them on the Colorex plate with the tin spoon, shooing away the mosquitoes obstinately perched on the rim of the empty glass. I ask the server what I owe her and she yells at her coworker, "Coffee with milk and a buttered roll!" I head over to the cash register, take out my leather wallet from my back pocket, pull out a crinkled note, and give it to her. The woman hands me back my change and smiles, "Have a nice day." "You too," I say, stuffing my wallet back in my pocket. I wish the server behind the bar a nice day and she smiles back. I head out into the punishing brightness. I walk halfway across the old bridge. Rio Pomba, an open-air sewer. Opposite, the new bridge. To the left, the tree-filled garden of the Hotel Cataguases; to the right, the tennis courts of Clube do Remo. Does anyone get ringworm anymore? What about swollen lymph nodes? Or scabies? Back in the day, all the kids had swollen lymph nodes—I got it several times, in the groin, the pits—and ringworm—my back was constantly covered in blemishes— while a handful had scabies—I used to tear out tufts of hair, my head an infestation. And then there were the sand draggers. Small boats pushed upstream by long bamboo poles. They'd plunge the shovel into the riverbed and pull up sand. Once full, the hull level with the surface of the water, they'd wade back to the riverbank and unload the sand, which dried in large mounds under the sun. I continue toward city hall. Businesses are opening their doors to another day of work and hosing down the sidewalk to settle the dust. At this hour, Mom would have been at home in the basement, surrounded by patterns and tracing wheels, ready to start working on a new garment. People used to come from all over to order clothes from her. The permanently cluttered rooms exposed our private life. We were a family without walls, which may be what drove us children to get out as fast as we could—first, Lígia...then, João Lúcio, Isinha, Dad, me, Rosana...By the time Mom fell ill, she hadn't made clothes in a long while. Having lost the fight against ready-made apparel, she focused on tailoring and mending. A black dog with silken fur wags his tail in front of city hall. I lumber up the steps, into the building. A security guard, tall and strong, intercepts me. "Can I help you?" he asks gruffly. "Good morning," I say, which takes him by surprise. Puzzled, he says, "Good morning. You'd like to..." "...speak to the mayor," I finish. "Do you have an appointment?" "No...I'm a friend...I've come from São Paulo...I just wanted to say hello..." The security guard scratches his head and leads me to a table with two white phones, a school notebook, and a set of matte acrylic pencil and paper clip holders. "Wait here." He cuts straight across the hall and walks through a side door. I stand and look around at the furniture—two frayed armchairs, a coffee table, a handful of magazines stacked in a basket—and the long, dark-wood staircase that leads to the second floor and the mayor's office. I wait patiently, the silence muddied only by the sound of a woman cackling in the room the security guard has just entered. I slowly make my way to the door, which is ajar, and push it open to find a cramped but spotless break room. The security guard and two women, one younger and the other older, glance at me in surprise. "Good morning," I say, and the security guard gestures, "This is the guy, Michele." Michele must be twenty-odd years old. She's beautiful, with long and soft straight black hair. "So, you're a friend of the mayor's?" The person asking this, with a sneer, is a short, slender woman in shorts, a sleeveless shirt, and open-toe sandals, with white strands poking out from her bouffant cap—no doubt the one with the hearty laugh. "Well," I say, "I knew him when we were both sixteen. Then we grew apart." "Uh-huh," she mumbles, like she's won a bet. "The mayor doesn't see anyone without an appointment," Michele explains, circumspect. "I already told him," says the security guard, as if apologizing to her. "Have you had breakfast, mister?" asks the older woman. "Yeah, I've just come from the bakery by the old bridge." The security guard stuffs a piece of cornbread in his mouth and downs the rest of his coffee. "That's a shame," says the woman, "I guess you can't try Michele's cornbread," she adds, cattily, making her coworker blush. The security guard smothers a laugh. "So, you're a friend of the mayor's, huh…" the older woman insists. "Is he a good mayor?" I ask. "We're small potatoes here—easy to keep in order," she howls. The security guard sets his empty cup on the sink and leaves. "Are you really from here?" she continues. Michele's nails are painted red and her pinkie finger juts in the air as she holds her mug. "I am, but I've been living in São Paulo for years." "Your family's from here, though…" "Yeah… My sister Rosana is a school principal… And my mother was a seamstress… In

Beira-Rio…" "I was born and raised on this side of the river. Matadouro, Pampulha. Ring a bell?" "You bet. I used to ride my bike over there. That's where the city ended. There was nothing at all past that point…" "Michele," she begins, "Can Dona Iara not find him an opening?" "Good God, Dona Ivete! You know that's not how things work around here!" Michele leaves her mug in the sink and storms off. Dona Ivete whispers, mischievous, "The mayor comes in through the back. At around seven, seven thirty…Wait there, ambush him…" I thank her with a smile and say goodbye. She switches on the battery-operated radio, turns on the faucet, and begins to do the dishes, humming. I walk up to Michele, sitting behind her desk. "Any chance I could leave a message for Marcim?" Without a word, she grabs a notepad from her drawer and a pen from the acrylic pencil holder. "Write a note here and I'll give it to Dona Iara. She's the one who can reach the mayor. I'm just the receptionist." I scribble: 'Hello, Marcim. It's Peninha, we knew each other as kids. I wondered if we could get together sometime, catch up. I'll come by again tomorrow.' I fold the piece of paper in two and hand it back to Michele. "If you see him, would you say Peninha was here? That's me, Peninha. Peninha's a nickname. He wouldn't know me by my given name, Oséias. At least, with my nickname…" Michele says, "Yeah, sure." She answers the phone, "Good morning, mayor's office!" I shuffle to the door, say goodbye to the security guard, and head down the stairs. The black dog dawdles up to me, tail wagging. I greet him with excitement, scratch his head, and cross the street. He follows me. I cross Santa Rita Square. The lighted fountain is dry. Trash collects in the basin: leaves, a sneaker, cigarette butts, plastic bottles, beer cans, shards of glass, a toy car, a blue bag filled with trash, a doll's head. Mothers and nannies shepherd children around the playground. I head to the church, and realize the doors are locked. Saddened, I look down at the black dog. He wags his tail. The sun scorches the neglected flower beds. I walk up to an old man. "Good morning." Cagey, he turns to face me. "Do you know why the fountain's dry?" Surprised by my ignorance, he says, "Because of dengue, uai...The mosquitoes..." He keeps walking, his shoulders domed. I sit on a bench and the dog flops down at my feet, rests his head between his front paws, and shuts his eyes. Dad used to bring me here sometimes to eat popcorn and watch the colorful lights dance around. Mom hardly ever left the house, always busy sewing. She mended through Christmas, New Year, Carnival, and all night, the machine's hum right below the floor of the room I shared with João Lúcio. Next door, Rosana had her own bed, while Lígia and Isinha shared a bunk. Mom only let herself take time off in July, when she traveled to the Rodeiro countryside to see her Italian family, whom she missed terribly, and above all, as she never tired of saying, to relive the happiest moments of her life. She became a different person then, sloughing off her stern husk and resurfacing as someone new and almost unrecognizable—fun-loving, chatty, radiant. She loved when the pigs were slaughtered because it took all weekend, from daybreak, when Uncle Paulino stuck a dagger in the barrow's heart, until the following day, when they finished sealing the tins of meat brimming with animal fat. In the endless hustle and bustle—hours passed between laughter and anecdotes—it was as though the world, which was so distant, did not exist. But that time was short-lived. As soon as Rosana became a teenager, she refused to step foot in *those backwoods* and Mom didn't want to leave her alone, so she stopped traveling there. João Lúcio, as a young boy, was the one—A pastor! I can tell from the black clergy shirt. Jeans, flaky Bond attaché case, worn-out shoes. I get up and tap him on the left shoulder. He swivels around, startled. "Father," I say. "Could I have a moment of your time?" Without stopping, he glances down at his watch, and anxiously says, "Of course, my son. Let's walk though, I'm in a hurry." "Father, the church is closed." "For security reasons," he says. "Come back during mass." "But it's urgent." He comes to an impatient stop and eyes the black dog tailing us. "What seems to be the problem, son?" "I'd like to confess, Father." "Now? Can't it wait?" "I don't have much time left, Father…" He comes to a stop a little farther ahead. Hog plums are spattered on the Portuguese pavement. The pastor checks his watch again, unsure of what to do. His cell phone rings. He pulls it out of his pocket, an old, compact model, and says, "Ten minutes, tops." We walk at a clip, in silence. The pastor is much younger than me, with copious black hair and an athletic build. We make our way to a dusty Volkswagen Gol, and he says, "Look, son, I'm not from this parish. I have a meeting to get to, so I can't help you right now. But let me leave you..." He opens the car door and rummages through the mess in the glove compartment. He grabs a yellow scrap of paper, takes a pen from his pocket, and jots something down with the Bond attaché case propped on his leg. "Look, I'm going to leave you a phone number. For Dona Juscelina, the church secretary at São Cristovão, in Taquara Preta. Do you know it? Call her to make an appointment. That way we can speak at leisure. All right? Now, if you'll excuse me, I'm already late. God be with you." He tosses his attaché case in the passenger seat, shuts the door, and drives away, turning right at the corner. I wipe my glasses with the edge of my shirt and read the number—nice handwriting. On the back is a supermarket receipt: wine, toilet paper, deodorant, detergent, eggs, flour, butter. I stuff it in my pants pocket. The black dog had retreated to a corner but now pads toward me assertively, tongue hanging out of his mouth. It's hot. Sweat douses my head, drenching my hat. I cross Santa Rita Square and head down Rua do Pomba, steering clear of Tamires's deli. The places, trees, and houses are the same as when I was a kid—but not the faces, or the cars, or the motorcycles. I'm a frightened ghost barreling into bodies that move restlessly through the past. Dona Júlia was a loyal client. She'd suffocate you in fat arms heavy with perfume. One time, while my mother was upstairs looking for change, Dona Júlia stood in front of me half-naked as she tried on a dress, and my eyes fixed on the unruly hair bristling from her panties. João Lúcio used to keep a dirty magazine under his mattress. Now and then, Dona Magnólia would take Rosana to Clube do Remo to get some sun. She took me with them once, and I saw asses and breasts on the edge of the blue-watered pool that smelled of chlorine. Malu wore a red bikini...The first naked woman I ever saw was Cidinha, on the Island, the red-light district. Six of us boys paid to watch her strip— saggy breasts, blemished skin—I went back across the wood bridge on my own, retching, and was bedridden for three days with a fever and pains...To escape the sun, I enter a bookstore that's actually a stationer, and the black dog lies down at the door in resignation. As I pretend to skim the titles of the few books they have—a row of bestsellers lining a tiny shelf—I hear a familiar voice chatting amicably with the shopkeeper. Her back is to me, and thin white hair sweeps down her shoulders. I edge up to the counter and give her a quick, sidelong glance. Marilda, my first girlfriend! She's buying newspaper for her dog. At least that's what the sign says, Newspaper for Dogs. Wanting to make conversation, I ask, "Pardon, but do your dogs read?" She doesn't recognize me and snaps back, "No, they shit!" I turn red and instinctively step back as she says goodbye to the shopkeeper, slips on her sunglasses, and stomps irritably down the aisle with the bundle of old newspaper and an enormous bag. I muster up the courage to intercept her.

"Marilda, don't you recognize me?" I ask. She stops, hesitates. "Have I changed that much?" I insist. Wanting to be polite, she says, "I'm sorry, but—" "Oséias...Peninha..." I say, a little brusquely. "Goodness! Peninha!" Marilda drops her package, takes off her sunglasses, squares her hands on my shoulders, and studies me with her light-brown eyes, now nestled in wrinkles, "My God...It really is you!" Touched, she takes me in her arms. "I'm so sorry I didn't recognize you." "It's not your fault. I haven't aged well..." "You're much slimmer. Aside from that, you haven't changed one bit." "May I?" I ask, picking up the bundle of newspaper for her. "You're the one who hasn't changed. I recognized you immediately," I say as I search for the black dog who, fickle, has gone elsewhere. She puts her sunglasses back on. We walk a few meters, brushing past people cluttering the sidewalk. "Have you moved back?" she asks, pressing the car key and unlocking her red EcoSport. No, I say. "I'm visiting my sisters." She opens the trunk. "Ah, your sisters..." I place the bundle of newspaper in the back. "What were they called again?" She closes the trunk. "Rosana and Isabela." "That's right! Rosana and Isabela!" We linger for a moment by her car, not knowing what to do. "So you moved back?" "Yeah..." she says, studying the paving stones. Another uncomfortable silence. All of a sudden, she asks, "Are you up to anything now? I've got an idea. Why don't you come over for lunch?" I say nothing, and she interprets my silence as agreement. She presses the key again, locking the car doors, and pulls me by the hand.

"Let's go to the grocery store. I'll cook for you." And we're back on the sidewalk, cluttered with people. "Did you ever get married?" "I did." "And are you still married?" "Divorced." "Oh." Though I can't see her face, I can guess her expression from the sinuousness of her voice. "Kids?" "One." "Boy or girl?" "Boy...I mean, a young man...or rather, a man... twenty-eight this August." "Oh, he's almost the same age as my...Rôney." "Just the one?" "No...I've got a girl too... Sabrina. She's a young woman now. How long has it been since you got divorced? *Are* you divorced? Or did you just separate?" "No, no, we got divorced." "So how long?" "Eight years, give or take." "I see. I bet you immediately found a new squeeze," she presses, letting out a forced laugh, "Hahahaahahaha." "No...Nobody wants an old lemon like me..." It's a good joke, I think—lemon, squeeze—but Marilda either doesn't get it or doesn't like it. She grows quiet, pensive. We reach the grocery store, also cluttered with people. She takes off her sunglasses, tells me to fetch a cart, and starts wandering down the aisles. "How do you feel about spaghetti?" she asks as she stares at the pasta display rack. "It's all right, isn't it? I make a killer shrimp pasta." She grabs a pack of Italian spaghetti—"the trouble is, it's hard to find decent shrimp in Cataguases"—and three cans of peeled tomato. "Hmm...I've got olive oil, garlic, and onion at home. Let's keep going. Excuse me, mister, but have you got shrimp? You do?! Where? Let's go see if it's any good." In the frozen food section, "What do you think? A bit small, aren't they? We'll make it work, though." She tosses the bag of shrimp in the cart. "I think that's it! Anyway, do you come to Cataguases often?" "It's been almost…" "Oh, the wine! You drink wine, don't you? Wonderful! I adore wine. I've got to be careful, though. If you let me at it… It's just so glorious. That feeling of… of… I don't know… of… you know… languor! That's it! Languor. Wine… Wine… Wine… Mister, excuse me, would you point me to the wine? Ah, thank you! Well, Peninha… Oséias… It feels weird to call you Peninha. But I can't get used to the idea of calling you Oséias either. Anyway, what I mean is, what kind of wine do you drink?" "Whatever's good." "Hahahahaaha! Whatever's good! Well, let's see… I like dry wine myself. Not Brazilian though! I always get a splitting headache from Brazilian wine! Christ Almighty, it's like death. Chilean… Hmm… I'm not sure… I don't recognize any of these names… Help me out, will you, Peninha… Oséias! Are you familiar with any of these?" I pretend to study the shelves. I grab a bottle, scrutinize the label. She takes it from me—"Nope, no Carmenère for me, thank you, too acidic"—and hands the bottle back for me to put back on the shelf. She continues to study the selection. "Aha, here we go! Nothing like some good old Portuguese wine, don't you think?" She flashes me a bottle of Monte Velho. I approve, with the air of a connoisseur. "It's excellent. And the price is reasonable. Grab four bottles, will you?" she orders, and charges on, steered by the shopping cart. We get in line at the cash register. "Soon we'll be using the priority lane, isn't that right?" she asks with a chuckle. "Not you, Marilda, no one will buy it. It's like you don't age...If it weren't for the white hair..." Pensive, she says, "Ah, the white hair..." I take the groceries out of the cart and place them on the conveyer belt. The cashier absently scans each item while chatting with her coworker in the next lane. "...A fever... Almost forty degrees! I'll call daycare again in a second. The doctor says it's viral. Everything's viral here...Will that be all, ma'am?" Marilda nods. I stuff my hand in my back pocket, but she immediately stops me, "No, no, it's on me. I insist. It's my pleasure." Marilda riffles through her enormous purse for her wallet and pulls out a credit card. She sticks it in the machine and taps in her PIN. Taking the receipt, she slides it into the same compartment as her money, puts away her credit card, and walks away. A skinny teenager hands me four plastic bags. On the sidewalk, Marilda puts on her sunglasses and grumbles, "It's true." "What is?" I ask. "These days, everything's viral." "Oh," I mumble. I pick up on our earlier conversation. "And when did you move back?" "No, first tell me why you never met someone else. Was it out of fear of commitment?" "No...It just didn't work out. After being married all those years..." "How many?" "Twenty-two." "Twenty-two, wow. Did you get along all right?" "As well as we could..." "Why split up after twenty-two years?" "The truth is, our marriage ended long before." "What do you mean?" "After a while, you start to sort of settle...You don't go out anymore...Then you stop...You stop having sex...You stop sharing a bed..."

"True," she said, with a sigh. "Did you fight a lot, though?" "Not me. But Marília..." "Marília?! Her name's Marília?" "That's right." "Ha! It's nearly identical to mine..." "I'd never noticed..." She stops and unlocks the car, teasing, "I got you hooked. Admit it, you never got over me... Hahahahaha... You had to go and marry someone with practically the same name..." She opens the trunk and I set the grocery bags next to the bundle of old newspaper, but Marilda rearranges everything before closing the trunk. We get in. She switches on the AC, connects her cell phone to the stereo, and turns on the engine. A song I don't recognize floods the car. "So, this Marília character... Was she... Is she... pretty?" she asks. But before I can answer, the *Star Wars* theme song starts playing on her cell phone, and Marilda smiles, "Rôney, my boy..." She unplugs the device and picks up. "Hi sweetie!... Yeah. I got some newspaper, then I went to the grocery store... Just a couple of things we needed... No, I'm headed back... Late evening? All right... No, honey, I'm going to stay... Love you." Marilda's smile has been wiped from her face. She says, stone-faced, "That was Rôney, my son," and once again connects her cell phone to the stereo. "Anyway, what were we talking about?" "Were you married long?" "Almost twenty years." "How old's your son?" "Rôney? Twenty-five." "So you've been back for five years?" "No, three. After my husband and I separated, I moved to Salvador, but that didn't work out..." "Salvador? Why Salvador?" "Now that's a long story," she says in a mournful tone, and changes the subject. "How long has it been since you last visited Cataguases?" "About nineteen years." "Nineteen years?! Wow! What kept you away?" I take a deep breath. "It's a long story..." I answer. "Seems we've got plenty to talk about, haven't we?" she says, once again relaxing as she drives down an empty avenue that appears to lead outside the city, the two of us enveloped by the sounds of a mellow tune I can't identify. "Where are we going?" "Don't worry, I promise I'm not kidnapping you," she says with a laugh. Before long, a few houses pop up after a bend in the road. "Where are we?" I ask. "Bela Vista." "Bela Vista?" "Formerly known as BNH." "Right..." "I bought some land here when I was still living in Bahia. As an investment... I never thought I'd use it. Then, all of a sudden... You'll see, it isn't even finished yet." She presses a button on the remote, and a heavy gate sluggishly draws open at the end of the street. "Here we are!" Marilda parks her car in the garage, the gate hums shut, and frantic yaps torment what little remains of the morning. "My little shitbags," she says incisively, and asks me to grab the groceries from the trunk. I reach for the bundle of newspaper and find that I'm surrounded by two tiny dogs snuffling at my pant leg. They snarl and growl, yowl and tremble, mean and territorial. "Let them sniff you. They'll quiet down in a second," Marilda says. And then, softly, in a baby voice, "Mommy's back... This gentleman here is Mommy's friend. Be nice now. He's just helping Mommy out." I am escorted by the bowwow of the two dogs as I round the house behind Marilda and set the package on the floor of a veranda filthy with shit and piss. I feel queasy. In the vast, meticulously turfed backyard are a spattering of fruit trees—lime, jaboticaba, papaya—a grill, and a table with four white chairs. I return to the car with the crazed duo on my tail, grab the grocery bags, and circle back to the veranda. Marilda has cleaned the poop and is now washing the pissed-up floor, jetting water from a rubber hose. "Put it on the kitchen table, will you?" she says, pointing at the door. The dogs snarl and growl, yowl and tremble, bark and yelp. The kitchen is bright and spacious. I place the bags on the table. She yells, "Go on into the dining room, grab a bucket from the shelf, fill it with ice, and stick the wine in it to chill." I walk through the door into a hallway, and falter over an ashen wool rug that ends in a wide room dimmed by thick curtains hanging shut. In the center of the room, a dining table of solid dark wood dressed in a bright white tablecloth with floral embroidery sits on another ashen rug—this one shaggy. On the table are three tin candlesticks arranged by size. Framed photographs of Marilda at different times in her life, with and without her children, are displayed around the room. I spot the bucket on a shelf of the same style as the dining table, next to various knickknacks standing on a swath of white lace fabric. Back in the kitchen, I take three ice trays from the freezer, fill the bucket, insert a bottle of wine, and leave it in the sink. Marilda pops back in. "I love these little guys. But boy are they hard work!" she says with affection as she glances over at the now-calmer dogs. She takes the ice bucket, sets it on the table, pulls out the cans of peeled tomatoes and the bag of shrimp and leaves them in the sink. She puts the three remaining bottles of wine in the fridge. She balls up the grocery bags and stuffs them in a cloth casing with the words Puxa Saco embroidered in red. "Okay. Now let me introduce you to the cutest little duo in the world," she says, picking up the dog with a pink ribbon on each ear. "This one's Angelina. Angelina Jolie. Go on, give her a little scratch." I reach anxiously for the dog. Just as I'm about to touch her, she snarls, and I gently draw back. Marilda laughs. "She doesn't bite, she's just testy." Wanting to be congenial, I ask, "What breed are they?" Marilda sets Angelina Jolie back down on the floor, picks up the boy and says, "Lhasa apso. They're excellent companions!" She rocks the dog as though he were a baby and explains, "This one's Brad, Brad Pitt. Aren't they just darling?" She sets Brad Pitt down again. "Oh dear, where've I left my purse? My cell phone's ringing!" she exclaims and runs off. "Gosh! Five missed calls. Make yourself comfortable, I'll be right back." Brad Pitt turns to face me and begins yawping without further ado. Angelina Jolie, who had left with Marilda, comes back and joins him in barking at me, already a touch hoarse. I stand stock-still, nauseated by the funk that lingers in the air. Ten to noon, reads the white wall clock. The second hand advances furiously. The dogs finally quiet down. I hear Marilda purring on the phone. Disconnected words, loose like soap bubbles: "worse," "do," "nobody," "everything," "tired." Birds twitter in the backyard. João Lúcio would know what they're called. Even though Dad had been born in the countryside and only moved away a married man, he could never tell a thrush from a seedeater. Mom used to say that he did know the difference but pretended otherwise so that people wouldn't peg him for a hayseed. João Lúcio had liked old things ever since he was a kid, and it pained him to live in the present. He loved food cooked over a woodstove, places without electricity, going to sleep early and rising before dawn, life under the thumb of daybreak and nightfall. So much so that—"I'm so sorry, Peninha, Oséias… Goodness, I've got no idea what to call you!" Marilda bemoans, her eyes moist. "Is everything all right?" I ask. She answers in a fluster, "Of course, why do you ask?" "No reason," I say. "Okay. Let's hop to it." She claps as though to shoo away a negative thought. She grabs a corkscrew, a foil cutter, and a wine pourer from the cupboard, places them on the table, and says, "Open the bottle. I'll take care of the rest." She heads down the hall and returns with two glasses. The dogs circle us, discombobulated by the havoc. I pour some wine and hand a glass to Marilda, who sets a pasta pot filled with water on the stove top. She theatrically swishes the wine, sniffs it, and then takes a sip. "Exquisite," she proclaims. "And it'll be even better once it's had time to breathe." I pour some more wine in both our glasses. "To us," she toasts, looking me square in the eyes. "To us!" I echo. After a long sip, she says, "Let me change into something cooler, more appropriate." Marilda gives me her hand, damp, cold, pulsing. "But, first..." She tugs me behind her. We cross the dining room into another room that is equally large, equally somber, then stop in front of a dark but modern piece of furniture that suggests a vintage dresser. "There are about a thousand CDs in here...Music's my passion. Remember? Choose something," she says, pulling open an enormous drawer. "They're organized by country, except for Brazil, the U.S., and England, which are organized by genre. For example..." She pulls open another drawer. "Here, we've got rock, pop, et cetera." And another, "And here we've got Asia—China, India, Japan, Middle Eastern music, et cetera. Got it? All right. Now find something cool for us to listen to." She adds, proudly, "There are speakers all around the house." Angelina Jolie follows her mistress to the bedroom, while Brad Pitt keeps watch from the sofa. I wipe my glasses with the edge of my shirt. I open a drawer and read the spines at random. I become bored after the first few rows. But I know Marilda. She'll ask why I've chosen one CD over another...I study the spines and once again lose focus. I persist. Telenovela soundtracks...Ah, here's something: *Estúpido Cúpido*— Nacional. It's from back in our day. Now, how do I get this thingamabob to work? I pick up the remote. Switch it on. A light shines green. I manually open the tray, place the CD inside, and close it. No sound. I press a few buttons. Nothing. I give up. I sit in the armchair. The last time I saw Marilda she was about to move up north, to Acre. Rio Branco. She'd been offered a job at Banco do Brasil. We were no longer seeing each other. She threw a going-away party, and I was invited. She drank too much and left the party before it had ended. The last thing she said to me was, What about you, Peninha? Which I took to mean, My life's on track, but *What about you, Peninha?* I was eighteen and she was nineteen. We'd been together for two years. Until she got it into her head that she needed to get out of Cataguases. She studied day in, day out for her public service exam. Our relationship cooled. We fell out of touch. Here comes Angelina, growling in anticipation of Marilda's return. Brad Pitt gets up and begins to harass me too. Marilda has changed out of faded, ripped jeans, a billowing white shirt, and sneakers into a light, patterned dress and sandals. A clip fastens her sparse white hair. "Have you picked something for us?" "You look lovely!" I say. She smiles, flattered. "I put on a CD but there's no sound," I confess in dismay. She takes the remote control and Wilson Miranda starts screaming: "Alguém é sempre bobo de alguém / Se amor não há entre os dois." She blushes and turns down the volume. I stare in rapture at the fuzz on her neck. My face becomes flushed. "Where'd you find this album?! It's so corny! Put something else on, now." And as she crosses the dining room with Angelina Jolie shimmying behind her, she shouts, "Put on something more...more, like...contemporary...I just hate nostalgia!" I take out the CD. My fingers idly rake through various names. "The Cranberries?!" I yell. Marilda yells back, "Sure!" I walk back into the kitchen to Dolores O'Riordan's singing. Marilda sports a beige apron with a map of Italy and various types of regional pastas. Her glass is empty. I refill it. She dices an onion. "Marilda, could you point me to the restroom?" She stops, says, "There's one that way," and gestures at the hall with her knife. I walk into the bathroom. The whiteness of the tiles lining the wall and floor is blinding. I lift the toilet cover, pee, flush, wash my hands, head back to the kitchen. Marilda is dicing garlic. She sees me and says, "Grab a saucepan for me, will you? In the cupboard. Not that one... The other one." She sets the pan on a burner and slops in a generous amount of olive oil. "The secret is low heat," she explains and takes a long swig of wine. "What does your wife... or rather ex-wife... Marília... do?" she asks. "I don't know what she's up to now, but she's dabbled in a bunch of different things. When we split up, she was a partner at an event-planning company that specialized in children's birthday parties." "Wow, how unusual!" "What about you, Marilda?" "What about me?" she dumps some onion into the pan. "What do you want to know?" she insists, amused. "Everything," I say. "Everything?" she shoots back, cheekily. "Yes, everything," I insist. "Hmm... Where should I start?" "At the beginning," I tease. She slides the garlic into the pan with the onion and stirs both with a large wooden spoon. "Pass me that pepper grinder, will you? Thanks. All right. So, I applied to work at Banco do Brasil. You remember that, don't you? And I was posted in Acre. I asked to be relocated, I wanted to come back to Minas, or as close as I could get to Minas..." She tears open the bag of shrimp and empties it in the saucepan. She adds black pepper and a pinch of salt. "I was able to get transferred to Barreiras, in Bahia. Next stop, Minas Gerais. Except..." Another long swill of wine. "What happened in Bahia?" I ask. Marilda grabs the cans of peeled tomato, opens them, and dumps the sauce into the pan. "The trick to seasoning this..." She heads to the cupboard, takes out a white sugar bowl, and sprinkles sugar into the sauce with a small teaspoon. "Cuts the acidity," she explains. "Well... in Bahia... Barreiras was growing fast. Out-of-staters were setting up soybean plantations in the Cerrado... That's where I met my husband, a Gaúcho. There were tons of southerners up there. Tall and handsome, green eyes and brown hair. A prince," she concludes, with a touch of sarcasm. "All right, now we wait for the water to boil." "Then what happened?" "Oséias, my glass is empty!" she laughs. The *Star Wars* theme song plays and startles Marilda, who reaches for her cell phone. "Just a minute," she says, heading out to the veranda. Dolores O'Riordan sings, "There was a game we used to play." A pleasant smell takes hold of the kitchen. I edge up to the stove and watch the red sauce bubble like lava in a volcano. My head, light, seems to want to sever itself from the rest of my body, slow and bone-weary. Brad Pitt snores under the table. Angelina Jolie monitors the door, alert. The water comes to a boil. Time evaporates. Marilda returns, her face puckered. She dabs sauce onto the back of her left hand with a wooden spoon, tastes it. "Is there more wine?" she asks, with a touch of impatience. I show her the empty bottle. "Well, open another!" she orders. I head to the fridge for another bottle of wine, remove the foil, uncork it, insert the wine pourer, fill Marilda's glass and then mine, and set the bottle in the ice bucket. "And your parents?" I ask. She dumps spaghetti in the boiling water and sighs. "Dad died more than ten years ago. Mom lives in Betim with Paco, my brother. Do you remember him?" "I do... Works for Fiat, right?" "Right." "My mom and dad passed away years ago... It's funny, isn't it? That feeling of being an orphan..." "Yeah..." she mumbles, preoccupied, as she pries loose the strands of spaghetti. "Time is ticking out," Dolores O'Riordan reminds us. There is a long silence, then Marilda whispers, "Bastard broke two of my ribs." "Huh?! Who?" I ask, confused. "Prince charming..." "Oh," I mutter, taken aback. "Do you mind if we eat here, in the kitchen?" she asks, arranging a couple of bamboo placemats on the table. "Do you think you might ever move back, Peninha?" she asks, placing a pair of small bowls over two plates. "No... It wouldn't make any sense..." I answer. "Do you think you'll remarry?" she asks, folding the cloth napkins. "No... That wouldn't make much sense either," I answer. "Well damn, nothing seems to make sense to you, does it!" she says, exasperated. I stand there in silence as Marilda sets a pair of forks and spoons beside each plate. Sore, she asks again, "Does anything make sense to you?" She takes a long swig of wine. She takes the strainer out of the pasta pot and holds it under the faucet, beneath a stream of cold water. She scoops spaghetti and sauce into the two bowls and then puts them on the plates. She washes her hands and takes off her apron, hanging it on a hook by the oven, and sits down. The music has stopped. She tops up the glasses with wine and gives a half-hearted toast, "To life!" We dig in. "The food's delicious, Marilda. Not just delicious, exquisite!" She smiles sadly and asks, "Do you still find me attractive?" I look up at her light-brown eyes. "Marilda, you're a very attractive woman. Like I said, I don't think anyone would guess your real age. And if you were to dye your hair, well…" "Again with the hair!" "I'm sorry, Marilda," I say, stuffing a heaping forkful of spaghetti in my mouth. She polishes off her plate. "Peninha, why did we split up, huh?" "You wanted to get out of here, remember?" "And you didn't?" "I think I did… I just didn't have the initiative… You sort of egged me on without realizing." "Do you think we did the right thing?" I remain quiet. "Sometimes I think… Sometimes I feel like we go round and round… But we're still just stuck in place. It's all so strange…" she says. We fall silent. The only sound is of the cutlery scraping the ceramic. There is still a small amount of spaghetti on my plate but I can't eat any more. I wipe my mouth with the napkin. Marilda asks, "Did you not enjoy the food?" "I did… It's just that… lately… I've been unwell… Everything upsets my stomach…" I explain. She sets down her cutlery too. "Sometimes I think life is all about regret…" she says, abruptly rising to collect the plates, the forks, the spoons, the napkins. I get up to help her and she stops me. "No, no, that's all right. I'll stick it all in the dishwasher later. Some more wine?" "I'm good, thanks," I say, my head aching. "How about a cup of coffee?" "Some coffee would go down nicely." She grabs a box from the cupboard and opens it. "Strong or aromatic?" she asks, showing me various capsules of extravagant flavors. "Something strong, I think." "Ristretto?" "Sure," I answer. She starts the machine, takes me by the hand and guides me to the living room. "Sit down, I'll be right back." Angelina Jolie pads behind Marilda. Brad Pitt plops down next to me on the sofa, diligent. The heavy drawn curtains make the room heel like a moored boat. Marilda returns and sets her glass of wine, which is once again full, on the coffee table. She then reappears holding a silver tray with a demitasse of coffee, a small spoon, and two small packets— one sugar, the other artificial sweetener—on a white cloth, and places it next to the glass of wine. She sits in the armchair opposite me, Angelina Jolie splayed at her feet. I pick up the cup of coffee, add sweetener, stir. "Migraines," she says. "Huh?" "Migraines, I get migraines. Hence the curtains…" "Oh!" She takes a long swill of wine, says, "He used to…the…the bastard used to beat me! The scumbag. I did everything for him, everything…But he still cheated on me…He went around with other women…Drank… Did cocaine…Hit me in front of the kids…And then he'd come crying and apologize to the high heavens. I believed him at first. I thought he could change…Then, I started counting the days, like I was serving time." I don't know what to say. "I'm so sorry," I mutter, but I don't think she hears me. "When Rôney turned eighteen, his dad agreed to let him study in Salvador. I convinced him to let Sabrina attend high school there too. Meanwhile, I secretly filed for retirement at the bank. The moment it was approved, I climbed into my car and drove away. I didn't look back. I didn't say goodbye to anyone. I left everything behind—my house, my furniture, my clothes, everything. He tried to make things right with me, in Salvador. I filed a restraining order. I don't know why I'm telling you all of this..." I'm still holding the cup of coffee in my hand, unsure of whether I should say anything. She takes a long swill of wine. Gets up and makes her way to a large abstract painting hanging on the wall. "Rôney—that's his name, right? What does he do?" I ask. "He's a lawyer. He's trying to set himself up here. But it's not easy. He hates the city... The people... He never got over the divorce..." "And..." "Sabrina? She's at school in Viçosa for environmental engineering." "Uh-huh..." Her eyes are red and her words, bloated, squeeze past her lips. "Marília... Was she... Was she... the woman of your dreams?" she asks dolefully. "She was a good person," I say. Marilda pauses behind me. "The worst part is I don't get to regret marrying the bastard. Because that would mean rejecting my kids." She circles back, shoves Brad Pitt out of the way, and sits beside me on the sofa. She grabs my right hand and presses it to her breast. "Firmer than most young women out there, don't you think?" I recoil, embarrassed. She downs the rest of her wine. "You know what, Peninha?

You could stay in Cataguases. Just imagine. We get back together, live here, in this house...We could be happy—for however long we have left. Say...Twenty years? Who cares! Twenty years is a long time. We may not be able to change the past, but we can determine the future. Don't you think?" The *Star Wars* theme song rings out. Marilda glances at her cell phone. "I gave birth to a monster, Peninha, an actual monster! I have a spy living under my own roof. A spy that came out of my own body...Look at my nails...I'm not allowed to paint them...My hair...Do you think I like wearing it white? I'm not allowed any makeup...Or earrings, bracelets, necklaces...I may as well be a nun! I left home to get away from a jealous husband... But my son's just like him...Maybe even worse..." The *Star Wars* theme song continues to play. "You know what I want to do right now? I want to sleep with you...I'm single...I'm fifty-five years old...Independent...But my son won't stop calling me...He's suspicious of everything...He can tell I have someone over...He'll turn up here soon enough. You'll see..." I stand, say, "Let's make sure that doesn't happen, Marilda." She remains seated. "I don't want to get you into any more trouble," I insist. The dogs are agitated; they snarl and growl, yowl and tremble. She gets up, wraps her arms around me, whispers, "I thought things would be different, Peninha...So different..." and her lips reach for mine. I wriggle free and thank Marilda for lunch. She shushes the dogs, who immediately fall quiet, and opens the door in silence. The light blinds me. My feet follow

Marilda's unsteady steps. "I'm a pale, white shadow, Oséias," she says as she throws open the door. "Bye, Marilda," I say, unable to meet her eyes. I rush down the sidewalk, the sun beating down on my head. Shit! I forgot my hat! I stop and turn to check if Marilda is still there, but she's disappeared behind the wall. What now? I'll have to buy a a new one. I can't go around without it. Another pointless expense... When had I taken it off? I think it must have been in the kitchen, right when we arrived. Or had I left it in the car? Maybe it was in the car. Or when I took the groceries out of the trunk. Those nutty dogs. It's insane! Everybody bosses her around. Her ex-husband, her son, her dogs. The stench permeates everything. And the filth caked on the veranda. She's terrified of this Rôney character... Angelina Jolie and Brad Pitt... What a joke! No, we can't determine our futures, Marilda. The future is only a projection of the past. We are what we once were. We make our own path. We design our own course. When we choose one direction over another, we set the boundaries of what will come later. Her breasts... She's still attractive... Though she's let herself go... It's hot. Sweat pours down my armpits, drenching my back. My skin smarts. Would things have turned out better if we'd gotten married? Different, sure, but better? Can anyone know? No one knows. What I'd give to start from the beginning, from scratch. And still... Still, I haven't got long left... Jesus, I'm going to die and never... It isn't my body they'll bury—what is a body?—but everything I once was, my memories, the people who live inside me

and who I can visit by closing my eyes. They'll disappear
with me forever, as if they'd never existed... Just like
Lígia... How many people still remember Lígia? Yesterday,
a body; today, a name; tomorrow, less than... I need some
water, I feel dizzy. I pass roads that lead to fallow plots of
land, arid brush, and see no one except for a rangy horse
gazing out at the afternoon with downcast eyes. I glimpse
Estação Square in the distance, the anarchy of the city.
Women at bus stops freshen themselves with makeshift
fans, their foreheads misted and their bodies slack. Heat
ripples up from the paving stones, scalding my legs and
warping the landscape. I walk into a diner, order a bottle
of water, unscrew the lid, drink half of it in a single swig. I
ask how much I owe, stuff my hand in my back pocket,
pull out my wallet, glimpse a photograph of Nico, pay and
leave, hands trembling, body careening, feet sinking into
the churning waters of the Rodeiro marshes, my hips brace
against a stand chock-full of underwear, "Buy two, get one
free!" yells a young guy, and I almost knock him over,
apologize, keep on walking, as though asleep, bumping
into people and things, ignored by some and cursed by
others, until I find myself on Avenida Astolfo Dutra, where
I collapse onto a concrete bench under the shade of a
couple of oiti trees. I empty the rest of the water over my
head. Wipe my glasses with the edge of my shirt. The
digital clock reads 16:27. 31°C. I grab my wallet from my
pocket, slip out the photograph of Nico. He must be
around nine years old here. Jet-black hair, big blue eyes,

anxious to get back to playing. I wonder who took that photo. Was it me? Marília? Marília ran a gift store on Rua Orfanato at the time, but she felt restless and was considering a change of career—she was on the hunt for new opportunities, as she liked to say. She later ended up working as a manager for a company that organized parties and events, and then founded her own event-planning business specializing in children's birthday parties. I slide the photo into my wallet, which I stuff in my back pocket. Was Marília already cheating on me then? Probably. You moron, she'd spat, rolling her Rs and drawling her Os, an accent she slipped into when nervous. It's all your fault anyway. You leave me at home on my own all week. Then when you're here, all you do is bitch and moan, I'm tired, I'd rather stay home. You're constantly bitter and unhappy. Nothing's ever good enough. No one can live like this, in the gloom. People need light, joy, fun. At first, I was overwhelmed with shame and devotion—I bent over backward trying to please you. I even made you pierogis, your favorite. But your apathy got under my skin, so I cheated on you out of spite. As payback for marrying a man too goddamn dumb to see what's going on right under his nose. At first she'd tried to disparage me. She'd feigned jealousy and accused me of entertaining lovers in every city I went to. She made up plots, dreamed up intrigue. Weekends were hell. But all her stories—and she knew this—got her nowhere, because I had neither the time, the occasion, nor the

desire to add to an already colossal mess. Our fights and
quarrels and misunderstandings were so persistent I decided
to throw myself into work. Coming home to São Paulo on
Fridays started to feel like a burden. One sweltering
afternoon just like this one—a Saturday in December, the
twelfth—Marília asked me to take her to a motel,
something we had never done before. Though I didn't
understand why, I figured it might be a good idea. A new
beginning. Christmas was around the corner. We could
make peace with one another and do away with the
constant fights, which were exhausting and pointless on top
of being bad for Nicolau, who was becoming increasingly
aloof and aggressive. We climbed into the car and chose a
random, discreet, and clean-looking motel on Avenida
Sapopemba. I inspected the room—huge TV, jacuzzi,
enormous bed, chandelier. Marília said, Sit down, Oséias,
we have a lot to talk about. Calm and firm, her eyes
averted, she confessed her infidelity to me. She'd been
seeing the same man for five years, she said. They were in
love and had finally decided to separate from their
respective spouses—that's the word she used, stammering,
after a short pause, *spouses*—and get married. I watched
Marília's reflection in the various mirrors hung around the
room. It was as if she—unreal—were performing onstage or
in a movie, reciting words that had been written for her by
someone else, and as if we—she and I—were enacting the
end of a marriage that wasn't ours but instead belonged to
some other couple. Then she got up and grabbed her bag. I

asked in shock, Why did you bring me here, Marília? And she said, Because I didn't know how you'd take it. Before she left, slamming the door behind her, she said, Your stuff's in the trunk of the car. Please don't step foot in the house ever again. I fell back on the bed, exhausted, and slept without dreaming. I awoke several hours later, disoriented. After settling up, I climbed into the car and drove through the night on Raposo Tavares highway until I couldn't keep my eyes open anymore. I pulled into the parking lot of a gas station. Sunday awakened me with rain pitter-pattering on the windshield. I was somewhere near Ourinhos. All I had was a suitcase of dirty laundry and a cardboard box filled with clean clothes and a few personal effects, grabbed in a hurry. We saw each other in person only once after, the day we signed our divorce papers. She looked a little puzzled, almost regretful . . . I got nothing but the car I used for work. I handed over the apartment, our only joint asset. I never saw Marília or Nicolau again. He never tried to contact me and I never tried to contact him. We weren't on good terms. Neither were he and Marília, for that matter. He was almost twenty and still hadn't finished high school. He spent his time cooped up at home, on the computer, chain-smoking, probably doing drugs. Sometimes he disappeared for a whole week and then came home covered in filth. No matter how much we pressed him, he refused to explain his sudden disappearances. I'd spend days on the road, working, then come home to that nightmare. At first when I scolded him, he would hang his head low and stick his tail between his legs. But as he bulked up, he began to stand up to me. One time he went so far as to push me. Another, he raised his fist and only held back because I turned away from him. Things went downhill after that. We grew apart. By the time Marília and I separated, I hardly knew what he did with his time, only that he alternated between locking himself up in his fetid room— pizza boxes and Coke bottles strewn across the floor—and going out into the world. What had happened to the boy? We'd had such high hopes. We used to spend whole nights listing the various professions he'd be able to choose from, fantasizing about the happy moments we would have together once he grew up...Nicolau...Niquim...Nico... For what? My bladder hurts. I get up. I cross the avenue and walk along the footpath, knocking into people who sweat and pant. The sun burns my bald spot. I've got to buy a hat. I walk into the same diner I'd gone to the day before, on Rua da Estação, and start toward the bathroom when the young man behind the counter intercepts me, "Where are you going?" "Bathroom," I answer. "You've got to buy something first," he says. "This isn't a public restroom," he adds, embarrassed. I'm neither hungry nor thirsty. I scan the pastry display—sfiha, pão de queijo, empanada, coxinha, kibbe, rissole, croquette, sausage rolls...I feel queasy. "Juice and a...pastel...Have you got pastels?" "We fry them on the spot." "All right, a juice and a pastel." "What kind of juice?" he asks. "Doesn't matter...How about...that red one over there?" "And the pastel? Meat or

cheese?" "Cheese...I'll have cheese." I rush to the fetid
bathroom and try to keep my sneakers from touching the
yellow puddle that oozes along the rutted floor. I hold my
breath and empty my bladder. Not a single drop of water
trickles from the faucet in the small, grimy sink. I sit at a
table. The deafening fans in the four corners of the diner
circulate the muggy air. By the door, a man with a half-full
tulip glass of beer, the same one as the day before, is
entranced by the movement on the street. The server
hands me a very thin plastic cup and a paper plate that
holds a pastel sticky with grease. I take a sip of the juice,
which is sweet, watery, and so cold I feel it scrape down my
throat. I hold the pastel with my fingers wrapped in
napkins, and bite one of the corners. The steam burns my
lips. Fuck! The lone man turns and greets me, solemn. He
takes another sip of his beer, which I assume is now warm,
and carries on watching the monotonous parade of cars and
hurried people. I bite the opposite end of the pastel and am
met with a piece of bland, rubbery cheese. I take another
sip of my sugary beverage. Mosquitoes buzz round and
round, then land on the thick and greasy sheet of
semitransparent plastic that sits over the checkered
tablecloth. Marilda...Marília... She's right. I'd never
noticed the resemblance...Kindred names...Marília is
taller, stronger—though both are bossy, dogged, willful.
Dr. Alper said, It varies from patient to patient. The disease
evolves depending on the energy you're willing to put into
fighting it. The psychological burden is considerable and

should not be discounted. I leave half a pastel. I collect the paper plate, plastic cup, and dirty napkins, then throw them in the trash. I ask what I owe him, pull my worn leather wallet from my back pocket and take out a bill. He goes to the cash register and hands me back a few coins. I leave the diner. Sweat runs down my forehead, face, stomach. I amble aimlessly in the shade of marquees and gazebos. After we separated, I lost all interest in my job. The head office called me, warned me, took my circumstances into consideration, made allowances, and then, two years later, they let me go. They tried to make it look like I hadn't been fired. Like it had been an… honorable…discharge…They threw a small party on a Friday after work. The sales director gave a speech praising my dedication and honesty, and gifted me a watch with my name engraved, incorrectly, on the back— Oséias with a zee—and a check for four months' salary. My colleagues greeted me with indifference, and a half hour later I was sighing on my own in the boardinghouse room where I still lived, near the Minhocão. I withdrew the remainder of my pension fund, most of which had been sunk into the apartment renovation, and slowly lived off that money as I wore through two pairs of shoes going from door to door in search of work—but who wants to hire a bitter, crabby, and fussy old man? Can I still catch Marcim at this hour? I quicken my pace, legs burning. I need to buy a hat ASAP, while shops are still open. I wonder where I can find something like that. Bakery, bank, stationery, fuel reseller, boteco, bank, diner, ice cream parlor, city hall! Spotting me in the distance, the black dog immediately wags its tail. He approaches me, gently sniffs my hand. "You again! Left me high and dry, didn't you, you bastard!" I say without bitterness. The dog seems happy to see me, and follows me up the steps of city hall. He sits restless in a corner as I shuffle up to the big-bellied security guard. "Good afternoon." "Good afternoon." "I'd like to speak to the mayor, please, Marcim Fonseca." "Do you have an appointment?" "No, I'm a friend...A childhood friend..." Solicitous, he takes me to the receptionist. "Valéria, this gentleman here would like to speak to the mayor." The guard circles back to the entrance, confident of having fulfilled his duty. "How can I help you?" she asks, perfect teeth drawing an earnest smile. "Thank you, Valéria. I'm a friend of Marcim's—the mayor, Marcim Fonseca—and I'd like to speak with him. Just a quick chat." "Personal business, then?" "Oh yes. Personal business, all right, we're childhood friends...He used to know me, or rather, he knows me by the name Peninha... Because of my... build... Back in the day... I mean... I was like this back then too, skinny and..." "Mr. Peninha, is it? Let me have a word with his secretary, Dona Iara. I'm just the receptionist, there's not much I can do to help... But I'll have a word with her, leave it to me." "Is he... Is the mayor around?" "I couldn't say. But write your name down here, yes, right here, and I'll make sure to pass it on to Dona Iara." "Thank you very much, Valéria...I left a note for him this morning...with your colleague...Michele, is that right? She probably gave it to him…" "I see, okay. As you've done that already, you'll have to sit tight until he calls. He makes a point of responding to every…constituent." "So he'll call?" I ask, not so much ironic as resigned. "Definitely," Valéria confirms, with confidence. I draw back and hear footsteps clipping down the dark-wood staircase that leads to the mayor's office. The features of the older of the two men remind me of Nem Ladeira, a classmate from Colégio Cataguases. The men materialize before me, then vanish down a hallway to the side. I circle back to the receptionist's desk and wait for her to finish her call. "Valéria, the gentleman who left just now, who is he?" "Dr. Domingos Ladeira? Oh, he's a service provider." "What sort of services does he provide?" "Waste management." "Oh…And is he a doctor?" "When you're poor like us, all rich men are doctors," she says, disarmingly. I thank her. "Happy to be of service, Mr. Peninha," Valéria responds. I leave the building, and the stray cheerfully gets up to follow me. I cross Rui Barbosa Square—what time is it now? The streetlamps switch on. Rows of cars honk frantically, their racket muffled by the trilling of thousands of sparrows swooping back into the trees, where they perch on branches to wait out the long night. Nem Ladeira…Doctor… Service provider…Waste management…Through all three years of high school, Nem Ladeira sat at the desk next to mine so he could cheat on tests. He knew nothing and never studied, but his father was Dr. Ladeira, acting pediatrician for most of the children in town—though his real passion was drinking cachaça and eating mocotó on the weekends in botecos on the outskirts of town. When he drank, he turned bell-pepper red and indulged in samba circles. Nem was the teacher's pet because his father, as a doctor, commanded respect. I never thought he'd amount to anything, and, now look here, Galego, I'm going to call you Galego, you no-good mutt. You up and left me all alone. Though that's got nothing on what happened to me after, a real travesty...Women!...Women are terribly complicated, I'm sure you know what I mean...Hold on, though. Are you a stud or a bitch? Let's have a look. Aha, a stud! Looks like I'm among equals. Galego...Galego was the name of a dog we had at the farm...Galego...He had a long life, that dog...Uncle Paulino was crazy about him. And how could he not be? When the sun went down, the dog would herd the cattle on his own, steering them to the corral. He'd fetch the horses from pasture and lead them to the stable, scare away the forest foxes and oncillas that came down from the woods. He used to escort the family into town, always watchful as he padded ahead of the wagon. He looked after the kids. The only thing he didn't do was talk...Nem Ladeira. Who would have thought... He didn't even recognize me...Walked right on by, like I was a post...I mean nothing to him...Or to Marcim Fonseca...He must have gotten the note...He doesn't remember me...Does anyone? Galego does—let's be fair. We may have met only once, but you took an immediate shining to me, didn't you? These sparrows are making a goddamn racket! You don't happen to hunt birds, do you? What do you eat? How do you get on? I wish I were like you, free, just traipsing around, accountable to no one. I guess I'm sort of like you already. But believe me, there's nothing good about this life... If I were you, boy—you look young, you've still got that twinkle of joy in your eyes—if I were you, I'd find a partner stat, mark my territory, start a family, and then take it easy. Because otherwise, you reach a certain age and find you've got nobody beside you... What can I say, buddy? It's tough... A damp breeze slips through my shirt, faintly sweeping the dead leaves off the footpath, scattering sand from between the paving stones and kicking up dust. It's probably going to rain. Drawn faces brush past mine, each of them seeming to suspect what a mess my life is. Galego?! I guess he's off. I look for him up one street and down another, but find nothing. Fleet-footed, he's melted away like a mirage. When all's said and done, he probably does have a home, and is on his trusty way there now, like everybody else, after a hard day's work. Except for me... With no home, no ground to stand on... I heave my feet along the pitted footpath. Nothing's worked out, Galego... Nothing. How come? When did things take a turn for the worse? What shortcuts had my legs led me down without my knowledge? This constant discomfort... I actually had prospects... But nothing came of those either, small as they were... Night has fallen once and for all. A packed bus pulls up. Men and women squeeze in, glowing with exhaustion and leaving the bus stop empty.

The windows of buildings flicker intermittently to the color of flashing television screens. Side by side, two motorcyclists have a chat. In the shade of the fig trees, a young man with his hood up and both hands in his jacket pockets comes toward me, and for a moment I'm scared I'll be assaulted—but he walks past, without disturbing. I wonder if Rosana's home yet. I can't tell from outside, the front of the house is hidden by the gate. I stop by the tall rough-concrete wall, press the intercom buzzer, and wait. I guess no one's home. Now what? I'd have liked to go to the bathroom, shower, rest. Though I don't expect a response, I press the intercom buzzer again and Rosana's voice rings out almost instantly. "Who is it?" "It's me," I hear the click. "Did that work?" "Yes!" The door is slightly ajar, casting light on the hood of the red Duster. I walk along the concrete path, enter the empty kitchen, and make my way to the bathroom, skin covered in goose bumps. I lower the toilet cover and sit, relieved. I turn on the faucet, wash my hands and face— the mirror shows features that are aged and pallid—turn off the faucet, wipe my hands and face—I'm as yellowed as the pages of an old book—and sweat, legs aquiver, hang up the towel, unlock the door. "Over here, Zézo." I follow Rosana's voice to the living room. Zézo...A family nickname...It's been years since I've heard anyone use it...Zézo...Rosana's slender and elegant body is draped over the sofa, all but a shadow in the faint lamplight. On the coffee table are two glasses—one empty, the other half full—a bottle of wine, and a charcuterie platter. "Won't you join me?" Still sore from the abuse I'd been put through that afternoon, I accept her invitation. "Were you expecting someone?" I ask, serving myself and settling onto the sofa. "Yeah, you. You still owe me an explanation, remember?" "I thought the glass might be for Ricardo..." She smiles wickedly. "Wednesday's our day off..." "What do you mean?" "Today's our day off from each other. Ricardo spends the night somewhere else." She raises her glass. "Cheers!" "Cheers!" I echo, taking a sip of wine that claws down my throat. "I don't mean to pry, but...What...What does he...get up to...exactly?" "I don't know. He says he spends the night playing poker with friends. I don't care." "You don't care?" "No, I don't care." She fills up her glass again. "Rosana, do you not love your husband anymore?" "Jeez! You sound like a teenager, Zézo. Love...what is love anyway? An emotional attachment that deteriorates year after year...I was practical about it. I married without the emotional attachment. Ergo, it didn't deteriorate. What usually happens is people put up with each other. Since I've always been happy to just put up with Ricardo, I haven't gone through all the other stages—disappointment, reconciliation, frustration, reconciliation, depression, resignation, et cetera. I went straight to the end." The half gloom highlights her pearly teeth, which weren't so white when she was a teenager. I take another sip of wine. Gesturing at the charcuterie platter, she says, "We've got an excellent spread here. Parma ham, Emmental cheese, Chilean olives...All of it from Tamires's shop." "And where is she at the moment?" "Wednesdays are when she sleeps with her boyfriend..." "So, she does have a boyfriend!" I exclaim, spearing the prosciutto slices with a toothpick. "No, she doesn't. She's just pretending," Rosana counters, sarcastic. "What do you mean?" "She's made him up." "Made him up?" "That's right," Rosana continues, in the same tone. "She goes to a motel on her own...And comes back in the morning so we'll think she spent the night in her boyfriend's arms." "And how...How exactly do you know this?" I ask, devastated. "I've got my spies..." Indignant, I prod Rosana. "And what do your spies have to say about your husband?" She answers without blinking, "That he cheats." Feeling vindictive, I decide to goad her. "And do you know who this lover is?" "I mean, he hasn't got *one* lover. He's always switching it up." "Doesn't that upset you?" She laughs. Takes a long swig of wine, chews on a cube of Emmental, says, "I know Ricardo, Oséias. He's got diabetes, high blood pressure, angina...The man hasn't screwed anyone in a looooong time. Those tramps he parades around are just for show." Rosana gets up and says, "I'm no saint myself," then cackles and disappears into the kitchen. The wind has picked up, and now rattles the windows. Thunder claps in the distance. Day off...I wipe my glasses with the edge of my shirt. I wonder if Rosana knows Nem Ladeira. I'll try some of this Emmental...I've got to visit Tamires's shop...Poor thing...I'll go to city hall early tomorrow and ambush Marcim...Per the suggestion of the woman with the coffee...It's a good plan...I need to buy a hat...Rosana, wiry-bodied, returns with a new bottle of wine and sets it on the coffee table. She fills her glass and has a sip. "Delicious!" She clicks her tongue, an expert. Since when does she know anything about wine? "Since when do you know anything about wine, Rosana?" "I took a class. In Juiz de Fora." Changing the subject, she asks, "What did you get up to today?" "I bumped into Marilda. Remember her?" She shakes her head disinterestedly. "My first girlfriend." "I had no idea you'd dated someone here, before moving to São Paulo..." "Well, I did...Marilda." "Ah," she sighs. For a few moments, lightning floods the room with light. Seconds later, thunder rattles the walls. "It's going to rain," she declares. "Rosana, what are people saying about the mayor, Marcim Fonseca?" I ask as I take a fat olive to my mouth. "The usual: some say he's decent, others that he's no good. Everybody agrees he's a crook..." "Did you know he was a classmate of mine at Colégio Cataguases?" "Oh, really..." she sighs, again disinterestedly. "Do you remember Dr. Ladeira?" "Dr. Ladeira? You mean the pediatrician?" "Yeah. Better known for drinking cachaça and eating mocotó with common people on the outskirts." The wind capers outside. Rosana stretches out on the armchair, sipping at her glass of wine as though lying on a divan at a Roman feast. I take a long drink of wine and whisper, "There's isn't a day I don't think of Lígia..." "Huh?!" Shocked, Rosana topples out of her languorous fog. "Fuck, Oséias," she jumps to her feet, wineglass in hand, and flips on the light. "Are you still

obsessing over that?! Stop dwelling on the past, Oséias!"
She paces around, her voice unsettled. "We've got to live in
the present. In the moment! You keep looking back. You
can't see what's around you, much less what's right under
your nose. No, nobody can take that kind of weight. That's
why you're the way you are—no wife, no kids, no friends...
Estranged from your family... I'm sorry to put it like this,
but it's my right. I'm your older sister. I worry... If you carry
on like this... If you carry on, you'll end up just like Dad...
Dad wasted away under all that guilt... And Mom... Her
cancer... I got over it, Oséias. Not long before I became
pregnant, something strange started happening to me. I
wasn't sleeping. I heard voices, saw things. I visited a
Spiritist Center and put myself through a disobsession
treatment, to persuade Mom that she wasn't part of our
world anymore. It wasn't easy. At first, she refused to accept
it. She was so tormented... But I broke free from her...
Then, when Tamires was around ten, eleven years old, I
had another rough patch. Insomnia, anxiety, depression. I
was falling again, when someone—I can't remember who—
told me to see a psychologist. I started therapy. It was a
godsend." The blue glare of lightning flashes against
Rosana's silhouette, which hovers in the darkness like a fish
skimming the surface of an aquarium at night. Thunder
makes the entire house rumble. Rosana fills her wineglass,
sits on the sofa, and picks up where she left off. "Our sister,
God rest her soul, was... sick... The more I think about it,
the more I realize it was no one's fault. The truth is that

what she did, that...reckless...act...It destroyed our family. It hurt some more, others less, but everyone suffered...enormously...At first, instead of guilt all I felt was hate. But I don't think about it anymore. I've forgiven her. My conscience is clear." The lights suddenly turn off, and the world plunges into a primordial darkness. "Power outage," she says. Damn it, how am I meant to shower now? Silence. Fat drops crackle at intervals on the roof. Then, all at once, a thick curtain of water pours down from the sky. Rosana's voice, tender and a little slurred, shoots through the gloom. "On nights like these, when it storms, I think of Mom...She would've lit a candle by now and had us all praying on our knees to Saint Barbara..." "Saint Barbara, your courage is much stronger than the forces of hurricanes and the power of lightning," I begin. Rosana joins in and together we continue, feigning contrition, "be always by our side so that we, like you, may face all storms, wars, trials, and tribulations with the same fortitude with which you faced yours..." We laugh. "And she used to burn something too..." "A holy branch that hung on the wall." "That's it! She used to say it'd protect us from lightning." I hear the clattering of glass. "I still have nightmares about that house, you know," Rosana says. "I dream that the river is rising and no matter how quickly we try to get everything out, the water is much stronger and sweeps through every room...Suddenly, I can't see the ceiling anymore, everything is underwater...I hated that house. Would you believe I once found a snake on the stove?" "I remember."

"You remember? But you were so small..." "It was a vine snake." "Was it?" My hands fumble through the darkness for my wineglass. I drink the last sip. My mouth is bitter, my head aches, my body tingles. The rain ebbs but does not stop. "Rosana, are all the windows shut?" She laughs. "Yes, all the windows are shut, Zézo. I knew the weather was going to turn... A habit I picked up back in the day... I always check everything before leaving the house. In case it rains and all the furniture is wrecked... Like when the river used to overflow... Those things, they get into your blood," she asserts, tragicomically. "And Isinha?" "What about her?" Rosana asks. "It'd be so nice if we could get together—me, you, Isinha, João Lúcio... Wouldn't it? Like the old days..." "There you go again with the old days... There are no old days, Oséias. It's all in the past! Dead. Over!" she spits out. "Does everything have to be that way?" I mutter. "I haven't seen Jôjo in years, I know nothing about his life. We fell out of touch. Isinha and me, we still talk now and then, on the phone. Sometimes months will pass, but I always call. She can't even do that... You know how difficult Isinha can be... She's terribly jealous of me... And proud... Last time I was there, I asked if she needed anything, and she became furious. Said I could visit anytime as her sister, but if I planned on playing the social worker, I'd better stay the hell away... So, I did. No one wants to be treated that way..." "I feel sorry for Isinha," I sigh. Rosana glowers. "Sorry? She chose that life. Nobody forced her to marry her good-for-nothing husband! He's a

little shit…A washout…" Washout. Marília had used the
same word to describe me. Hurt, I say, "I'm a washout too,
Rosana." She falters, then continues. "You're not a washout,
Zézo. You left, you fought to get where you are…" "And I've
got nothing to show for it…No home, no family, no
friends…You said so yourself…" Rosana immediately asks,
"Are you broke, Zézo?" This is the only thing that really
moves her, offering financial help as a form of humiliation,
what should be an act of compassion manifesting in her
hands as pure condescension. Rosana had clawed her way
out of the muck and now had the resources to rescue her
needy relatives, as she liked to tell anyone who'd listen. It
was a way for her to counteract malicious rumors about the
suspicious origins of Ricardo's properties and possessions.
When they talk about me behind my back, they're wolves,
but when they need our help, they dress in sheep's clothing,
she threw in the face of the world. Bunch of hypocrites, I
could picture her screaming, finger raised. "No, Rosana, I'm
not broke. I told you already." The rain falls harder. Water
roars down the gutter. "Why did Marília never visit, Oséias?
Was she embarrassed?" "Embarrassed? Why would she be
embarrassed?" "Who knows…Maybe because of how poor
we were." "Her family was just as poor as ours, Rosana."
"Then why did she never want to meet us?" I say nothing, I
don't have an answer. "Isinha's difficult…Always has
been…" she grumbles. A car drives down the road,
honking convulsively. "I know why you're here, Oséias,"
Rosana says now, haltingly. "You've come to stoke a dying

ember... You're a creature of shadows, feeding off the suffering of others..." I need to get up, my body is beaten and can't take it anymore—my hands tremble, my legs wobble, my heads feels light. "One time..." A hoarse voice rises faceless from the depths of the dark, faint and ragged. "It was Saturday and I'd come home late. I was fifteen or sixteen at the time. I threw myself on my bed to cry. I was miserable, torn by everything my godmother was offering. I felt this sudden hatred for our house and everything that tied me to it—Mom, Dad, all of you. I was scared. I kept wondering what would become of me, what my future would hold. I lay in bed sobbing, quietly. I was sure no one could hear me. Lígia and Isinha were usually asleep at that time of night. Like I said, it was late. But then someone lay down next to me and held me firmly in her arms. She stayed there, silent and still, until little by little I calmed down. The sadness bled out of me and I was filled with a sense of peace so enormous I immediately fell asleep. Me, the insomniac with huge bags under her eyes. I slept like a rock. When I woke up the next day, the sun was already high in the sky. The bunk beds were empty, and the girls had left for mass. I never had a chance to tell her how much it had healed me to be held in her arms, because it wasn't long before...she...That thing...happened...How I wish she...she were here...so that I could...I could..." Rosana falls silent. I can picture her made-up face desecrated by small tears. She's right there. I could hold her in my arms, say something, anything, offer a word of comfort. Instead I get up and grope the walls until I reach my room. I've turned to stone, to steel. I feel nothing. I fumble with the lock, put my glasses on the nightstand, lie down over the blankets with my clothes on, close my eyes

i wake up. I've probably slept an hour, if that. I get out of bed and try the light switch, still no power. I unlock the door. I make my way to the bathroom, pee, flush, wash my hands. I glance into the living room, Rosana's gone. I head back, lock the door, take off my sneakers, my socks, nudge them under the bed. I slip off my shirt and pants, hang them on the coatrack. I turn to the window. A breath of humid earth strikes my face. The rose-apple tree resembles a wet dog. I strip the bedspread and get under the sheets. I have to buy a hat tomorrow i'll wake up early have a shower maybe i'll be able to meet marcim ambush him per that lady's

thursday,
    march 5

i need to close the window the window's still open the window

hat where have i left my hat marilda strips lies on top of me marcim fertilizer i need to close the

the window mom tell him to stop nicolau is going to be when he grows up he answered my god what a clever boy the sun is poison look right there in the corner go take care of your

i need to close the window the window's still ope

i wake up in a sweat. Get out of bed. I lean into the dead of night. The sky is a tank of blue water and white saplings.

I wonder if Dona Eva is still alive. She was already old
back when she used to come to the house once a week to
launder and iron clothes. She had a grandson, Valtim, and
we shared a birthday. We were one year apart, and I was
younger. One day Mom was on her way—she was taking
me to a portraitist in the center—when Dona Eva stopped
by with him. She said with pride, It's Valtim's birthday
today. A little embarrassed, Mom responded, How adorable!
Let's take a portrait of the two boys together. In the only
photograph I have of myself as a child, I am standing
side by side with Valtim, our full bodies in view, visibly
uncomfortable. Dona Eva brought him with her a couple
more times, but he rebelled and gradually freed himself
from what he regarded as a punishment, and disappeared.
His grandmother used to always tell my mom, An angel,
Dona Stella, a perfect angel! Just like Zéia. Zéia was what
she called me…Their faces—they look alike, don't you
think? Valtim moved to São Paulo—I heard he worked in
the metro—but I never saw him. Names that flicker with
faces, like neon signs over ordinary roadside motels. I leaf
through a catalog of stories. My head spins, I feel nauseated.
I open the door, cross the hall into the bathroom, switch
on the light, turn the lock. I sit on the floor, stick my head
in the toilet bowl. Shove my fingers down my throat. A
stream of sour vomit gushes out, and I buckle. I rise. Flush.
Rinse my mouth. Wash my face. Moisten the back of my
neck. My hands tremble. My legs tremble. I pat myself dry.
Switch off the light. Cross the hall into my room. Lock

the door. I collapse on the bed. Somewhere a cat mews
anxiously at the window i forgot the window

the gate creaks

i wake with a start. The sun, high in the sky, sears my left
leg, which is uncovered. I wonder what time it is. My heart
races, I try to get out of bed. My head is reeling. I put on my
glasses. Make my slow way to the coatrack, pull on my shirt
and pants. I sit on the bed, slip on my socks and shoes. I've
got to buy myself a hat, no excuses. I grab my toothbrush
from my backpack. Unlock the door. The only sound is the
humming of the fridge. I head into the bathroom, lock the
door. I pee. Wash my face and hands. Brush my teeth.
Towel myself off. The mirror shows a creased face with
forehead wrinkles and crow's-feet, gray hairs bristling
chaotically from my dried skin. I cross the hall back into
my room. Put away my toothbrush. Only then do I spot
Rosana's teacherly scrawl on a piece of paper on the floor.
"Oséias, I'm afraid this situation can't go on. Ricardo has
been patient, too patient. I don't want to get into a fight
with him at this point in my life. He'd appreciate it, we'd
appreciate it, if you could find some other place to stay.
Rosana." I stuff the note in my pant pocket. All right,
Ricardo. You bastard! You little shit! All right! You may be
on top today, but tomorrow...Death will come for

everyone. We're all pilgrims—rich men, poor men, black men, white men—headed for the same destination, a hole where we'll be eaten by maggots. Sure, I'll go first, but I'll be waiting for you. Contempt, vanity, arrogance, and pretense will get you nowhere there...It's tears, regret, remorse, and grief that matter. I close the window. Sling on my backpack. On the kitchen table, another piece of paper. "Oséias, eat something before you go. There's turkey ham, bread, and cheese in the fridge. And oranges. The juicer is in the old cupboard. Keep in touch. Rosana." I leave. I slam the side door, don't look back. Where will I go? I need to buy a hat; the sun is a malagueta pepper. I zigzag down the cracked sidewalk. I need coffee, my stomach's growling. What time is it? At the bus stop, a teenager talks on her cell phone, an old man with a hunchback holds a grocery bag, and two boys chat animatedly. Back to square one, the snake eating its own tail...Cataguases...These trees have guarded me, and the paving stones have marked my steps...The walls have ears but no mouths. Otherwise, they would tell the story of a skinny boy who'd soared through the city on his green Caloi bicycle, taking in the landscape. Master of my own time, I had expanded my horizons further and further, not realizing that in this new, massive space I would lose my way, lose my wits, only to end up right back where I had started—a place so changed that it seemed to hold no trace of the person I'd once been. Just as in old photographs we often don't recognize the faces around us. I cut through the city like a specter. This is

where Dr. Armando Prata, mayor, once lived. Dr. Paschal
Cannabrava—Lawyer, Philosopher, Author, it says on the
lead placard, lived here. This was the home of Dona Diana,
wife of Dr. Manuel Prata, who'd send my mother expensive
clothes to mend. Here lived Patrícia and Denise, twins—
one blonde, the other brunette—daughters of Dr. Pelágio
dos Reis Antunes and classmates of mine at Colégio
Cataguases; I was in love with them, though they never
knew it. Here was the office of Dr. Gilson Machado, who
gave me a prescription for Tryptanol when Lígia...she...
when it...that...when that happened. Dead memories.
The houses have become fortresses. The neighbors used to
post their chairs on the sidewalk to enjoy a breath of cool
air and watch the gloaming. Women stride by, clasping
purses to the fronts of their bodies. The tumult of cars and
motorcycles clogging the streets deadens voices scattered
across time. A digital clock reads 10:40. 28°C. Sweat
drenches my shirt, feet, and head. I can't eat, or else I'll
have to skip lunch. I walk into a bakery, order a bottle of
water and an espresso. The ceiling fan whirs impotently. I
sit on the stool, feet dangling. The server hands me a bottle
of water. I open it, then down half of it at once. He
immediately brings me a brown demitasse, liquid sloshing
onto the saucer, also brown. I pour in the sugar and stir it
with a wood stick. It's disgusting. Watery, too hot; tiny
granules stick to my tongue. Damn it. I don't finish it. I ask
the server how much I owe him, fish out a few coins
forgotten in my pant pocket, count them, and leave him

the exact change. I slide off the stool, tuck the half-empty water bottle into my backpack, and leave. I walk down cluttered sidewalks, sidestepping the surge of people and the raucous cries of street vendors. I need to find a vendor that sells hats. Glasses, watches, cell-phone cases. Dishcloths. Cigarettes. Cleaning products and burlap sacks. Toys. Junk jewelry. Mom, bent over her sewing machine, battery-operated radio tuned in to Rádio Cataguases, runs the family. A foreman in the textile room of Industrial Cataguases, Dad gives her an unopened manila envelope with his month's wages on the tenth day of every month. A recruit at basic training, João Lúcio flaunts his spotless olive-green uniform—gleaming boots, kepi, and his nom de guerre, Moretto, embroidered on his puffed-out chest—stirring in me both admiration and envy. A student at Colégio das Irmãs, Rosana tutors in the evenings, after which she disappears into Ricardo's arms. Isinha, Lígia, and I attend morning sessions at Colégio Cataguases. Isinha is timid and passes the time quietly, dressing her dolls in scraps of fabric on the damp basement floor in the company of a cat, Duvalina, who gives birth to a litter of kittens twice a year without fail. Mom loves to harp on and on about how docile her youngest daughter is, She's been like this since she was a baby. Never made a peep when I put her down in the cradle so I could work! At night, the two of them watch telenovelas with rapt attention. Lígia is a whirlwind. One moment, she's spending every day cooped up in her room, lying on her belly in the top bunk and immersed in the pages of a hefty tome, so abstracted she's even got Dad worried; Dad, who never notices these things. Next, she's off with her friends from the Nossa Senhora de Fátima youth group, attending rehearsals with the church choir and evangelistic meetings, cycling to waterfalls, having picnics in open fields, visiting nursing homes, distributing food, clothes, and blankets at the Sociedade São Vicente de Paulo, so involved she even has Mom puzzled; Mom, who considers community service the apex of religious life. Because she's smart, she gets a scholarship from Rotary to learn English at the Yázigi language school; because she's sensitive, she learns guitar from Father Honório; because she's persistent, she takes free secretarial classes at the school of Dona Emerenciana Duarte, Mom's client. There are misunderstandings. Among the more minor are disputes over who gets to play their favorite songs on the Philips tube radio and record player—an enormous morado-wood cabinet. On Sunday mornings, Dad liked to listen to crooners like Nelson Gonçalves, Orlando Silva, Frank Sinatra, and Johnny Mathis, much to the dismay of João Lúcio and Lígia, who poked fun at what they called his *stodgy drivel*. João Lúcio had bought both volumes of the compilation *Músicas Inesquecíveis*, which, when he wasn't away at boot camp, would sound breathlessly through the windows of the house. Lígia used to bring home borrowed MPB records—Chico Buarque, Caetano Veloso, Milton Nascimento—and Rosana favored rock music, though she never took part in our tiffs; not even these sorts of

family matters seemed to concern her. Ricardo…What a
blockhead…I can't believe it! Loping down the road, tail
wagging, eyes bright with joy—Galego! I pat him on the
head. "Where were you hiding, buddy?! Some friend you
are! Vanishing like that into thin air…" Let's take a walk,
sweet boy, walking helps to organize your thoughts. I need
to buy a hat, and find a hotel or a cheap boardinghouse. A
muggy gust licks my face. The weather is turning. Moments
ago blue and sparsely clouded, the sky is now a swath of
gray hospital sheets. Vendors of umbrellas and clear-plastic
rain ponchos begin to pop up. It's going to rain, Mom
would announce the moment we woke up, My knee is
killing me. The dampness of the basement, where she'd
spent most of her life, had gotten into her bones. Though
in terrible pain, she kept on climbing up and down the
stairs to see the clients, who grew scarcer by the year. Aha!
A bunch of hats hooked to a shop door. I stop and enter a
small room chockablock with merchandise. Galego waits,
darting through the legs of passersby. The shop attendant
smiles and asks if she can help. She follows me to the
sidewalk, "I'd like one of these. How much are they?" She
grabs a metal pole, unhooks the net, and unfurls it over a
counter covered in children's shirts. "Go ahead and choose
one." I ask her for the price again and she quotes it. I pull
out a black hat with a Nike logo, clearly a counterfeit. She
gathers up the hats, lofts the pole, and hooks the net back
to the shop door. She scribbles numbers on a piece of paper
and points at the cash register, a small nook at the back of

the shop behind a lattice metal plate. A pair of dried, spotted hands take my money and give me change. "Is this for security?" Irritated, the old man says, "There were two robberies last year, and one attempted robbery. Can you believe it? Two robberies and one attempted robbery!" I fit the hat on my head and step back onto the sidewalk. Galego gets up and nudges my hand with his snout. I pat him on the head. "Let's get going," I say. Ricardo...One time, he'd ambushed me. I'd been shopping around for a blender to give my mother for Christmas. The streets glinted with string lights, and the heat kept nightfall at bay. I heard my name being called and glimpsed his fat hand waving from the deck of Hotel Bevile. I pretended not to see him, but he got up and intercepted me, huffing, a few steps later. Hey, Oséias! Trying to get away from me, are you? he asked, half-friendly and half-teasing, his shirt unbuttoned at the chest, exposing a thick gold chain. He gripped my arm, stopped by the table where he'd been sitting, and said, You'll have to excuse me, I've got to have a word with my brother-in-law, then dragged me to the back of the bar. The moment we sat down, he took a small hand towel from his pant pocket and ran it across his forehead, face, and jowl, wiping away the sweat leaching from his pores. A graying waiter appeared with a half-empty glass of whiskey, the ice almost entirely melted, and asked, Can I interest you in some more? Yes, thank you, he said and then to me, Do you want anything? Whiskey, beer, Coke, juice...I said no, and he swished his glass, downed the rest of the diluted whiskey, and started his song and dance, speaking in his usual halting manner. I know you don't like me, Peninha. And that's okay. Not even Jesus got on with everybody. All that said, I'm your niece's father. We're family now. So it's only decent for you to take my side. Whatever happens to me, affects you. And whatever affects you, will no doubt become a problem for me. Do you follow? Your sister's upset. She keeps on crying… We're such a small family… And there's so much conflict… The only time Dad and João Lúcio ever agreed on something was when Rosana finally broke the news of her relationship with Ricardo, the day of her debut. Mom congratulated her, What a wonderful choice, honey! Dad's face clouded over, I don't like it. That family's money is dirty—they never broke a sweat to get where they are. João Lúcio slammed his fist down on the table, Dr. Normando's no good. Everybody knows he's in bed with the worst characters in town. Dr. Normando lives off his rental properties, Mom, ever the diplomat, insisted. It's all Dona Magnólia's fault, she's gone and filled the girl's head with nonsense, Dad argued. People say all kinds of stuff, João Lúcio, Mom pressed, trying to smooth things over. When she and Rosana were alone, she would tell her, What matters is for you to be happy, sweetie! Rosana didn't seem to mind all the talk. After years at her godmother's, she coveted the easy life she and her sons seemed to enjoy. Pudgy Ricardo in his avocado-green Puma convertible; scrawny Roberto in his black Opala, which he had nicknamed the Skull, and the infamous parties he threw with his cousin Netinho at a country house in Paraíso; Dona Magnólia and her carefree spending. Dr. Normando died in a car crash on his way to Juiz do Fora, his cár hurtling down a hillside as hc drove up Caieira, somewhere near Argirita. They say some die murdered, others from heart attacks, and still others because they lose control. Widowed, Dona Magnólia moved to an apartment she bought in Rio de Janeiro, and hardly ever stepped foot in Cataguases again. She even refused to be buried there. In her will, she asked to be cremated and for her ashes to be scattered in the ocean in front of the building where she lived in Copacabana until the very end. The brothers divvied up their father's business. Ricardo, the more discreet of the two, was put in charge of the properties, a series of modest rental homes and a few office spaces— though he also, people said, bought and sold dollars, loaned money on interest, pawned jewelry, seized merchandise... Roberto, who was more aggressive, used jogo do bicho, or so folks said, as a front for a drug-trafficking operation. Roberto was killed... Six shots... Day has turned to night. A damp wind jerks the trees around, felling dry branches and dispersing dead leaves. People begin to rush, knocking into one another. Cars roll forward with beaming headlights. The streetlamps turn on. Lightning strikes once. And again. Thunder rocks the ground. I need to find cover. Aha, a buffet! I look around for Galego, but he's gone. I walk in, the server hands me a piece of laminated paper with the number fifteen on it. The reddish glow of the woodstove pierces shadows that lumber through the half darkness of the restaurant. I grab a plate and file past casseroles of food. White rice. Black beans. Steak. Zucchini. Collards. Grits. A woman in a bouffant cap weighs my plate. I grab a knife, fork, and napkin. I set the plate, cutlery, and napkin on a table off to the side. I slip off my backpack and set it down on a chair. I sit. Thunder makes the floor shudder. I hear clattering on the roof. A young man asks me, yelling, if I'd like anything to drink. I still have half a bottle of water left. With a gesture I tell him I want nothing. I chew slowly. Rain crashes down. Where has Galego gone off to? He's no fool, he's probably hiding somewhere, hiding safely away. It's a popular restaurant. Most of the clients are old retirees. The commotion stunts their conversation. They remain mute, though sullen, sunken in the half gloom. Here and there cell phones appear as bright spots. To Rosana's despair, the weather remained overcast on the Saturday of her wedding, though the party went according to plan—a memorable affair at a farmhouse that some monied relatives had loaned to Magnólia for the occasion. The dress had a long train and had been made in Rio de Janeiro. The chapel was blanketed in flowers and resembled a painting. There was a glut of food and drink. Mom had sewn clothes for Isinha's children. I'd bought a black suit. Dad refused to attend. João Lúcio sent a telegram. Wellington got sauced. A boom! What was that?! My heart goes off the rails. We all rise as one and rush to the door. Oh, a tree's fallen, causing a traffic jam. "At least nobody got hurt," they remark. Water rushes into the restaurant and the cashier tries to force it out with a squeegee, but it's no use. A woman dressed in white arranges bowls around the room to catch the water leaking from the ceiling. I head back to the table. Polish off my food. Take the bottle out of my backpack and drink the rest of the water. I wipe my mouth. Burp discreetly. I sling on my backpack, shove the laminated card into my back pocket and head to the bathroom. There is a thick stench of urine and cresol. I pee. Brush my teeth without toothpaste, put away my toothbrush. I take off my glasses. Wash my face and arrange the sparse hair on the sides of my head with my damp hands. The mirror shows tired eyes. I dry off my face and my head with a paper towel. I cross the dining hall, which is now a little brighter. I hand the cashier the card. He examines it. "Nothing to drink?" "No," I say. He reels off what I owe. I take my wallet out of my back pocket. Pay. Fill a small plastic cup with coffee. I take a sip. It's treacly and weak. I toss the cup in the trash can. Join the people clustering at the entrance. I peer outside to check the rain, which has started to fall softly. "... the one in 2012 ..." somebody says, in front of me. "2012? What do you mean 2012! More like the flood of 1972. The river rose ten meters during that storm!" "No, the worst one was in 2008. Just look at the photos. The water got places it'd never been before!" A white head intercedes. "You're too young, so you won't remember, but it was the flood of 1950, 1951, I don't know what year it was exactly. That one really showed us. It was a flood like you've never seen before. Dead bodies floating downstream. Animals by the dozen…" "Yeah, but…" Some have already ventured outside and walk past with umbrellas, dodging puddles and stopping to admire the fallen tree. I reach the marquee in long strides, shirt spattered with water. I catch my breath and zigzag to another marquee through fallen branches and publicity boards. Water cascades from the gutters. A hotel! Hotel dos Viajantes… An elegant establishment when I was a kid, and always fully booked. All I have to do is skirt the old, vacant station. I fill my lungs with air washed clean by the rain. People begin to march out of the anthill, a little dazed. It's much cooler now. I wipe my glasses with the edge of my shirt, but the lenses fog up again. Another mad dash. I parry the cars—one practically runs me over and a collective honking ensues—and reach the footpath intact, with only my feet and the hem of my pants drenched in water. I walk at a brisk pace and burst into the hotel lobby, just about knocking into a man smoking at the threshold as he watches the commotion outside. "Sorry," I say. He grunts back. There's no one at reception. I ring the bell, following instructions, Please ring bell & wait. I wait. The old wall clock reads one thirty in Roman numerals. Behind the counter hangs an old black-and-white photograph of Cataguases, already quite faded. Snapped from up high, maybe from the hill behind the building: the train station, the wagons used to transport merchandise, a parked Ford, a motley of men in hats and drab clothes. I wonder what year the photo was taken. High ceilings. Worm-eaten floor. The two red napa-leather armchairs with white frieze look greasy. The voice of a television broadcaster filters through the curtain of colorful plastic strips from the room next door, discoursing on the mounting frustration with government corruption. "How can I help you?" An individual more or less my age, cross-eyed and thin as a rake, emerges while drying his hands on a rag. "Good afternoon. Have you got any rooms available?" "How many nights?" he asks, opening the enormous black notebook sitting beside the vintage cash register. "Two," I say. "A single?" he asks, running his index finger down the list of bookings. I nod my head. "I've got something for you. Number nine. Shared bathroom." I ask for the price and he cautions, "Payment's up front." "Up front?" "House rules," he says, unyielding. I edge away in search of a discreet angle. I take off my backpack, zip it open, reach my hand into one of the compartments, grab a tube of Cebion, uncap it, pull out a roll of cash, unfurl the money, count it, roll up what's left, stuff it back in the tube, cap it, slide the tube back into the compartment, and zip the backpack up again. I return to the counter and hand the money to the desk clerk. He checks the amount, presses a couple of buttons on the cash register, and pulls the crank, making the drawer shoot open with a ring. He slides a stub toward me—"Fill in your name, address, and phone number"—and shuts the drawer, ring-ring. Address? Rua...Rua...I make something up...Rua...Oiapoque.

Number...number...100. City: São Paulo. State: SP.
Telephone. Hmm...011 followed by a random series of
digits. The man skims the stub and asks to see my ID. I pull
my wallet out of my back pocket and show him the
document. He glances at the photograph and measures it
against my face. "All right," he concludes. He fishes a set of
keys hanging from a corkboard and passes it to me. "First
floor. Breakfast's included and is served..."—he walks out
from behind the counter, shifts the colorful plastic strips
out of the way, and points—"...here, from six to nine
thirty." Chipped red Formica chairs stand empty on the
worn floor. The TV is on and hangs in the middle of the
back wall. "We also serve lunch, if you're interested, from
ten thirty to one thirty. It's a set meal, you'd have to pay
separately. Dinner is from six to eight thirty." I thank him,
we head back into the lobby and I plod up the wood
staircase, which creaks beneath my wet sneakers, then turn
into a dark and stuffy hallway. I scan the small blue signs
on the doors for the number nine, painted white. I
maneuver the key into the lock. Walk in. It reeks of
mildew. I throw open the window, the commotion on the
street lurches inside. A single bed and two towels—a face
towel and a bath towel—folded over coarse blankets
pungent with laundry powder. In the tiny wardrobe, a fleece
blanket that stinks of mothballs. I take off my hat and
leave it on the chair by the window. I drop my backpack. I
try the mattress. Stiff. I sit down, pull off my shoes and
socks. The feel of my damp feet on the dusty floor sends

shivers through me. I lay out my socks and shoes on the windowsill. I take off my rain-spattered shirt and hang it off the back of the chair. I have to visit Isinha... I stuff my hand in my pant pocket... What's this? Oh, Rosana's note... "Oséias, I'm afraid..." I crumple it and toss it in the plastic wastebasket. In the other pocket, a single *real* bill, two coins, and a small yellow supermarket receipt... 3421... the number of the church... I lie down. Taquara Preta, was that what he'd said? And what about his name? How ridiculous... Hello, I'd like to speak with Father... Who may I say is calling? It's... a man he met yesterday... On Santa Rita Square... He said that I should call this number... to talk to him... Completely ridiculous... I don't know the pastor's name. He doesn't know mine... I crush the piece of paper and place it on top of the nightstand, next to the bill, two coins, and my wallet. What would I ever say to him? Father, I'm dying. And the pastor would glance impatiently at his watch and say, We all are, son. But I'm dying right now... Son, go see a doctor. What you need is a doctor, not a pastor. I've already been to one, Father. He gave me six months... Well, then all we can do is pray and hope your soul finds its way to a better place. But, Father, there are things I want to understand before... Like what, my boy? he would ask, glancing at his watch again. One afternoon when I had nothing to do—a light, deceptive rain was falling, the kind that keeps children cooped up indoors—and needed to find a way to entertain myself, I remembered that Dad would buy copies of *Reader's*

Digest every month from the Italian at the kiosk on Rui Barbosa Square, because he enjoyed some of the sections. Such as, Laughter is the Best Medicine, Jokes for Every Branch, Work Stress, My Most Unforgettable Character, and above all, Word Power, which he cited as proof that he'd received a better education than we had; though he'd only completed fourth grade, he knew far more words than we did, like derisory, mansard, credulity, perfidy . . . I shoved open the door to the room where Mom and Dad slept, which was always left ajar, and went looking for the magazines, usually stacked in a corner. I leafed through them one by one and was frustrated to find I'd already read them all. So I decided to explore the wardrobe, which smelled of Phebo soap from all the dark-brown bars Mom layered between the clothes, a strategy she had devised to ensure things always smelled nice. I found a hatbox, put it on top of the bed, and opened it. Portraits, just a couple. A manila envelope, birth certificates, marriage certificate, diplomas, immunization records. A white envelope with receipts for various payments. I closed the box and put it back where I'd found it. I shuffled through hanger after hanger, pressing at the pockets of pants and shirts to see if they held anything interesting. I put on Dad's suit jacket, which fell to my knees. Rain ran drearily down the shutters. Maybe there was something on top of the wardrobe? I carefully dragged over the nightstand, its drawer kept locked, probably to hide money. I climbed onto the chair and then onto the nightstand, so that the top of the wardrobe was at eye level. There were cobwebs and two shoeboxes. I grabbed the first one, which was very light, placed it on the bed and opened it. Inside were colorful glass ball ornaments for the Christmas tree. I climbed on the chair and then on the nightstand, and put the shoebox back. The other one was farther away and difficult to reach. I stretched my arm as far as it would go and dragged the box, which was heavy, to the edge. I put the box on top of the nightstand, climbed down, picked it up again and placed it on the bed. Inside, I found a piece of green felt wrapped around something hard. My heart raced. I had the sneaking feeling I was about to embark on a thrilling adventure, like the ones in *Reader's Digest*. I unfurled the felt, revealing a chrome revolver with a wood handle. I was so startled, the gun slipped out of my hands. I shook all over and broke into a cold sweat. Without thinking twice, I wrapped the gun back in the green felt, placed it in the box, closed it, got on the chair, then on the nightstand, shoved the box toward the wall, got down, dragged the nightstand back, put the chair in its place, left the room, shut the door halfway, and threw myself on the bottom bunk of the bed I shared with João Lúcio; legs weak, heart in a riot, mouth dry. Outside, the afternoon light slowly faded, driven away by the gray rain. Even though it was April, I got under the covers, and was soon shivering with fever. I tried to yell for my mother, but my voice wouldn't come out. Paralyzed, my body seemed to float. The train whistle, the sound of the sewing machine, the music playing on the neighbor's radio, the rain tapping on the roof, the barking of a dog feet squelching on the sidewalk voices honking cars whistling trains hair nuzzled Mom

i wake up to yelling, "Get him!" "Get him, thief!" "Thief!" "Hold him!" "Hold him!" "Did you get him?" "Ow! You're hurting me!" "I've got him!" "He's got him!" I rise, put on my glasses, and rush to the window. Right beneath me, a lanky guy in a white woven shirt, jeans, and flip-flops clutches the twig-thin arm of a scraggy boy who comes up to his hip and is flailing furiously. "Let go of me, you asshole! Let go!" Soon they are surrounded by a crowd of rubberneckers. An elderly, well-dressed man spits out "You little shit!" and slaps the boy over the head. A pregnant woman walks over in tears in the company of another woman slightly older than her, who asks, "Did you get him? Have you got him?" The circle, more numerous by the minute, breaks open, and the lanky man displays the boy's puny body, which he holds in his thin hands. The pregnant woman screams, "He stole my cell phone! Where's my cell phone, huh? You little fucker! Where is it?" The lanky man jostles the boy, "Where's her cell phone, kid! Where is it?" The boy, who had been trying to shake loose from his captor, now stands mute, indifferent, staring blankly. "Search him," someone suggests, and right away a man begins ruthlessly patting down his torn shirt and dirty shorts, only to be disappointed, finding "there's nothing here." The pregnant woman despairs, "Oh my God, I never finished paying!" Someone ventures, "He probably handed it off to one of his buddies." Another offers, "They always work in pairs. Never alone." Yet another adds, "Yeah, that's exactly how they do it." Finally someone concludes, "Pros, aren't they?!" The friend of the pregnant woman yells, "She's not feeling well, someone call an ambulance, for the love of God, call an ambulance!" A man takes the keeling pregnant woman into his arms and leads her to the hotel lobby, where they probably seat her in one of the red, greasy armchairs. "Did somebody call the cops?" asks the voice of a woman filming the scene with her cell phone. "They're on their way!" says a man. The boy remains withdrawn. Sweat runs down my forehead, temples, chest. "He's a minor, tomorrow he'll be out stealing again," growls the old woman with the umbrella. "Smack him around a bit," cries a teenager with gym-sculpted muscles. "Someone should kill the lot of them once and for all," says someone else. All of a sudden, the cross-eyed desk clerk hurries out of the hotel lobby, followed by a man with the pregnant woman in his arms and by the slightly older woman. They all squeeze into a Monza Classic. For a second, the crowd is distracted by the pregnant woman. The boy looks up and our eyes meet, and for a moment he radiates such intense hatred and disdain, so much frustration and resentment, that I step back from the window, scared and ashamed. I need a shower. I open my backpack, take out my last pair of clean underwear and my last clean shirt, a toothbrush, drape the towel around my neck, unlock the door, and walk barefoot down the dusty floor to the end of the hall. I lock the bathroom door, hang my clean shirt and underwear on the ceramic bath hook, and arrange the towel over the curtain rod in the shower. I gaze into the face in the cracked and rusted mirror—five o'clock shadow, yellowed eyes. I brush my teeth. I need to get toothpaste. I carefully set my glasses in the sink. I pull down my pants and underwear, sit on the toilet to relieve my bladder and guts. The white wall tiles are soiled. The white floor tiles are soiled. Cobwebs cling to the corners of the ceiling. There are dark splotches of mildew. I wonder if the commotion downstairs is over. I'll go visit Isinha. I'm out of clean clothes. Behind the door, a notice: Be quick. Leave the bathroom clean for the next person. That next person might be you. I get up. Flush. The water, meager, trickles down without force. I take off my pants and underwear and put them on top of the toilet cover. The plastic shower curtain, once maybe blue, has hardened and faded. I turn the left tap, the one with the letter H on it, and wait. I flush again. Several of the holes are blocked, and cold water spits this way and that in thin slivers. I turn the right tap, the one with the letter C on it, and wait. The water is still cold. I get in anyway, my body covered in goose bumps. The small bathroom window shows a hill behind the hotel. I need to buy soap. And shampoo. And conditioner. I run my hand over my wet skin. Malu...Malu...You know what I'd like to do right now? I'd like to sleep with you...

Marilda...I've been cheating on you for years, Oséias. Years! Marília...Marilda...Marília...Marilda... Have you ever seen a naked woman? Really? Cidinha says she'll show us her tits and her pussy. But it'll cost us. Tufts of pubes bristling out from Dona Júlia's panties...The woman standing at the entrance to the hotel...Was it in Pirassununga? Black, timid eyes. She'd walked upstairs in silence. The doorman, who probably took a small cut, had turned a blind eye. Seconds after entering the room, she was pulling off her clothes. When I came out of the bathroom, I was met with the starved body of a young girl with bird legs, and hardly any breasts. She shivered from the cold. How old are you? Over eighteen, she lied. I sat on the edge of the bed. A girl...I said, Look, get dressed, I don't want anything from you. She turned to face me, wary. I took money from my wallet, put it in her hand, and again said, Get dressed, go home, it's late. She dressed in silence, went downstairs. Shortly after, as I smoked out the window, I saw her hanging off another client. Her legs and shoulders bare in the cold July night...I turn off the shower. Grab the towel, pat myself dry. I pull on my underwear, shirt, and pants. I'm sweating again. I need to buy deodorant. There's so much I need to buy...I put on my glasses. Oh, the squeegee. I push the water back into the shower, soaking the hem of my pants. I rest the squeegee against the wall. I look in the cracked and rusted mirror, now also fogged up, and comb what little hair I have left with my fingers. I grab my dirty underwear, the wet towel, and toothbrush, and leave the bathroom. I head down the hallway. Dust sticks to the soles of my damp feet, setting my teeth on edge. I unlock the door, walk in. Toss my toothbrush on the bed. Grab my sneakers and socks off the windowsill and stretch out the towel. I rummage through my backpack for my last pair of clean socks. I sit on the bed. Wipe the soles of my feet with my dirty underwear, then slip on my socks and shoes. I get up and tuck into my backpack the toothbrush, underwear, and dirty socks. I grab my hat and put it on. I gather up the money and my wallet and place them in various pockets. I wipe my glasses with the edge of my shirt. Take a deep breath. I lock the door, head into the half darkness of the hallway, and lumber down the stairs. "Good afternoon," I say to the man behind the counter. He raises his black eyes. "Good afternoon," he echoes, his voice nasal, his teeth crowded, his nose large and covered in sunspots. "Nine. Mr. . . . Nunes?" he hazards, hanging the key back on the corkboard. "Very well, Mr. Nunes, I should explain, in case you come back late at night, hehehe, not that you look like the kind of guy who'd come back late at night, hehehe, but, house rules, as Pereira likes to say, hehehe, I should explain, in case you come back late at night, what the procedure is—" From behind the counter steps a scarecrow, white long-sleeved shirt and baggy black slacks hanging off his body. "This is a good city, a great city, but you know how things are these days, hehehe, so, if for any reason, any reason at all, you find you have to come back late, just be careful, it's not that the city is perilous, hehehe, but I should warn you, alert you, there are a good deal of vagrants around these parts, and a lot of crackheads, yeah, lots of crackheads, hehehe, it's the crisis, you know, hehehe, and whores, tons of whores, and where there are whores there are transvestites, hehehe, so, if you happen to come back late," he lingers at the doorway, just outside, "There's this little doorbell here, see? All you've got to do is press it. Hehehe, Cleber, the night clerk, he'll come and open the door for you. This is a good city, it really is, but these days, hehehe, drugs, you know, they're targeting everybody, am I right? Hehehe. Just today, right here, right outside, I don't know if you saw, one of those little mulato boys swiped a cell phone off a pregnant woman, he had a rough time of it, he did, hehehe. Pereira's the one who helped her, if it wasn't for him she might have miscarried. He hauled her into his Monza and took her to the ER, the man treats his Monza like it's his bride-to-be, the car's just like new, spick-and-span, that's Pereira for you, systematic, but if you need him, hehehe, he's an angel, spares no effort, available around the clock. Spiritists are like that, you know, hehehe, they live to help their neighbors, hehehe. Well, Mr. Nunes... You see, I managed to memorize your name on the first try, hehehe, if I was to bump into you again in a year or ten, I'd say to you, Good afternoon, Mr. Nunes. I'm like that, I've got the memory of an elephant, as they say, hehehe, though I've never seen an elephant before, have you? Like in real life, hehehe." I shake my head no, and say, "You'll have to excuse me, I have an

appointment to get to." And he says, "Of course, Mr.
Nunes, I don't mean to intrude, hehehe, if you need
anything at all, just say the word. The name's Morais, Paulo
Henrique Morais, at your service, hehehe." I shake his hand
then disappear into the passersby crowding the sidewalk.
The sun is burning, even though it's... What time is it? If
asked, I could pinpoint the day everything started to fall
apart: February 23, 1974. A Saturday night during Carnival.
Isinha was hell-bent on watching the samba schools parade
down Avenida Astolfo Dutra, and Dad, irritated but
amenable, called Miguel Carroceira early that morning to
help him haul three chairs from the house to the sidewalk,
right next to the judge's box. He sat there all day long,
saving us a place. Around lunchtime, I took him a ceramic
plate covered with another plate, wrapped in a kitchen
towel. He gave me some change to buy two Americana
guaraná sodas, one for me and one for him, and then
grudgingly ate the rice and beans, grits, collards, and steak
and onions that Mom had fixed up for him. Then he drank
a whole reused Scott's Emulsion bottle full of cold and
treacly watered-down coffee. After returning the soda
bottles to the bar opposite, I'd raced back home on my
green Caloi bicycle. Mom had given me an old pillowcase
to wear as a mask with three tears cut in it, two at eye level
and one near the mouth. I'd put on a dress Lígia had gotten
from her godmother for her thirteen birthday but never
worn, a red dress with huge black polka dots exactly like
the one Little Dot wore, and in my bare feet joined an

improvised procession drumming at the entrance to
Paraíso. We were having fun messing around, spritzing
water out of a plastic tube that looked like a perfume bottle
and showering passersby with talcum powder, at one
moment eliciting laughter, the next curses, and then
threats. Rosana had set off early to Dona Magnólia's
because that evening, she and her godmother were going to
attend a dance at Clube do Remo. João Lúcio had taken
the bus from Viação Marotti to Rodeiro the day before and
would only be back after mass on Ash Wednesday. Lígia
was at a spiritual retreat at the Seminário da Floresta in
Juiz do Fora. Mom, an introvert, appreciated the Folia de
Reis and bate-pau, but didn't like the crush of Carnival,
claiming she found all those people suffocating. Still, she
donated a couple of outfits she'd made to the Luzu Samba
School, which residents from Vila Teresa all the way to
Saudade held in high regard—They asked, I can't right
turn them down, she explained. That year, Isinha felt she
was all grown up and insisted on watching the parade.
Mom gave into her in no time at all, and Dad, as ever, said
neither yes nor no and instead just skulked about the
house, grumbling to himself. At around six o'clock, Mom
and Isinha, who was dressed as an Indian, and an excited
Sino all headed out onto the street. Around ten, a rumor
made its way around the neighborhood and finally reached
my ears. Some men had burgled a house and the cops were
on their heels. I took off in the direction of the incident,
and imagine my surprise when I spied a patrol car parked in

front of our house... Trembling from head to toe, I yanked off my mask, and, stammering, asked the soldier what was going on. He look at me, dressed as a girl, and said, Why? Do you live here? I nodded and he grabbed me by the arm and dragged me down the street. Sarge, this boy here lives in that house, he said, unable to contain his laughter. The sergeant held back and asked where my parents were. I told him, in tears, and sat on the curb. Our neighbor, Dona Arelene, took me by the hand to her house, where she served me coffee with milk and Marie biscuits. Mom, Dad, Isinha, and Sino arrived shortly after. Mom grabbed the key, hidden in the electricity meter, and swung the door open. A mob of people—cops, snoops, gossips, smart alecks—flooded the room. The burglars had jumped over the wall and forced open the kitchen door. They'd emptied the wardrobe, shifted the furniture, made a mess of everything, and even eaten the ubá mangoes we had picked from our yard and that would have soon been sweet enough for us to enjoy. Mom was given Maracugina and fennel tea. Though she didn't shed a single tear, those of us who knew her could tell she was beating herself up inside, Why'd I insist on that darned parade? Why? Dad was beside himself. He paced this way and that, speculating on who had sounded the alarm and who had seen someone or something. But it was the night of costumes and of chaos, and no one knew who'd called the cops. Scared and weepy, Isinha clung to Mom. The house only emptied after daybreak. We slept in a pile on the bed, Mom, Isinha, and

me, while Dad and Sino kept watch. The next day, we
found unfiltered Paquetá cigarette butts on the floor—Dad
smoked filtered Continentals—and footprints by the lock
on the kitchen door as well as by João's lettuce beds. For a
long time, we kept finding new things that had gone missing.
The jewelry box, which was what Mom called her little
Memphis soap box, was found empty, and from it disappeared
the never-worn, thick gold chain and small "R" pendant
Rosana had received from Dona Magnólia on top of the
simple gold chain we each got from our parents for our First
Communion; Lígia's gold earrings; all our baby teeth nestled
in cotton pillows; Rosana's pearl necklace; Mom's
engagement ring, whose small gemstone was apparently
emerald; Dad's prized pocket watch, an Omega, with
eighteen jewels. A red lacquer purse. Three of Dad's
polyester shirts. The Keds João Lúcio wore to play indoor
soccer at Senai. The money hidden under the mattress.
Two of our four hens, one of which was broody. For a
month Dad visited Deputy Aníbal Resende, to get updates,
and though they'd beaten a couple of well-known, hard-up
pot dealers in town, and squeezed a couple of crooks,
they'd come up with nothing. They must be from out of
town, Dr. Aníbal would justify, in a rage. Desperate, Dad
bought himself a revolver, which he told no one about. I sit
on a bench on Rui Barbosa Square, shirt drenched with
sweat. I take off my hat, run my hand along my sopping
bald spot and dry it on my pant leg, put my hat back on. I
wipe my glasses with the edge of my shirt. The digital clock

reads 16:46. 29°C. The sky is blue, cloudless. Now and then, in the masses of people, I think I recognize a face from the old days, or a face from the present with features from the past, probably the children or grandchildren of someone I once knew. A strong stench wafts from the bandstand, where a vagrant sleeps on a square of cardboard, flanked by a stray dog with brownish fur. To city hall! Who knows, I might get lucky. I walk toward Rua do Pomba, avoiding the strip between Rui Barbosa and Santa Rita Square, where Tamires's deli is located. I have no interest in seeing anyone in that family. What a disgrace! Ricardo...Rosana...João Lúcio was right. He quickly realized it was a trap, got out and struck it rich. Everybody envies him. João Lúcio had been Uncle Ítalo's pride and joy, and he used to go with him to the countryside, near Rodeiro, every chance he got. Uncle Ítalo, our uncle on our mother's side, only had daughters, three of them—one, Verônica, was lame from having polio as a child—and out of frustration had sort of adopted João Lúcio, who felt like he was more his uncle's son than his own father's, a man he got along with about as well as water and oil. Mom also showed a clear preference for him. One day when it was just the two of us at the hospital, I asked her why she loved João Lúcio more than the rest of us. Lying on her back, voice thinned by the disease, she'd hemmed and hawed, and insisted she didn't, it wasn't true, before finally admitting that even if she may not love this child more than the other, there was always one son or daughter who expressed more tenderness, more devotion, more affection to their parent and found a special place in their heart, though this didn't mean, it certainly did not mean, that she loved the others any less, To mothers, all children are equal, she concluded. Yes, João Lúcio was special. As soon as he completed his military service, he grabbed his stuff and moved in with Uncle Ítalo, who by then had ditched the country for Rodeiro, where he ran a small, foundering sawmill he'd bought from one of the Bettios. I stop in front of a bakery. Walk in. Scan the items by the cash register. "How can I help you?" asks the server. Cigarettes. Gum. Candy. Chocolate. Oh, bonbons! I ask for two Sonhos de Valsa. He slips them into a small white paper bag. I stuff my hand in my back pocket, grab my wallet, pull out the exact amount of money, pay. I put my wallet away, walk outside, and keep walking. Isinha and Wellington were married the following year. A shotgun wedding with Isinha pregnant in her veil and garland, at São José Operário Church. Mom had been uneasy, while Dad had thought it was absurd for a woman who wasn't a virgin to wear white at the altar, They can fool people but they won't fool God, he'd said, smacking the table with his open hand and retreating to smoke on the sidewalk, shaking. I walk up the steps of city hall. No sign of Galego—I wonder where the old dog's hiding? I greet the potbellied security guard and tell him I'm going in to have a chat with Valéria. He gestures in a way that I take to mean Go ahead. I cross the empty hall and beeline to the reception desk, on which there are two phones and a set of matte acrylic pencil and paper clip holders. "Hi, Valéria. Remember me?" She squints her jet-black eyes. "Peninha, the mayor's friend. I was here yesterday," I say as I pull out a bonbon from the white paper bag and slide it toward her. "Is that for me?" she smiles, surprised, perfect white teeth contrasting with her red lips. "Thank you so much! How are you doing today?" "All right...Is Marcim up there?" I asked, pointing at the ceiling. "Oh, no, Thursday's when he goes around the city visiting different neighborhoods, his voter base, you know?" And then, as though she's had a sudden thought, "Has he called?" "No, not yet." "Don't worry about it, I'm sure he'll call." "I'm sure he will. I appreciate your making the time." I cut across the hall. I hear the sound of her opening the bonbon wrapper. I knock on the half-open door to the break room, "May I?" "Only if you come in peace," answers the short and slender woman in open-toe sandals, laughing loudly. "This is for you." I hand her the bag with the other bonbon. "For me, really?" She peeks inside. "In case you're wondering, I'm married, and happily!" She howls with laughter. "Could I bother you for a glass of water?" "Sure thing!" She pulls a plastic cup from a freshly opened sleeve and asks, "Cold or room temp?" "Room temperature." She fills the cup at the watercooler. "Is the mayor working today?" I ask. Planting her hands on her hips, she says, snidely, "No, today is when he visits his sidepiece in Muriaé," I drain my cup and toss it in the wastebasket. "She's a nurse. Thursdays are her day off," she adds. "Is that right?" I ask, taken aback. "Yeah!

Everybody knows, even his wife." "Who's his wife?" "Dr. Patrícia Antunes, a dentist." Gawking, I ask, "Does she have a twin sister?" "As far as I'm aware, she's got one sister, Dr. Denise, a physician. But one of them is blonde and the other brunette, so they're probably not twins..." Dizzied, I keep mum. Marcim...Patrícia... "And she doesn't... mind?" "Goodness knows, those rich folks are a whole different breed. If it were me, I'd already be two-timing him back. Hahahahaha..." The security guard had stopped silently behind me. "Dona Ivete, you'll get yourself in trouble if you carry on like that..." "Carry on telling the truth, you mean? Sweetie, you see this white fuzz on my head?" She points at her bouffant cap. "I'm upwards of sixty now. They'd be doing me a favor by sending me home." She takes the kettle off the cooktop, asks, "Coffee? You may as well, it's the last one. My shift's up." The security guard hands her a ceramic mug with the Flamengo club shield. "What about you?" she asks. "Sure," I say. She pours out fuming-hot coffee and hands the mug back to the security guard, who returns to his post. She passes me a cup and confides, "If you really want to meet the mayor, do what I said, come in the morning, at seven, seven thirty, through the garage. Wait for him there... You can't go wrong." I set the mug in the sink, thank her for her kindness, and head back across the hall, "Bye now, Mr. Peninha," Valéria, congenial, waves. I nod at the security guard and walk down the steps, welcomed bitterly by the dregs of the afternoon. Where should I go? What should I do? No sign of Galego. Walk, walk, walk... As though walking fixed anything. At least it tires me out. Patrícia... Marcim... Denise... Patrícia, dentist... Denise, physician... Marcim, mayor... They all did well... Turned things around for themselves... And here I am, without a pot to piss in. What have I ever done with my life? Maybe if I'd stayed here... Maybe... No, I couldn't have stayed. No, not after everything... João Lúcio was right... As a young boy he started hiding out in the country near Rodeiro with our Italian family... As soon as Uncle Ítalo bought the sawmill and moved to the city, João Lúcio stopped visiting Cataguases. Claiming he had to play ball for Spartano's B team—he was a left fullback—he spent every weekend in Rodeiro, where he learned to turn logs into planks, boards, laths, rafters, and timbers. The moment he completed his military service, he used the confusion at home to move out once and for all. Uncle Ítalo was always bemoaning the fact that he only had daughters—who would inherit his business? He urged João Lúcio to marry one of his cousins, that way they could keep everything in the family. But then Uncle Ítalo was paralyzed by a stroke and needed money for treatment, so João Lúcio took out a loan from the bank and bought part of the sawmill, which he gradually turned into a furniture workshop. One day at a kermis, he met a young woman who was studying nutrition in Ouro Preto and spent holidays with a classmate from Rodeiro, and they became attached to one another. He didn't think twice before backing out of the deal he'd made with Uncle Ítalo and marrying her instead. The young woman, Maria Teresa, dropped out of school, and her father, a man of means and a relation of the Barboza Vieira family, which at one point had even boasted a senator, invested in João Lúcio's company, which in no time at all went from being a modest fabricator of beds and wardrobes for regional purchase to a national corporation with an enormous warehouse just outside the city: Pádua Furniture. Toffee-nosed Maria Teresa brought along Prazeres, the nanny who had looked after her from the moment she stopped nursing. Maria Teresa was spoiled, mean-spirited, and despotic. When Prazeres died, she asked to bury her in the Moretto family plot, a black granite tomb with photos of Nonno Anacleto Moretto and Nonna Luigia Peron. The Morettos put their foot down, refusing to entertain such *insolence*, and though she pushed, fought, and screamed, she ended up losing. Disgruntled and spiteful, Maria Teresa commissioned another tomb in white marble that was larger than ours and bore the turgid inscription "Barboza Vieira Netto and family"—she'd had Nunes struck from her daughters' surname because it was *too vulgar*—and buried Prazeres there. I feel light-headed. I enter a boteco, and flop into a chair. The server, a young man, stalks toward me. I gesture to explain I'm not feeling well. He asks if I'd like a glass of water. I say no. I take a deep breath. "It's the heat," somebody says. "Yeah, it's the heat," another person chimes. I take a deep breath. Remove my hat, fan myself, and put my hat back on. My hands and legs are trembling. I'm queasy. My vision darkens, I think I might faint. The server rushes back, "You're really pale!" he says. I take a deep breath. Open my eyes. Mumble, "I'm all right, thanks." On the television, a TV presenter, elegant in his suit and tie, is in the middle of a diatribe about criminals, crooks, and hooligans. A man, dressed in blue serge pants, Rider sandals, and a white open shirt that reveals a prominent, hairy gut, stands with a beer in hand remarking loudly on the news. At the other table, with a tulip glass of draught beer, a paper plate holding rounds of salami speared with toothpicks, and half a lime, is a man with a long gray mustache, in oil-blue shorts, a green polo shirt, tennis shoes, and aviator glasses, staring longingly at the street. Leaning against the bar, an older guy with white hair and beard, a T-shirt with political slogans, threadbare jeans, and roughed-up flip-flops sips cachaça. I wipe my glasses with the edge of my shirt, slowly get up, thank the server, and walk out. Still a little unsteady on my feet, I watch a bus pull up to the stop on the opposite sidewalk, direction Taquara Preta. A sign! I hurry across the street, climb the first step, and the door closes. I walk into the bus, reach into my back pocket for my leather wallet, pull out a bill, give it to the fare collector, and push through the turnstile as he hands me some change. The bus speeds across the new bridge, down below it, the dark and fetid waters of Rio Pomba. I sit next to a man in a once-black suit, yellow tie, and shoes splitting at the seams. Bible in hand and index finger marking a page, he nods in greeting then looks back down at the book, his eyes grazing on the chapters and verses of the Sacred History. What am I doing here? It's a ridiculous idea to go looking for the pastor! What am I going to say to him? Hello, I lost your phone number...The bus stops, and in plod the workers who clocked out at six from Industrial Cataguases. Perspiring, they squeeze into the aisle and cling to the handrails, their faces drawn. I'll get up and get off. The city multiplies like cancerous cells. A supermarket now stands over landfill where the Island used to be. The houses, erected right on the sidewalk, now have metal bars on the windows. The bus bucks like a wild horse into Beira-Rio, and a hot breeze drifts through the window. Botecos, bars, botecos, bars, butcher, pharmacy, bakery. Our house is coming up soon. No, I can't get off here...There it is...We sold the place when Mom died. We thought of letting Isinha live in it—she needed the help—I didn't mind, Rosana had agreed, but at the eleventh hour, João Lúcio, or rather, his wife, kicked up a fuss, wanting revenge on account of her nanny, Prazeres, since Isinha had insisted it would be ridiculous to bury a stranger in the family plot, adding, Especially a colored person! Maria Teresa never forgave Isinha. Dad hadn't approved of Isinha's relationship with Sizim, her first love, because Sizim was a mulato, and he was convinced mixed-race marriages never ended well. She retaliated by getting pregnant and marrying Wellington, who was blond and a member of the Scarano family, from Leopoldina. The rest is history. Maybe, if she'd stayed with Sizim...He has his own taxi license, a nice house in Imê Farage, is well liked, and once ran for city council. Though he may not have won, he certainly racked up plenty of votes. Meanwhile, Wellington...We enter Santa Clara. The man with the Bible excuses himself and gets up; the bus empties out. I have no choice now but to visit the pastor. When I get there I'll say, Father, you probably don't remember me. We met on Santa Rita Square and you gave me a phone number...for Dona...I forget her name...Dona...Never mind...The number for your parish secretary. Well, I'm afraid I lost the piece of paper...Careless of me, I know. Ridiculous, even. And he'd say, in that annoyingly mellow way of his, Mister, et cetera et cetera et cetera. No, I've got to get off! As I sit by the window, the fiberglass seat hard and uncomfortable on my back, my body clammy and rattling like the metal exterior of the bus as it speeds down the crooked paving stones of Reta da Saudade and melts into the twilight, I spy beaming streetlamps and the beaming headlights of cars rushing in the opposite direction. The military barracks, The price of freedom is eternal vigilance. No pleasant memories there. Sublieutenant Cortes and Sergeant Martinez treated me like Moretto's Brother, the perfect soldier—obedient, responsible, fearless, honorable, combative, committed, an example for classes to come—not me, of course, but João Lúcio. I found it all insufferable: the physical exercises were brutal, the marches were stupid, the monitors were servile, Sergeant Martinez was sadistic, the combat boots gave me callouses, the sun burned, and my fellow citizen-soldiers were frivolous. The silhouettes of huge abandoned warehouses rise against the shadow of night, which stretches gently over the industrial zone. Old factories and mills—furniture, textile, metallurgy, apparel—that went bust, courtyards now overrun by wilderness, walls gouged by rain, roofs ripped up by the wind. Time, unrelenting, furtively gnaws at the passing present, like moths at a book. How many times had I ridden my green Caloi bike through that part of the city? It was nothing then but a dusty dirt road—on one side the occasional tree, stunted and shameful, while on the other, marshes along the banks of Rio Pomba, which flows so drowsily here it's like an arrow at rest. Silence. Solitude. The bell tolls, I glimpse the church. I get up, shirt and hat drenched with sweat, and stand with my hand firmly gripping the back of the seat behind three women, the one right in front of me carrying a nylon bag heavy with groceries. The bus stops and I get off. I rush along the unpaved sidewalk and anxiously reach the gate. It's locked! I breathe a sigh of relief. It's for the best... I'll take the same bus back. To hell with the pastor! I would've made a fool of myself... I walk across the street and into a boteco with a spring in my step. "Good evening," I say to no one in particular, the half-light barely sketching the bodies scattered across the three or four red metal tables that boast ads for a popular brand of beer. I ask a man holding a filthy rag if I can use the restroom, and he grudgingly points at a closed blue door—WC painted in enormous, sloppy white letters—with a wire that fastens to a hook. I unhook the wire and the door opens, letting out a cloying scent of naphthalene that turns my stomach. I flip on the light, hold the door closed with the sole of my shoe, unzip my fly, and pee, unsteady on my feet. On the wall are drawn penises and disconnected phrases: I fucked Tatiane—below it, in different handwriting, Who hasn't fucked her?—Uesli's Aline sucks cock, Ratão's a fag, I wasn't put out after putting out / Have you put out? Romaria to Aparecida—Talk to Ninho, Shit here motherfucker, with an enormous arrow pointing at the bowl. Disgusted, I pull the chain, flip off the light, fasten the wire to the hook. No sink. I thank the boteco owner, who is carrying a bottle of beer by the neck, and ask him where I can find the bus stop. A man seated at a table gets up. "I'll show you." His breath is sour with the smell of cachaça. We go outside. "Walk to the end of this street then turn left," he explains. "Thank you," I say. I begin to make my way, then hear "Remember, left!" The night is muggy and smells of night-blooming cestrum and jasmine, of rice and beans. Broken lampposts form glades of darkness. Though the houses are hidden by tall walls, the light from the glowing television sets makes the tree branches shading the sidewalk shudder in spasms of green, red, and blue. Light spills off the fat moon onto the bodies of cars parked along the curb. A stray dog hungrily sniffs the air. Aha, the bus stop! Fixed to a wood post, a white circle with a red outline and the word

Ônibus written in black, bullet holes in the O and B. On one side, a boteco, Beira Bar, its steel door shut. On the other, a vacant lot. I stand and anxiously wait. I need to wash my hands. Somewhere, there is the song and clapping of an evangelical service. The scent of ripe mango and cigarette smoke tickles my nose. I notice, then, an ember glowing at the mouth of a man leaning over a low cement-board wall. "Good evening," he says. "Good evening," I answer. "Hot, isn't it?" he continues, trying to make conversation. "Baking," I answer. "Imagine inside—it's unbearable! Practically a furnace. And then there's all those damned mosquitoes!" I feel as though I recognize his voice. "...*Aedes aegypti*, they're called. A couple of people in the neighborhood have died of dengue hemorrha..." But where from? I comb through my memories. "...dangerous...They don't look it, but they are!" A teacher...from school... "...You're not from here, are you?" "Huh?" "You...you're not from here, are you?" Mendonça! That's it! "Excuse me, but aren't you Mr. Mendonça?" "Why?" he asks, immediately suspicious. "I was a student of yours...at Colégio Cataguases. You were the art teacher." "Hell, you're right...How did you...How did you recognize me?" He flicks the cigarette butt into the distance, opens the gate, and steps toward me. It really is him! Tall, slender, a jet-black mop of hair, pajamas, flip-flops. I reach out my hand and he hugs me, reeking of smoke. "Wow, a former student! But how...How did you recognize me?" "I think it was the voice..." "Uh-huh, makes sense...At least that hasn't changed much, right?

Though I'm a little hoarser...From breathing in all that chalk dust. Hahaha...Aside from that...Never mind. What are you doing here?" A teenager chugs by on a motorcycle with an exposed exhaust pipe. "I came looking for Father..." "The pastor? Father Gil?" "I don't know his name...The one who serves the church around the corner..." "Father Gil. Is he a relative of yours? Do you know him?" "No...not at all..." "Father Gil...Father Gil is...He likes to spend time with the youth...If you catch my drift...Hahaha...Never mind, never mind. Hold on, though, you said you were my student?" "In fifth and sixth grade." "That must have been in..." "Seventy-one, seventy-two." "Right...What's your name?" "Oséias...Oséias Moretto Nunes." "Oséias?..." "Moretto Nunes." The teacher says: "Take off your hat." The teacher says: "Take off your glasses." Then he confesses: "I'm sorry...Maybe in other circumstances...Who knows if..." "Don't worry about it. Nobody remembers me..." I put on my glasses and hat, and he says, "Won't you come in a minute? For a cup of coffee...The bus won't be here for a while. They're few and far between at this time of night." "Thanks, but I won't sleep if I drink any coffee right now. Insomnia, you know...I'll take a glass of water though..." "Sure thing. Follow me." We cross a tiny front yard covered in a thin layer of crumbling concrete, where nutsedges push through the cracks and a rusty oil drum lies on its side over the gutter. Two small glass windows with metal frames hang wide open. "Come in, come in." The teacher ushers me through a door of untreated wood, the bottom veneer already half-rotten. He shoos away a fat black cat who's napping, stretched out on the patchwork chenille blanket draped over the sofa, and tells me to sit down. "Wait here and I'll fetch you some water." The stuffy living room with thick concrete flooring lets off a terrible smell—a mix of dampness, cigarette smoke, and cat. The walls, once blue, are bare. On a makeshift shelf, in terrible shape, are four art and design books lying on their sides, and four more books standing upright, their spines held together with Scotch tape—*Papillon, The Godfather, Jonathan Livingston Seagull, The Other Side of Midnight*—a picture of Our Lady—or is it Yemanjá?—a glass ashtray with a scattering of ash in it, a matchbox, and an open packet of Derby cigarettes. The teacher returns, in his right hand a small murky glass with water of a suspicious color, which he hands to me. Disgusted, I bring the glass to my lips and take the smallest sip possible. I sit in the wonky armchair. His face—moist and wrinkled, flaky skin and missing teeth—is half-lit by a dim lightbulb that hangs on a wire from the bare ceiling. I regret accepting the invitation. He ventures, circumspect, "I was just thinking. Your surname...Moretto, is that right? It just dawned on me...Wasn't Moretto the girl, the young woman, who committed suicide in Beira-Rio? About forty years ago..." My hands tremble as I knock back the rest of the water. My stomach turns. "Lígia...Lígia Moretto...My sister..." "Oh, I'm sorry...I'm really so, so sorry..." He places his hand on my leg with frank concern. Outside, crickets chirp. The teacher drums the armrest of the sofa with his left fingers, while with his right he pets the cat, now curled in his lap. I remember him in his classroom, teaching art. I say: "I remember you in your classroom, teaching us to draw." He smiles, sadly, "I wasn't such a wreck back then, was I?" He sighs, "I'm nothing but a poor old queen now…" His eyes probe the darkness, past the window and the yard. "I was handsome once. Do you remember? If only I had liked women… They were constantly throwing themselves at me… Even the married ones…" He waves his right hand as though erasing a chalkboard and says, his eyes roving, "Here, no one even knows I was a teacher… That I was important… I owned a house in Barridê… I had people of influence eating out of my hand… Do you have any idea what I've got to do these days to get someone to pay attention to me? I bring boys home, pay them to let me… touch them… I degrade myself… And you know what they do? They rob me, beat me, hurt me… I've got nothing left. You can see so for yourself… They've taken everything… the TV, the stereo, my cell phone… I use this thing now. Look." He pulls a small, old device out of the pocket of his pajamas. The bus is at the stop. I get up as if to leave but the teacher places his right hand on my arm and says, "Don't worry, there'll be another one soon." He rises, the cat springs to the floor and steals deep into the house. He takes the ashtray from the shelf and sets it on the left armrest of the chair. He pulls out a cigarette, lights it, puts back the packet and the matchbox, and sits down again. "It's not easy growing old," he says, blowing a cloud of smoke in the air. "Especially when you're poor and queer..." A car barrels past, music blaring. "I'm so happy you're here...No one ever comes into this house anymore, not unless they're paid to. They avoid me...My former students...It's like I've got AIDS... Christ! Generation after generation. Kids who are now lawyers, teachers, doctors, dentists. They all walk right past me like they don't know me. And some of them...Pff, never mind. Say, you don't live in Cataguases, do you?" He drags on the cigarette. I settle into the sofa. "No. I live... lived...live in São Paulo." "Ah, São Paulo...What a city, am I right? Afraid I've never been. Though I've wanted to my whole life. What about MASP, have you been to the Museum of Art? The city that never sleeps. Are you visiting someone?" "Me? I...Yeah...Just...My sisters..." "So they live here?" "They do." "I should have gone to São Paulo. The city of light rain...I'm not from here. I don't know whether I ever mentioned this, but I'm actually from Rio. Rio de Janeiro, born and raised. Actually, Santa Cruz, a suburb. It's still Rio though. I'm Carioca through and through...I wanted to be an artist, I even gave it a shot. I moved to the South Zone, but...When I realized I had no future there, I accepted an offer from my Aunt Noca, my father's sister. She was married to a man who owned a massive warehouse, the one that used to be in Vila Domingos, Casa Vouga. Do you remember it? I thought, I'll head over there and stay a little while. Soon enough a position opened up at Colégio Cataguases. I made friends with a bunch of oddballs who used to organize film festivals, music festivals, poetry festivals... Those were the years... It was totally wild... We had weed... Sexual freedom... It was the seventies, you know..." He takes a drag on his cigarette, then blows smoke up at the ceiling. "It wasn't the way things are now. This city, the whole damned country. Everything is so vulgar, the people, the men, the women, the music, their clothes. Everything. It's all vulgar and mediocre. I can say this because I'm a frustrated artist who used to paint small pieces to hang in the windows of Rua do Comércio. Christ, how embarrassing!" He stubs out his cigarette in the ashtray. "I could've had a better life, you know, but then... Love... *L'amour*, as they call it in French... Hold on, I'm so sorry, I haven't let you get a word in edgewise. Say something, man, for Pete's sake. Or else I'll just keep nattering on and on, and never stop! I never have anyone over, understand? Never." Stomach in a twist, murky water. The black cat pads back, glares at me, hops into the teacher's lap, and curls up. "Do you remember the... incident?" I say. "What incident?" he asks. "My sister... Lígia's... death? "Of course... Awful business... A devastating story... Your sister, huh?... Such a sad, devastating story... What year did... that... Did it happen? Was it seventy..." "Seventy-five. 4:30 p.m. on September 23, 1975. A Tuesday." "Goodness! It's been forty years..." "That's right... forty years! You close your eyes and when you open them... forty years have passed..." "And...

you...Did you ever find out...uh...Why she did
something so...so...drastic?" I get up and walk to the
window, caravans of stars glow in the deserted sky. The
song and clapping of the evangelical service...The scent of
ripe mangos...I'm sweating from head to toe. I hear a
match striking. The teacher walks past me, crosses the yard,
stops at the low wall. He looks from one end of the
sidewalk to the other. Drags on his cigarette. Walks slowly
back. Outside, I turn to face the house but remain standing.
The teacher sits in the armchair and lets out a puff of
smoke. He says, "Dear boy, listen carefully to this old man
who's been through all kinds of things in life. Don't let the
past consume you. The past isn't real. We've made it up.
What exists is the present. This moment, here and now.
Hic et nunc...Nothing else...There is no past, no future.
Just present. Carpe diem!" I watch as a trail of tiny ants
vanishes near the teacher's feet, his toenails cracked. "I died
with Lígia..." I say. "And this is what I've become. A body
without a soul. That longs for...and fears...the end..." He
drags on his cigarette, says, "I understand, I understand."
His right hand brushes away the ash fallen on his pajama
top. "Look at me," he adds, blowing smoke up at the ceiling.
"Do you think it makes me happy to live in this...hovel?
Do you think it's nice owing money to the bank, to loan
sharks? Do you think I like bringing little hoodlums home
to assault and humiliate me? I don't! And yet I can honestly
tell you right now: *I am happy*. You know why? 'Cause
there's no point crying over spilled milk...What's done is

done... I had a house in Barridê—gone. I had a car—gone.
I had money—gone. All because I believed in... In love..."
I turn back to the window and listen for the rumble of the
bus. My stomach turns, nauseated. I take a deep breath.
The teacher goes on and on. His words hover in the living
room and hit my ears like waves washing ashore, some loud,
others soft, while still others die before reaching the sand.
"(...) Thirty years younger than me... I fell in love (...)
Talented, you had to... (...) Practically in my house (...) I
signed him up for classes at Yázigi... (...) motorcycle? I got
him a motorcycle. He wanted clothes? I got him clothes
(...) stupid to invest in his career. (...) in Parque Lage, in
Rio (...) second mortgage on my house, would you believe?
Just so I could pay six months' rent on an apartment on
Rua São Clemente, in Botafogo (...) car and clothes so he
wouldn't feel embarrassed, the luxury! (...) canvases,
paints, paint brushes, all imported (...) at first he used to
come back to me in tears, claiming he missed me, but then
(...) an American art dealer boyfriend and (...) the son of
a housekeeper who lived in Dico Leite, a housekeeper! (...)
now in New York, they say he's famous (...) His mom still
lives in the area, in penury (...) he never looked me up,
which—" The sound of the bus shoots through the night.
"I'm going to catch that one, Mr. Mendonça!" I say. I hurry
through the yard and stand next to the sign for the bus
stop. He follows me. "Oh, you're really going? What a
shame... I'm sorry, I talked too much, didn't I?" The bus
pulls up. "Come visit again, when you've got more time." I

step in, the doors close. I shove my hand in my pant
pocket, take out some money, give it to the fare collector,
walk through the turnstile and down the aisle, then sit at a
window. Aside from me, there is also a religious couple—
the man in a suit and tie, the woman in a long skirt, both
with Bibles in hand—and a teenager with enormous
headphones jammed over her ears. Taquara Minimart. Bar
Vinícius. Todinho Filling Station. Povo Pet Store. The bus
is empty and bucks speedily down the uneven paving
stones of Reta da Saudade, the fiberglass seat hard and
uncomfortable, hurting my back. A cool breeze gusts
through the window. A slow fog settles, drawing a tulle
curtain across the landscape. The driver is chatting with
the fare collector, raising his voice over the clatter. "They
held up the guy who does the Leonardo–São Vicente
route." "Were they armed?" "Yep. A couple of young thugs.
The bus was coming into São Vicente when one kid
flashed a gun at the fare collector and the other stuck a
knife to the driver's throat. There were only four, five
passengers on board. They took the money and ran."
"Folks like that should get death row." "Yeah…Sounds
like they were minors though." "Minors? Sure. God forgive
me but as far as I'm concerned: you kill someone, you get
the noose. Remember that guy…" The bus plunges into
darkness and stops in Santa Clara, in front of the Church
of the Foursquare Gospel, "Hallelujah, brothers!" beams
the pastor. "Hallelujah!" echo his congregants. Three
passengers climb on. A man holding a package, maybe a

night watchman for some company on the way to his shift with a late-night snack, takes a timid seat next to me. A young man forces open the jammed window and his girlfriend, outside, whispers something to him. Another man, muscled arms covered in tattoos, growls into his cell phone, "...said I won't go.... Look, Jô, I've got obligations toward Maico, he's my son too. I don't even need the law to make me do it. But I ain't got none toward you, not one...You screwed around on *me*, and you've got the nerve to come to me with this crap?...Huh?! No fucking way, you hear me, no fucking way!...Sure, go wherever you like, but...No, not a chance...No, not even the—" I need something to eat. I feel light-headed, uneasy, and I can't tell if it's because I'm hungry or if my stomach's upset, if it's the dirty water or the filthy glass...Black dye sweating off Mr. Mendonça's hairline...A huge cockroach scurrying across the doorway... Beira-Rio! The streets are deserted. Everyone's at home watching the nine o'clock telenovela. The bus stops in front of another evangelical church, Life and Peace Christian Community—small door, white plastic chairs, half a dozen congregants milling around, saying goodbye. A drunkard climbs on, sits down, immediately nods off. Then, our house...Our old house...Across from it, Assembly of God. It's been there for as long as I can remember. Holy rollers...*Holy rollers* is what we called anyone who lived like they were still in the country—hayseeds, clodhoppers, hillbillies...Bunch of holy rollers, we would curse...*Holy rollers*...There's our house! They were like cats and dogs, Dad and João Lúcio. Fighting over any old thing. Mom always took João Lúcio's side. Dad picked on Rosana on account of Dona Magnólia, but they never argued. Even as a conceited, self-assured kid, she'd ignored everyone at home, without exception. But Dad and João Lúcio were like exposed wires. If Dad cheered for Botafogo, all of us kids would root for them too; except for João Lúcio, who'd support Vasco. If Dad criticized the government, João Lúcio would sing its praises. If Dad said stick, João Lúcio would say stone. But João Lúcio was the one with the temper. His outrage was so intense his lips would quiver the moment he heard Dad's voice. One Christmas, the Morettos had gathered in the country outside Rodeiro, the men had just slaughtered a barrow, and at some point Dad got into a row with Uncle Ênio, the youngest sibling, a blowhard who enjoyed pulling stupid pranks. The argument became heated, and Dad, livid, had grabbed Mom by the hand while she was busy cleaning intestines for sausage casings, and yelled, We're leaving, Stella. Now! Mom shoved Dad away and he flew into a rage, tried to drag her by the arm. Then, Uncle Ênio, Paulino, and Ítalo closed in on Dad, who started screaming, Grab the kids, Stella, we're leaving. *Now!* Mom turned away from him and carried on minding the intestines. Dad, immobilized by Uncle Paulino, barked, Stella, are you deaf? We're leaving, Stella. *Now!* Mom calmly faced him and said, Nivaldo, sweetie, you're all worked up. Go take a walk. We'll talk once you've cooled down. And Dad said, I'm not

spending another minute in this pigsty. And Uncle Ítalo
said, A pigsty, Nivaldo! What pigsty? Uncle Paulino let go
of Dad, who lost his balance and crashed on the ground.
He got up in silence, grabbed his hat, and headed toward
the road, screaming, Uppity fucking Italians! You're the
worst race on the planet. You'll pay for this! He never
stepped foot on the farm again, and never spoke another
word to any of the Morettos. The cousins had followed the
scene from afar—necks craned and ears straining—having
been herded away by Aunt Biquinha as soon as things
started to get ugly. João Lúcio was nine, ten years old at the
time, and knee-high. He soured on Dad from that day on.
The hatred he felt for him grew and grew until...when
that...thing...happened... the...the accident...he
blamed Dad, started a screaming match, caused a scene...
and decided to take Uncle Ítalo up on his offer. He moved
to Rodeiro three months later, right after finishing his
military service. At night, the city seems to shrivel...Next
stop, Rui Barbosa Square. A few passengers had gotten off
the bus without my realizing—the religious couple and the
drunk—while others had gotten on. The man I think is a
night watchman stands and pulls at the nylon cord, making
the bell ring. I stand too. The bus stops, and we get off. I
need to eat something, my body's shaking, my hands and
feet are sweating cold. I walk down the pedestrian way of
Rua do Comércio, through the fog. Everything is closed. A
teenager in garish makeup, jean shorts, with a huge tattoo
on her thigh, a red top hiding small breasts, and another

tattoo on her exposed midriff, steps toward me, "How's it going, stud?" she says as she grabs me by the neck and tries to kiss me on the lips. "C'mon, pauzudo, bring that big dick over here." Her eyes are red. I gently break free. Up ahead, another woman in practically the same outfit asks, "Want some crack?" I quicken my pace. Light spills from a door onto the pavement, the neon sign broken. I head inside. A man mops the floor with a damp rag; it smells of Pinho Sol. "Good evening," I say, queasy. He eyes me warily. I ask, "Anything left to eat?" He rests the squeegee against the wall, wipes his hands on his apron, hauls over his tired legs. "This is what I've got." He gestures at the mostly empty trays—two coxinhas, three croquettes, and one ham-and-cheese *cigarrete*—and stands behind the counter. "I'll take those two coxinhas to go." He slides open the display and slips two pastries into a white paper bag with a tong, grabs a handful of napkins and sets them on the stainless-steel counter. "Anything to drink?" "Have you got any Coke?" I ask, pulling my wallet out of my back pocket. He takes a can from the fridge and shoves it in a plastic bag, along with the small paper bag. He tells me the price and I pull out a bill. He opens the cash register and hands me back my change. "The neon sign..." I say as I put away my wallet. "Vandals." He follows me out. "It happened during Carnival. Owner said he won't fix it...That he's going to leave it the way it is...to set an example." He douses the rag in the bucket of water, wrings it, and curls it around the squeegee. "The city shows up to collect taxes, but when we

ask them to enforce security, they're nowhere to be seen…"
"Goodnight," I say, crossing the street. I enter a dark tunnel
of branches and fig tree leaves, which block out the light
from the streetlamps. The sharp smell of urine fouls up the
stilled air. My stomach turns. I walk quickly, scared
someone will accost me. My head spins. My legs vanish.
Back in the day, this stretch had smelled of horse piss and
horse shit from the wagons parked by the station, waiting
for the train, freight cars loaded with merchandise. The
funk of a vagrant lying on a square of cardboard makes me
woozy. I pick up speed, then come to a sudden stop. Unable
to hold back, I spray a knot of tree roots with a thick stream
of vomit. I hear voices. A drag queen clips up to me. "You
all right, mister?" "I'm okay, thanks," I say, still nauseated,
spying a pair of red high heels. "What's going on, Dô?" asks
another drag queen. "Just some man being sick." Their steps
recede in the darkness. I take a deep breath. I'm not far
from the hotel. I need to shower. I forgot to buy shampoo
and conditioner. I forgot to buy toothpaste. I'll look Isinha
up tomorrow. Roll out early. Try to ambush Marcim. I ring
the bell, which peals through the empty lobby. The glow of
the television in the dining hall spills out a side window
covered in a faux-lace white plastic curtain. The sound of
shoes shuffling along the parquet, hands lifting the latch,
key turning in the lock. The face of a young man, Cleber,
appears backlit through a crack in the door. "Good
evening," says a voice, groggy from having recently been
asleep. "I'm a guest here," I say. "Nunes. Number nine."

Bleary-eyed, he opens one half of the double doors, glances at either end of the sidewalk, closes it, drops the latch. He palms the key from the counter and hands it to me, and despondently reels off, "Breakfast starts at six." I thank him and plod up the wood steps, cross the half darkness of the hallway, struggle toward my room and open the door. I flip on the light, lock the door, tear off my hat and toss it at the chair. I left the window open! I take out the greasy paper bag, napkins, and the can of Coke, and place them on the nightstand. I edge my shoes off with my feet and push them under the bed. I take off my shirt, hang it off the back of the chair. Take off my pants, leave them on the floor. I sit on the bed and take off my socks. I take off my glasses, set them on the nightstand. I lie down. I need to pee, brush my teeth, shower. I haven't got the strength. Mosquitoes whir my legs itch my arms itch my belly shit left the window open the house is there just like it used to be except for the bars the soggy coxinhas need to shower my body's sticky my mouth bitter so the pastor so sleepy the coke is going to get warm take some laundry to isinha's tomorrow get up in a second to pee where has gale

friday,
march 6

i need to close the window the window's open the window

i need to piss to get up haven't showered brush tee—

what?" I wake up. The light stings my eyes. I grab my
glasses from the nightstand. Get out of bed. I pick my pants
up off the floor, get dressed. Riffle through my backpack
for the toothbrush. I take the towel from the windowsill,
drape it over my shoulder. Outside, dawn lies unmoving
in the fog. I wonder what time it is. I open, then close
the door. The empty hallway snores, sunken in gloom. I
grope along the walls to the bathroom. Flip on the light.
Lock the door. Drape the towel over the curtain rod in the
shower. I brush my teeth. Gray beard hairs creep across
my face. I take off my glasses, set them in a corner of the
wet sink. Red, sunken eyes. Sparse, unkempt hair. I look

like an old man. I pull down my pants and underwear, sit on the toilet. Be quick. Leave the bathroom clean for the next person. The next person might be you. The next person...is me...I am the next person. I've got to wake up early, ambush Marcim at city hall...I wonder what time it is. I relieve my bladder and guts. Get up. Lower the toilet lid. Flush. The water, meager, trickles down without force. I pull back the plastic shower curtain, turn both taps. Several of the holes are blocked, and cold water spits this way and that in thin slivers. I get under the water, my skin covered in goose bumps. I need to buy shampoo, conditioner, toothpaste...On the ceiling, cobwebs, and dark splotches of mildew. Through the rectangular window, I glimpse silent pastures. The next person could be you...Malu...Danton, Robespierre, and Marat were not the Three Musketeers. The Three Musketeers were four: Athos, Porthos, Aramis, and D'Artagnan...I turn the taps in the opposite direction. Wrap my body in the rough towel, which scrapes my skin. I grab the squeegee and push the water into the drain. That person could be you...That person...I rest the squeegee against the wall. Pull on my underwear and pants. Wipe my glasses with a square of toilet paper. I grab my toothbrush. Unbolt the door, turn off the lights. I cut across the dark jungle, which whistles, psssts, hisses, purrs, shushes, sighs, and moans. I push open the door to my room, lock it, and stretch the towel out on the windowsill. I tuck my toothbrush into my backpack. I need to find out what the time is. Otherwise, how else will I wake up early enough to catch Marcim? Aha, the clock in the lobby! I unlock the door, shut it gently behind me, head down the dark hallway. Slowly tread the steps of the wood staircase. The lights are off, and I can't make out the clock hands . . . I wonder where that young man . . . Cleber . . . sleeps. I shuffle across the parquet, through the curtain of plastic strips, and penetrate the dining hall. Nothing, only the quiet of tables set for breakfast. I circle back to the lobby. Slowly tread the steps of the wood staircase. Head down the dark hallway. Push open the door, lock it. Take off my pants, toss them over my hat on the chair. I switch off the light. Lie down. I should've brought a book with me . . . How long has it been since I read a book what was the last one again so long ago now

huuuh?! I get up, heart bucking. I make my way to the window. Fog cloaks the street past the foliage. I get back in bed. Lie down. I wonder where i put isinha's address ah my back pocket

i stir awake to the trilling of thousands of sparrows. Morning light fills the room. I jolt up in bed, take my glasses from the nightstand. The untouched coxinhas sag in the damp paper bag. The Coke is warm. The city rises. Cars honk and motorcycles honk. Beneath the window someone washes the sidewalk, armed with a bucket and broom. I grab my pants from the chair, pull them on. Get into a shirt. Put on my cap. Sit on the edge of the bed and slip on some socks, shove my feet into my shoes. I grab my backpack, rummage through it for the Cebion tube. I uncap it, pull out a roll of cash, unfurl the money, count it, fold some into my wallet, roll up what's left, stuff it back in the tube, cap it, slide the tube back into the compartment, and zip the backpack up again. I open the door to the hall and spy three people in line for the bathroom. I walk up to them, ask, "Excuse me, do you know what time it is?" "Ten after seven," answers the big guy, glancing at his watch. Ten after seven! "Thanks," I say and pad back to my room. I sling on my backpack, lock the door, hurry down the wood staircase. Pereira, cross-eyed and thin as a rake, says "Good morning." "Good morning," I answer, dropping the keys on the counter and striding to the exit. "No breakfast?" he asks and I say no, already on the sidewalk. Little by little, the fog lifts. The street vendors make a racket as they pitch their stalls. A woman with a large box hanging from her neck with six thermoses in it offers up "Hoooooooot coffee!" Buses roll by, packed with drowsy faces anxious for the weekend. Most of the shop doors are still closed. Street sweepers pile trash against the curb. A truck unloads fruit and vegetables at the supermarket. The botecos' first patrons eat breakfast with eyes fixed on TV screens. I enter the pedestrian way of Rua do Comércio, stride past a young couple—shorts, T-shirt, sneakers, fanny pack, cell-phone armband, water bottle—he wears a baseball cap and she wears her hair in a ponytail, both are red, panting, covered in sweat. I reach Rui Barbosa Square. At the kiosk, two old men discuss the news in a dither. The digital clock reads 7:23. 24°C. Cine Edgard stands empty. João Lúcio used to come here all the time. He was nuts about spaghetti westerns. Never missed a single one. *Blood for a Silver Dollar. My Name Is Nobody. The Good, the Bad and the Ugly. A Fistful of Dollars. Once Upon a Time in the West.* He only emerged after lunch on Sunday to exchange comics and pocketbooks. Western everything. Comanche. Zorro. Nevada. Coyote. Tex. Marcial Lafuente Estefanía. Silver Kane. Colt 45. He was fascinated by that world—the horses, duels, deserts, carriages, good guys, bandits, saloons, the sense of honor, the fearlessness and solitude. He grew vegetables in a corner of the backyard and on Saturdays wandered the streets of Beira-Rio, basket in arm, calling at house after house with lettuce, collards, vine spinach, taioba, endive, and dandelion, which the neighbors used to buy with delight. With the money he made, he'd get tickets for the six o'clock screening and for the Sunday matinee. Thrifty, he haggled comics and pocketbooks, and always turned a profit. I skirt city hall and stop at the entrance to the parking lot. The security guard eyes me with suspicion. What now? A Volkswagen Gol with a city hall logo pulls up at the sidewalk. A man, short, thin, clean-shaven, pushes open the heavy gate, which sluggishly gives way. That's when I spy him, Marcim, in the passenger seat; black

suit, blue tie, kempt beard, heavier and more dapper, but
Marcim no less. Before the security guard can see me, I
walk beside the car and wave at Marcim, who absently
waves back. The driver parks and Marcim gets out. I
approach him. "Good morning," I say. He reaches out his
hand, confused, "Good morning," he replies and starts
toward the side door that leads to the lobby. The security
guard takes a hesitant step toward us. "Marcim, it's me,
Peninha. Remember?" He stops, frowns, exclaims,
"Peninha?! Wow, you…" He starts walking again. The
security guard retreats. I enter the lobby behind Marcim.
"We went to Colégio Cataguases together…" "I
know… You've changed quite a bit, haven't you!" Then,
with a friendly smile, he says, "Good morning, everybody."
"Good morning, Mr. Mayor," Michele and the security
guard chime in unison from the break room, as a smooth-
faced youth, stiff in his black suit and red tie, hair parted to
the side, marches toward us. "Good morning, Mayor," he
says, looking me up and down with disdain. "Romim has
gone to fill up the car. We'll be ready to leave any minute
now." "Thank you, Jônatha," says Marcim. Michele and the
security guard slowly return to their posts. "I guess we
should have a quick coffee while we wait," Marcim offers,
making a show of walking to the break room. "Good
morning, Dona Ivete!" "Good morning, Mr. Mayor," she
answers. "Looks like somebody woke up on the right side of
the bed today…" She glances at me with complicity. "I left
a note, I'm not sure if it ever reached you," I remark to

Marcim. "Oh, of course, a note. Yeah, yeah, of course I got it...What's good today, Dona Ivete?" He turns to face me, "So where do you live?" "São Paulo." "Michele's cornbread," Dona Ivete answers, maliciously. "Michele? Oh, the young woman who works the phones...Hmm...Let's give Michele's cornbread a try then," he booms, so the receptionist can hear him. Dona Ivete places two mugs brimming with coffee on the small table. "Do you remember Mr. Mendonça?" "Mendonça?" "He was our art teacher." "Oh yeah, the gay one...Is that right?" Dona Ivete places another ceramic plate with two squares of cornbread on the table. "Sugar?" she asks me. "Sure," I answer. "None for me, thanks," says Marcim as he shoves a wedge of cornbread in his mouth. "I bumped into him yesterday," I explain. Marcim chews and then sips at his coffee. "This cornbread's to die for, Michele," he gushes. The receptionist smiles with feigned modesty. Marcim turns to face me. "Sorry, you were saying..." "That I ran into him yesterday...Mr. Mendonça." "Oh right, Mr. Mendonça...Uh-huh...Pretty thing, isn't she?" The man named Jônatha creeps toward us, half-arrogant, half-servile, and hands Marcim a cell phone. "For you, Mr. Mayor." Marcim takes the phone and steps away. Dona Ivete asks, "Are you off to Belo Horizonte again?" "You lot down here seem to know the mayor's schedule better than I do..." "Don't worry, hon, the rabble only pick at what they need to survive." She howls with laughter. I drink the last sip of coffee. Marcim comes back and returns the cell phone. He glances over at Dona Ivete. "Saying mean things about me behind my back, are you?" She howls. "Always! If I don't tell the truth, who will?" Marcim laughs. "Is there anything I can help you with? Just say the word." "No, no. Nothing. I just wanted to say hi, reminisce about the old days," I say. "Ah, the old days…" he muses. "Hey, Dona Ivete, tell me something. Any chance Michele is single?" "Now, Mr. Mayor. Do I look like a pimp to you? Does this place here look like a brothel?" She howls again. "That Dona Ivete…" Jônatha creeps up to us and says, "Romim's back." Marcim continues, "Peninha, I'm sorry I couldn't spend more time with you. I've got a meeting to get to in Belo Horizonte. Lunch with Congressman Carvalho Sá, I need to talk to him about increasing our budget." "Carvalho Sá?! Is he related to Mr. Carvalho Sá?" "His grandson. Good kid. Young, smart, he studied…" Marcim leans over to his advisor. "Jônatha, what did the congressman study again?" "He has a degree in economics from the Federal University of Juiz de Fora, and he got his MBA in Rio de Janeiro." "That's it, an MBA! Nothing to sneeze at, am I right? He was elected last year with almost twenty-five thousand votes from the Zona da Mata, all the way up the coast! It was the first time he ran…Quite the find, that kid. Before you know it he'll be working in Brasília." Jônatha taps his watch with his index finger. "All right, Peninha, I've got to go. It was great seeing you. If you ever need anything, just say the word! Michele, be good to my friend here, will you?" "Leave it to me, Mr. Mayor," she fawns. I walk them to the official state car, a black C-Class Mercedes-Benz. Marcim says, before sliding into the back seat next to Jônatha, "It was really great to see you, Peninha. You're looking well. We should do this again sometime! Look, if there's anything you need, anything at all, don't be shy, just let me know…" The driver starts the engine. The car rolls through the parking lot gate and a man—short, thin, clean-shaven— sluggishly shuts it behind them. I spot a bowl of kibble and another of water next to the guard booth. "Have you got a dog?" Slumped in the seat of an old van reading the *Jornal Cataguases* is the driver of the Gol, who answers, "Oh yeah, that's Pelé. A scoundrel who knocks around the neighborhood." "Black, shiny coat?" I ask. "That's him. Pelé is what we call him." "Is he yours?" "Pelé belongs to everybody," the driver answers. He folds the paper and lays it on a round table next to a red thermos and two glasses dirty with coffee. "He ain't nobody's," says the clean-shaven man. "We feed him here, someone else feeds him there. Nobody knows where he ends up at night. But he's gotta belong to someone. He always looks nice, like he's being taken care of…" The driver lights a cigarette. "Every Thursday he up and disappears. It's crazy! Dona Ivete says he takes the day off to see his sidepiece in Muriaé…" They both howl with laughter. After saying goodbye, I walk back into the lobby and head straight for the break room. "Thank you so much, Dona Ivete." "No problem, honey. I'm still good for something, aren't I?…More coffee?" "No. But thank you. Is there a bathroom around here I could use?"

She slips out of her cubicle and points, "Right there, you see, just around the staircase." "Thanks," I say. So that good-for-nothing Galego is actually Pelé... I enter the bathroom, unzip my pants, piss in the urinal. I zip my fly, open the tap, take off my glasses and hang them off my shirt. I wash my face. Wash my mouth. Wipe my hands on a paper towel. Wipe my glasses with a paper towel. I leave, stop at Michele's desk. "Thank you, Michele." She turns to face me, puzzled. "The note...He got the note, just like you said..." I explain. "Oh, yeah, the note...Don't mention it." I cut across the lobby and say goodbye to the security guard. As I walk down the steps, I gaze out at Santa Rita Square—nannies and new mothers strolling through the park with enthralled babies—and cross the street. Michele really is attractive. I wonder if Galego...I mean, Pelé...belongs to anybody, or if he just wanders from house to house—independent, sovereign, and free. I stuff my hand in my back pocket, fish out a piece of paper, unfold it—Rua José Custódio Araújo, 470, Ana Carrara—fold it, and slip it back in place. I walk down Rua do Pomba, making sure to steer clear of Tamires's shop. It's not her fault, poor thing. Maybe I should visit her...Businesses are already open. So, Mr. Carvalho Sá...His grandson, a congressman... MBA...I would've liked to visit Belo Horizonte. People say it's beautiful...In Rio de Janeiro, I went to the beach, took the tram, visited Christ the Redeemer...Three times. Marília loved it. Nicolau was a kid—little plastic bucket and shovel, splashing around in the water...I didn't mind it. Rio...A man tore Marília's gold chain off her neck...We didn't even see it happen...The chaos...So many people packed together...Rosana used to go all the time. She'd spend New Year with Dona Magnólia in Copacabana and come home toasted from the sun...Oh, Rio! she'd swoon, gloating. You simply must go, Isinha! And Isinha, who had three kids to bring up, would say, I've seen it in telenovelas. But maybe one day, God willing. I'm not sure she ever did. She won't now. João Lúcio visited once and hated it. I don't know whether he ever went back. He found it filthy, foul-smelling, expensive. Mom never visited. She only ever traveled to Rodeiro, to see family. She ventured farther once on a pilgrimage to Aparecida do Norte, when we were still small. Somewhere there's a sepia portrait of Mom and Dad standing by a grotto...Instead of taking us to the countryside to stay with family, they had Grandma Luigia look after us in Cataguases, I'm not sure why. Quick-tempered, she spent the whole time swearing at us. *Stupido! Maledio! Buèlo!* The digital clock reads 28°C. 9:18. There's the bus! Chácara Paraíso–Ana Carrara. Five people get on. I plod up the steps, fish some change out of my pocket, count it, and hand it to the fare collector. I head through the turnstile, take off my backpack, and sit down. The woman behind me taps my shoulder. "Mister, I don't mean to bother, but you shouldn't walk around wearing your backpack on your back like that. The streets are crawling with thieves. They lift things and you don't even realize. I experienced it firsthand. They slashed my purse, and when I got home, I thought, Goodness, where's my wallet?" I thank her. The woman beside her agrees. "That's right. You can't be too careful these days." The man in the seat in front of me says, "Drugs...Drugs will be the end of this country..." "My nephew," says the first woman. "He was wearing his backpack on his back, just like you are, when he got home from school one night and thought, Well, that's weird, my pack feels really light. He looked inside. Huh! Where'd all his stuff go? They'd lifted every single thing...To this day he—" People arrange themselves, settle down...Congressman...Mayor...Ricardo... Rosana...João Lúcio...I wonder where Nicolau is right now. Dr. Alper...Oséias, I have your test results...I'm afraid...The prognosis isn't good. Is there anyone in your family you'd like us to talk to? We offer support services for—I never saw the point of circuses. Dowdily dressed clowns, clothes that reeked of sweat, measly circus rings carpeted in sawdust, sad, pink dogs in tutus, monkeys forced to behave like humans, startled tigers, tents riddled with holes...The globe of death, the din, the stench of gasoline. The doctor said, You've got six months, maybe more, maybe less. Try to live life to the fullest. Do something you've always dreamed of doing. Is there anything you've always dreamed of doing? That day, I was a trapeze artist mid–triple somersault with no safety net. A dead-end street, one mistake leading to another, fifty-three years down the drain. Is that any way to live? The young man excuses himself and tugs at the nylon cord; the bell rings. He gets off. I take his window seat. The Rio Pomba riverbed...Louro Ice Cream Parlor...Malu...Malu had said to come by Saturday morning to borrow the book I needed for my project on the French Revolution. I hopped on the saddle of my green Caloi bike, pedaled through the city, and rolled to a stop in front of the house of Mr. Guaraciaba dos Reis, in Granjaria, feeling intimidated. Mr. Guaraciaba dos Reis—stern, venerable, uncompromising— was the Colégio Cataguses principal. A white-painted metal fence separated the well-tended garden from the Portuguese pavement. Two pairs of V-shaped columns on the veranda supported the second floor, its walls light blue. I plucked up some courage, dismounted, and rang the doorbell, rousing the dogs. A slight woman soon appeared in a spotless gray uniform and headscarf. I introduced myself. I'm a student of Malu's. She said to come by to collect a book for a school project. The woman slowly turned back and walked through a door next to the garage. The sun punished my skin. There was the sound of classical music, the orchestra enfolding the radiant morning. I prayed Malu wasn't home. I could do something else with my day, cycle across the Sabiá or Matadouro bridges...I enjoyed those rides. The solitude...The quiet...The woman returned holding a bunch of keys. Oséias, is it? she checked. Wow, I thought to myself, Miss Malu knows my name! I asked where I could leave my bicycle, and she pointed at the garage. You can leave it there, nobody's going anywhere right now. We walked through a side door into a long hallway with high windows to what I imagined must be the kitchen and living room. We entered a large yard, on one side a low, ivy-covered wall that hemmed the orchard and on the other five or six steps that led up to a deck. Wait here, said the woman, disappearing again. A medium-sized pool, perfectly blue water reflecting the perfectly blue sky, two wood lounge chairs, and a pergola with a sink, two armchairs, a wooden coffee table, and an old hutch. I stood frozen in place, unsure of what to do. Then there was the sudden sound of barking and two massive dogs with shaggy reddish fur started jumping and playing around me. And in the middle of all that racket I saw Miss Malu step toward me, colorful sarong fastened over her red bikini, oversized straw sun hat with a red ribbon, mirrored sunglasses, a jug in one hand and a straw bag hanging off her shoulder. Good morning, Oséias, she said, warmly—white teeth, short black hair, golden skin—as she half-heartedly shooed the dogs. Don't worry, she said, they just want to please you. I stood frozen in place, blushing, unsure of what to do. Lemonade? she asked. Dona Elisa made it just now. It's ice-cold. I followed her, legs shaking, heart pounding. She placed the dewy jug on the table, grabbed two glasses from the hutch, and filled them with juice. Irish setters, she explained, brushing her fingers through their long fur. They're a couple, Carlos and Rosa. After Marx and Rosa Luxemburg, she said with delight. Even though Daddy thinks I named them after Uncle Carlos, his brother, and Rosa, an old nanny I used to adore. I was so mortified, I couldn't take my eyes off the ground. She pulled out from her straw bag *Grandes acontecimentos da História—A revolução francesa*, placed it on one of the armchairs, and continued, So, Oséias, do you like studying? I must have nodded yes. How about history? Do you enjoy it? she asked, after drinking the last sip of lemonade. I couldn't get a single word out. I thought I might faint. With enormous effort, I managed to mumble, Yes, I do, and then stammered, I like *your* classes, ma'am. That's great! she said, satisfied, No need to call me ma'am, though. I'm not an old hag, am I? She smiled and stepped toward the lounge chair, bottle of Coppertone in hand. I emptied my glass and followed her, legs shaking, heart pounding. What are you going to do once you've finished high school? She asked, unwinding her sarong and lying back on the chair. I must have said, Get a job, because she grabbed the bottle of Coppertone and asked, Don't you want to keep studying? Her delicate hands smeared sunscreen on her legs. She said, You're clever and hard-working, you should continue studying. You can be whatever you want in life...doctor... engineer... lawyer...dentist...Maybe even a teacher, which is a great profession, don't you think? Yes, I could be whatever I wanted. An uncharted world unfolded before me, my fate was in my hands...I remember nothing else from that morning, now buried in time. Just Malu in her red bikini and oversized straw sun hat lolling in the lounge chair, the sky mirrored in her sunglasses, her delicate hands slathered in Coppertone, the bright pellucidity of the pool, classical music sounding through the house, the sun smarting my skin, the dogs chasing after each other, and her silken voice wending through my ears, You can be whatever you want in life…Whatever you want… Whatever you want…"Hey mister, it's the last stop. Everybody's got to get off," says the fare collector as he grabs the broom to sweep the aisle. I sling my backpack onto my back and get off. I ask the driver smoking at the door if he knows the way to Rua José Custódio Araújo. He gestures vaguely, "Round that way." I thank him and head down the narrow sidewalk that edges the more modest houses—front yards strewn with sheets of corrugated iron and plastic, clotheslines pinned with colorful garments, massive satellite dishes. I step around holes and bumps in the pavement, dogs splayed in the dust, half-naked children sucking on pacifiers, and teenagers gathered at the curb. I stop at a boteco. "Good morning," I say, and then ask if they know Isabela. "Wellington's old lady?" a man queries, his belly firmly stuck to the bar. "Straight on for as long as you can. Second to last, on your left. The house with the almond tree." I thank him and trade the sidewalk for the road, a thin layer of crumbling asphalt where all I have to dodge are bicycles. My hat is drenched in sweat. There isn't a cloud in the sky. Wellington's old lady…A young woman mops the floor of a small room with two towers of plastic chairs—on the outside wall, handwritten in red over yellow are the words Truth in Christ Pentecostal Church—as the soapy water forms puddles in the gutter choked with trash.

If she were alive, Lígia would be...What?...Fifty-four years old now...And seven months...A parked van booms: "Ladies! Gather round so I can tell you about a new homemade detergent. Not only is it the real deal. It smells like roses and it's a steal!" A young man pulls out a cardboard box of plastic PET bottles filled with green, pink, blue, orange, white, and purple liquid, and shows them to his customers. Oh look, there's the almond tree. A red Fiesta is parked at the entrance. A low wall and a small wood-slat gate front a narrow, unfinished cinderblock house with another metal gate to the side. Two boys around three or four years old, one blond, the other dark-haired, race toy cars in the front yard—small mound of sand, roof tile shards, and broken bricks leftover from an old build—under the watchful eyes of a small mutt that barks cloddishly when he sees me. I clap. The dog advances and retreats in wild excitement as the children eye me with curiosity. A bowed, weary shadow, glasses hanging from a cord around her neck, in an apron the color of jerky, appears backlit at the living room door. "Well! As I live and breathe," says Isinha as she opens the small front gate and pulls me into a firm hug. "Here I am," I say. "Come in, come in," she says, ushering me into the house, where she introduces me—"These are Diego's boys"—and scolds the dog—"Shut up, Hulk!" We cross the tiny living room—torn-up yellow pleather armchair and two-seater sofa, thirty-two-inch plasma TV, black-and-white photograph of Guanabara Bay and Barcelona pennant tacked to the yellow wall—and cross the tiny kitchen—gas range, fridge, sink, rusted white-steel cupboard, light-blue Formica table for three—and head out to the backyard, where a heap of unbranded jeans sit on a worm-eaten wood table in the shade of a cow's-foot tree. Under the lean-to is a brand-new motorcycle, a plywood cupboard, a concrete tank, and a washing machine. A cockerel, leg tied by a rag to the wood stake holding up the clothesline, forages unperturbed. Beside an annex with a corrugated iron roof, birds peck at ripe guavas splattered on the ground. Isinha takes a seat. "Fetch a chair inside," she says as she grabs the scissors, puts on her glasses, and gets back to work. In the living room, I take off my backpack and hat and put them on the armchair. "Zana, who rarely calls, rang yesterday to say you were in Cataguases. Said you'd spent a couple of nights at her house then disappeared," says Isinha. I heft a chair over from the kitchen and settle down next to her. "She thought you might've come here... Told me to let her know if I heard anything." She nimbly finishes each piece, the ground beneath her strewn with scraps of thread. "I'd call if I had any minutes on my cell phone..." "I don't even have a cell phone..." I say. Shocked, she asks, "You don't?" I change the subject. "What inspired you to name a tiny, scrawny dog Hulk?" "It was Diego's idea," she explains. "'Cause he's always green with hunger." We laugh. "Coffee? There's some in that thermos over there." I get up. "Where can I find a mug?" "In the cupboard." I open the door of the steel cupboard and take out a large amber Colorex mug, then close it. I press the button on the red thermos, which lets out a stream of brown, almost see-through liquid. I sit back down and have a sip of coffee. Sweet and watery, just like Mom used to make it . . . "As soon as Daniel wakes up," Isinha begins. "He's still asleep 'cause he gets home late from school, see, and heads straight to his computer. He only crawls out of bed around lunchtime. Anyway, soon as Daniel wakes up, I'll see if I can borrow his phone to call Zana." I bristle. "The truth is I didn't disappear. She and her no-good husband turned me out." She peers over her glasses. "Is that right?" "Come on, Isinha, True-Blue Ricardo's a blowhard and you know it." Tentatively, she counters, "That's not the whole story, though, is it, Zézo . . ." I get up and almost yell, "Taking their side now, are you?" Isinha doesn't stop finishing her pieces and yet her voice quivers as she continues, "I'm not taking anybody's side, Zézo . . . But you've got to be fair. It wasn't me or you or Jôjo who looked after Dad when he was dying . . . It was Ricardo and Zana. I was busy with my own problems—and mind you, I've got plenty—and you were busy with yours . . . And Jôjo, well, after Mom died, he cut ties with the family . . ." I drink the last of the coffee and place the mug in the kitchen sink. "Remember, Dad wasn't even talking to Zana at the time. Still, she was the one who went over to his house to make sure it was getting cleaned . . . 'Cause they hired somebody to come by twice a week, you know. And Jiló, who works for Ricardo—you remember him, don't you?—dropped food off every day around lunchtime.

They covered the rent, electricity, water, paid for his medication…At the very end, they even got Dad a private room in the hospital, and that can't have been cheap." I sigh. Sunlight ribbons through the long leaves of the cow's-foot tree. The sounds of the two boys' shrieking ripples through the hot, still air. Skittish, the birds take flight. The cockerel, neck craned, scrutinizes the day. Wearing a simple, blue-patterned dress under a jerky-colored apron and flip-flops that reveal ragged feet, Isinha works the scissors tirelessly. "Is the pay decent?" I ask, sitting back down. "Pfft," she answers. "Couple of cents apiece. I break my back for chicken feed. The upside is that people come over to the house on weekends to get facials and mani-pedis…" With her gray hair held in a headscarf, wrinkled face, heavy circles under her eyes, dry skin, and arched shoulders, Isinha looks a good deal older than Rosana, born four years before her. "There are advantages," she continues. "Because I work as a finisher, I get pants at cost. I pop on a label—I've got a mini overlock in the room—and Wellington sells them to associates of his in the center." "How do you get ahold of the labels?" "From a guy in Muriaé called Jadson." "And does the company not mind?" I ask. "Mind what? The fabrics and patterns they use come from a firm in São Paulo. They cut, piece together, sew, slap on a label, and mail them right back. We're not involved with the same brands. There's no competition…" Isinha rises to shake off her apron, shedding a tangle of threads. "Where are you staying, anyway?" she asks as she sits back down. "Hotel dos Viajantes, the one near the station," I answer. "That old joint?" I nod. "What have you come to Cataguases for?" she continues. "No reason." I spy a singing thrush perched on a branch of the guava tree. "Seen much of Marília or Nicolau lately?" "More or less. I mean, no, not really... I..." "That's not right, Zézo. The boy's your son... Soon you'll get old. And you'll get sick... Who's going to take care of you then?" The two boys run in, the dark-haired one in front, crying—"Júnio hit me, Gramma, he hit me, Gramma!"—and the blond one at his heels, making light of the situation—"He didn't wanna give me the truck, Gramma..."—followed by Hulk, the dog. "Stop it, both of you! It isn't nice to fight! Go on now, go play. Grandma's got work to do." They threaten to keep whining and Isinha says, "Pipe down or I'll call Uncle Dâni!" The two boys immediately fall silent and scurry back to the front yard, Hulk trailing behind them. Isinha is proud and resigned as she remarks, "Diego gets the girls pregnant and I end up taking care of the babies..." "They look the same age..." "That's 'cause they are! Born twenty-two days apart. Except one is Ingrid's boy and the other one is Vivian's. My knucklehead son knocked up two girls at the same time. Can you believe it? And you know what the worst part is? Both of the boys have got the same name!" "What do you mean?" "You heard me. He registered both boys under the same name. Diego Nunes Scarano Junior!" "But that kind of thing can cause problems later on," I contend. "You think I don't know? Even Wellington, who's no Einstein, had a row with him over it. But Diego thinks it's funny... He's my son and I love him, but the boy's got no sense." "Do the kids ever see their moms?" "Tss! Diego takes them to visit sometimes, though they're not always home. But boy do they go at it on the phone! Their grandmas come by every now and then. Andréia—that's Vivian's mom—cries her eyes out every time, poor thing. I feel for her... You don't know the half of it, though. Diego's got another kid, a little girl, with a third woman... That one, Jessica, she's got her head screwed on right. Raising the girl all on her own. She has an office job at Irmãos Prata, makes good money. Don't know how he managed to trick her into it. Pretty girl, smart... Diego can't afford to pay child support, though, so she won't let him near the kid. I think they were a one-off. I haven't even met Tábata myself." "Goodness!" I say. "Now you see what a peach my life is," she concludes, resigned. Isinha gets up and shakes her apron off again. She drops her glasses, which bounce on the cord around her neck. "Right, time to clean the house!" She heads to the annex and pushes open the tin door. "Dâni! Wake up, sweetie. Daniel!" "Ma, gimme a break. Let me lie in!" says a voice groggy with sleep. "No, hon, I need you to wake up and go to the butcher for some meat. Your uncle's here." "What uncle, Ma?" "Zézo. Uncle Oséias... from São Paulo... Did you leave the computer on again, Dâni!" "Jesus, Ma. Cool down. I'm getting up!" he grumbles. Isinha cuts across the yard. "C'mon, Zézo! We can keep chatting while I tidy." She heads to the lean-to and opens the plywood cupboard, grabbing the broom and the dustcloth. I follow. She peers through the living room window at the boys, filthy and mucking around in the sand as Hulk sleeps in the shade of the wall. "Isinha," I say. "I've got two shirts, two pairs of underwear, and a couple of socks to wash..." "Toss them in the tank outside. I'll wash them soon as I'm done tidying the house. In this heat, they'll be ready to iron after lunch." I grab my pack and go to the backyard. I pull out my shirts, underwear, and socks, and toss them in the concrete tank. Daniel steps out of the annex—creased face, jean shorts, blue tank top, colorful sneakers, and tattoos on his deltoids and calves. He grumbles something, his voice pasty. "How's it going, Daniel?" I ask. Tall and lanky, light hair fine and spiked up, face riddled with pimples, Daniel disappears into the bathroom. Isinha sweeps the red, burnished-concrete floor, dustcloth hanging over her shoulder. The rooms are tiny, with chita curtains instead of doors. "This is where Diego and the two Júnios sleep." She shows me a space with three beds—one single, two bunks—and a closet. "Every night is mayhem." She stretches out the yellow chenille blanket. "Both Júnios want to sleep together in the top bunk... But they can't, can they, 'cause it's dangerous. Except my idiot son eggs them on. Then I have to intervene. They used to take turns. One in the lower bunk, the other in the single bed, Diego up top. Kids, the lot of them..." Daniel flushes. "Come say hi to your uncle, honey!" yells Isinha. "I already

did, Ma!" Daniel snaps back. She glances at me, as though
to confirm. "He's got school at night, poor thing. He's
awfully tired when he comes home." She smooths out the
sheets on the bunk bed. "What's he studying?" I ask. "He's...
uh...Accounting, I think...Something like that..." She
grabs the broom and sweeps the dust down the hall and
through the kitchen door, startling the cockerel. "And
Deliane, how's she doing?" I ask. "Oh, Deliane...Well, you
know, Deliane's found God, hasn't she...Universal Church
of the Kingdom of God...She doesn't visit anymore.
Ardiles, her husband, won't let her. Says our house is a den
of heathens." "A den of heathens?" "That's what he calls
it..." Isinha grabs a dustpan, sweeps up the rubbish, and
dumps it into a banged-up garbage can. Daniel, coiffed and
perfumed, says, "Ma, the money." He straddles the
motorcycle. "You're riding there, Dâni? The butcher's just
around the corner..." she says, still rushing to open the
metal side gate. He revs the engine, accelerates. I cut across
the kitchen and watch the scene from the living room
window. Isinha moves the boys out of the way—"Uncle
Dâni, where you going?" "Uncle Dâni, take me, take
me!"—crosses the front yard, flings open the wood-slat gate,
and ventures, discreetly, "A kilo and a half of topside. Tell
Corumba I'll settle up with him later." She shuts the small
wood gate, scolds the boys, locks the metal barrier, and
shuffles in her flip-flops to the lean-to. I cut back across the
living room and kitchen. Reaching over the concrete tank,
she turns on the faucet. I sit in a chair by the table strewn

with jeans. She soaps and scrubs the clothes. "Damn it, I forgot to call Zana... I'll ring her later. What were we talking about? Oh, Deliane... So, she doesn't visit anymore. But I go there to see the grandsons... Isaque and Mateus... One's eight, the other's ten. They're darlings... I've got a photo of them somewhere. I'll show it to you later. They're doing well, thank God. They've got a little house in Guanabara. Ardiles works in the air-conditioning business. He's got two employees. Deliane does the numbers. We never talk when I visit. All she does is try and convert me. Would you believe it?" Isinha rinses the clothes. "You've seen all I've got going on. To think I'd find the time to go to church to clap and sing and yell Praised Be, Hallelujah! Then on weekends, Sunday service, home visits, hospital visits..." Isinha picks up a plastic orange basket filled with pegs and hangs each piece on the clothesline. "I've got too much on my plate! Folks coming and going all day long. Looking for Diego, 'cause you know he's in the car business, right? Boy's always got two vehicles on the go, one for him to use, the other to leave outside on display... Then there's those who come fetch pants from Wellington... And the two Júnios... And Dâni... I take care of them all! Where am I meant to find the time to listen to a priest jabber on about what's right and what's wrong? I won't say never, 'cause you can't ever know what tomorrow will bring, but... See, the problem is... In this God-bothering country, if you're with them they'll move mountains for you. But if you're a heathen, as Ardiles likes to call us, they'll let you

starve to death. They don't give a damn." Isinha changes
the water in the cockerel's tin. "Wellington brought us this
little guy to cook up. But then the Júnios got attached . . .
They even gave him a name . . . Zé. Nobody's got the
courage to kill the poor thing. So the bird just hangs out
here, like he's a pet. The Júnios have just about forgotten he
exists. Joke about eating the cockerel, though, and they
turn on the waterworks." At the sound of the shrill
motorcycle horn—"It's Daniel!"—Isinha darts away,
unlocks the metal gate, cuts through the front yard,
grumbles, chides, cuts back through the front yard, locks
the metal gate, and walks in with a plastic bag. "The cell
phone!" She smacks her forehead and places the bag on the
kitchen table. "He'll be back soon for lunch. I'll ask him
then. He's gone to see some friends," she explains. From the
window, I watch as she opens the steel cupboard and pulls
out a saucepan, a casserole, a stockpot, and a skillet, then
sets them on the stove top. Sweat trickles down my temple,
forehead, chest, and underarms. "I'm going to use the
bathroom." "Go ahead," says Isinha, peeling garlic and
tossing it in a small wooden pestle. I push open the door—
it smells awful—and close the latch. A plastic, flower-
patterned curtain divides the room. I raise the toilet cover,
unzip my pants, pee. A gecko clings to the wall. The louver
window is jammed, one of its glass panes broken. A car
steers down the road. I gather snippets of conversation from
the Júnios. I flush. Take off my glasses and wipe them with
toilet paper, then slide them into my shirt pocket. I wash

my face and dry it on the damp towel. I avoid the mirror spattered with toothpaste. Put on my glasses, unlatch the door, open it. The scent of rice takes over the noonday. Isinha is tenderizing the meat with a wooden mallet. I drag a chair to the kitchen and sit down. "I took a cab the other day. You wouldn't believe who the driver was. Sizim's kid!" Isinha says nothing. The black beans gurgle in the stockpot. Isinha sprinkles salt and pepper on the steak. One of the Júnios, the blond kid, sprints in. "Gramma! Gramma! It's Grampa!" There is the sudden booming of Wellington's voice, Júnio's chortling, and Hulk's joyful, chaotic barking. Júnio clings to Isinha's legs and asks for water. Wellington enters the kitchen with a grandson at his hip and the dog at his heels. "Peninha! I'm always saying: they'll show up so long as they've got breath in them." He sets the boy on the floor and pulls me into a firm hug, eyes glassy and breath sour with booze. The dark-haired boy tugs at Isinha's apron. "Gramma, gramma, me too!" Isinha pours water from a clay bottle into a plastic green mug. "It's been forever! Look, Zinha, it's your brother! She was beginning to worry," Wellington says, edging near the stove. "Opa! Meat for lunch! Zinha didn't think you'd come...Rosana said you'd disappeared...What did I say? Well, here he is!" He mechanically stuffs his hand in his pocket and pulls out two candies to give to his grandsons. "Wellington! I've told you a thousand times, no candy before lunch! Hell, you never listen!" Wellington steps into the backyard and taunts: "Is today the day we finally cook Zé?" The two

Júnios start to cry. Isinha yells, "For Chrissake! What'd you do that for? Nobody's eating Zé. Y'all can stop now. Grampa's just teasing. Now get out of here! Go on, out with you!" He palms an Itaipava from the fridge—"Where's the bottle opener, Zinha?"—places it on the table, and grabs two glasses from the steel cupboard. "In the drawer," Isinha says, chopping onions. Wellington sloshes beer into a glass. He gets ready to pour another. I stop him. "None for me, thanks." "No?" he cries, as though I were confessing a sin. "Have you made a vow or something?" he queries, cautious and without irony. "I got out of the habit," I lie. "Years of traveling during the week without being able to drink... The constant driving and chatting with clients..." Wellington has emptied his glass; he fills it up again. "That's a downright shame. You see this?" He brandishes an unlabeled bottle that holds a golden liquid. "This here is top-quality cachaça, made in Rio Novo. Have a whiff..." He just about shoves the bottle up my nose. "Smells great," I say. "Want a taste?" he asks, pouring a shot in the other glass. "No thanks," I reply. He downs the cachaça. "Now that's some good stuff, sô!" He grimaces and slaps his thigh. The smell of sautéed steak permeates the house. Wellington—face bloated, hair sparse and gray, potbellied and skinny-legged, top three buttons of his shirt undone to reveal white chest hair, ill-fitting pants and frayed shoes— asks, proud and playful, "You see the grandsons? Dieguito and Juninho. They both have the same name..." Isinha cuts in. "I've already told him about it, Wellington." He laughs and knocks back his second glass of beer. The motorcycle horn screeches and the two Júnios barrel in, screaming, "Gramma, gramma! It's Uncle Dâni! It's Uncle Dâni!" "Open the gate will you, Wellington?" she asks. Wellington rounds the house, dog and grandsons weaving in and out of his legs. Isinha sets three amber Colorex plates, a glass baking dish with rice, a white ceramic bowl with beans, a steel baking dish with steak and onion, and an enamel dish with grits on the table, along with three sets of forks, knives, and some serving spoons. Daniel parks his motorcycle and heads into the annex, the boys tailing him like two smitten cats. Isinha belts, "Dâni, get over here. Food's ready!" Hulk posts himself at the kitchen door. Wellington sits down, I pull up a chair, Isinha sets a liter-bottle of Coke and two glasses on the table. "Gramma, gramma! Me, me!" says the dark-haired boy, pointing at the soda. "Me too," parrots the blond one. "No sirree! Y'all need to shower first," Isinha says as she herds the boys into the bathroom. Wellington heaps food onto his plate. I serve myself some rice, beans, grits, and a bit of steak and onion. Daniel takes a seat and heaps food onto his plate too. "Beer, Dâni?" asks Wellington. "C'mon, Pa, you know I don't like beer," he says, peevish. Isinha's cooking tastes just like Mom's. "Won't you look at that, Daniel. We get to eat meat today 'cause your uncle's in town," he teases. Daniel chews in silence, as though in a hurry to finish. Wellington knocks back another glass and shakes the bottle, which is now empty. Daniel downs half a glass of Coke with each forkful of food. Wellington gets up to grab another Itaipava from the fridge, tops up his glass, and slugs another shot of cachaça. Isinha steps out of the bathroom with one of the Júnios bundled in a towel; the boy shimmies his legs as he walks, leaving a wet trail on the red floor. I take a sip of Coke. "I saw Marcim Fonseca this morning," I say. "The mayor?!" Wellington's eyes glimmer. "Yeah... We went to high school together at Colégio Cataguases." "Hey, Zinha! Did you hear that? Your brother's pals with the mayor!" Wellington remarks. "I wouldn't call us pals..." I clarify, but he doesn't hear me. Isinha steps out of the bathroom with the other Júnio bundled in a towel; he also shimmies his legs as he walks, adding to the wet trail on the red floor. "What do folks say about him?" I ask. From the bedroom, where Isinha is busy helping her grandsons get dressed, she says, "He's a good mayor." "Good? The man's a crook," Wellington counters. The boy with dark hair, now fresh-smelling and clean, leaps into his grandpa's lap. "He does a lot for the poor," Isinha insists. "Does he now! What does he do, exactly?" Wellington stuffs a hunk of steak in his mouth. "He's revamped school meals, upped the value of workers' ration cards..." "We're workers though, aren't we? And we don't live off school meals, do we?" Wellington snatches a piece of steak from the floor and lobs it at Hulk. "The poor have good things to say about him... It's rich folks who don't..." Isinha insists as she releases the blond-haired boy, now also fresh-smelling and clean. He immediately wedges himself beside his half brother on his grandpa's lap. "Sure." Wellington has another sip of cachaça. "Those folks are so hard up that any old handout will make them sing." "I like him," Isinha says, trying to put an end to the conversation while spooning food onto an enamel plate for the boys. "You like him 'cause you don't have a mind of your own," Wellington continues, exasperated. "Are you all going to start again?" Daniel bursts out. Wellington turns to face me. "So, Peninha, seeing as you're pals with the mayor and all. Do you think you could get Daniel a job there?" "For fucks' sake, Pa!" Daniel shoves his empty plate to the middle of the table and gets up. "What? What's the problem? You're at school, aren't you?" Wellington nudges the boys off his lap and gets up too. "Wellington, cut it out!" Isinha says, squatting to stick spoonful after spoonful of food in the two Júnios' mouths as they pace restlessly back and forth. Daniel slams the door to the annex. "Jesus. You all can be real pissy sometimes! What's the problem with your brother helping Daniel get a job? He's his nephew, they share blood..." Wellington gathers up the rest of the plates. "But that's not how things work..." Isinha says. Wellington slides a mix of leftovers into a bowl for Hulk, who waits anxiously at the kitchen door. "It's not? Then how do they work, Miss Know-it-all?" "You have to take a public service exam..." "An exam?... Exams are for suckers! The smart ones get in through the window, Zinha. The window! If your brother wanted to, he could talk to the mayor tomorrow and Daniel would have a job." Isinha gets up and presses her hands into her lower back, which feels tender. She wipes her grandsons' faces. "Meantime, he's just bumming around...Did you see what time he wakes up?" Wellington asks me. "At his age, I had responsibilities. I paid my way." Isinha serves herself some food and eats on her feet. Wellington shakes the empty Itaipava bottle for the third time. "These days..." he mutters as he walks out. "Wellington, where are you going?" But he doesn't answer. The two Júnios burst into tears. "They're tired..." She leaves her unfinished plate by the sink. "C'mon, time to brush your teeth." Isinha shepherds her grandsons into the bathroom. She patiently squeezes toothpaste onto their toothbrushes and hands one to each of them while inspecting their ears. Hulk observes them, his eyes pleading. "Isinha, do you remember Sino?" I ask. "Sino?" "Yeah, the dog we had as kids. Small, black fellow..." "Sort of," she says, tuning out. She dries the Júnios' faces and walks them to the bedroom. I watch her place pacifiers in the mouths of the boys, who lie with cloth diapers in their arms. I hear her turn on the fan and close the jammed window. Hulk joins them, sheltering from the heat. Isinha softly shuts the door and tiptoes out. "Coffee?" she asks. I nod. "Won't you finish eating?" Isinha picks up her plate. "I'm used to it..." She scrapes the rest of the rice, beans, and grits into a reappropriated paint can, which she'd pulled out from under the sink and behind a pink curtain. "I collect swill," she explains. "I'm raising half a pig...It's cheaper...This way, we always have suckling pig for Christmas dinner." She turns on the faucet and fills the milk canister with water, then turns it off. She places the canister on the burner. Takes a glass container from the steel cupboard and dumps five spoonsful of sugar into the canister, then puts the container away. She sets up the metal dripper. Grabs a plastic container from the steel cupboard and dumps three spoonsful of coffee in the cloth filter, then puts the container away. She takes out two large amber Colorex mugs and places them on the table. She covers the pots and saucepans and arranges them in the fridge. The leaves of the cow's-foot and guava trees are still. Sweat leaches out of every pore. Someone in the neighborhood is listening to funk carioca, "As novinha tão sensacional / As novinha tão sensacional / Descendo gostoso, prendendo legal." Isinha used to love Roberto Carlos. She and Mom knew every one of his songs. They would cry when listening to the Rádio Cataguases program "Roberto Carlos em minha vida," and never missed his New Year's TV special. "Isinha, do you still listen to Roberto Carlos?" "Roberto Carlos?" she asks, abstracted. "You used to be crazy about him... You and Mom." She watches the water bubble in the milk can and says nothing. "You knew all his songs..." She pours hot water into the cloth coffee filter. "Oh, Zézo, I don't have time for that nonsense anymore..." "What about telenovelas?" "What about them?" "Do you watch any?" She fills two mugs with a brown, almost see-through liquid—"Nah"—and empties the rest of the coffee into the red thermos. I have a sip. It's sweet and watery. "Your coffee tastes just like Mom's," I say.

She sticks her hand in the pocket of her apron and pulls out a crumpled pack of Eights. She taps out a cigarette, strikes a match, lights the cigarette, and blows smoke without inhaling. "Uai, since when do you smoke?" I ask. "Clears the head." She adds, "Nobody knows...It's a secret." She laughs. "Have you really quit?" she asks. "Yeah," I answer, adding, "What about João Lúcio, Isinha?" "What about him?" "Any news?" "Nothing. He used to visit before Mom died...When her health took a turn for the worse and she moved in with us, he'd come by every week..." Leaning against the sink drinking coffee, Isinha lets her resentment shine through. "All Sunday he'd be at her side. He paid for the essentials, made sure she was comfortable... He hurt so much when Mom...went...He spared no expense for the funeral...The coffin was top grade, and we had flowers coming out of our ears...It was a classy affair...He even rented a bus for folks coming from Rodeiro..." Isinha turns on the faucet and wets the tip of the cigarette, then turns it off. She tosses the filter into the banged-up garbage can. "Next day he wakes up and decides we're not family anymore. You know he's just getting richer and richer, don't you?" Isinha turns on the faucet and squeezes dish soap onto the sponge, then starts doing dishes. "Do you think he's happy?" "Uai, Zézo. You know any rich folk who aren't? You've got to be dumb to be rich and sad. Goodness! If I was rich, I'd be the happiest person in the world." She sighs. "Anyway, I hear that snooty, fuddy-duddy wife of his is depressed..." "Depressed?" "You see... Word is Jôjo cheated on her... Serves her right, the cow!..." "Really?!" "You didn't know? He's got a whole other family..." "You're joking!" "Cross my heart... It was about three, four years ago... Wellington was in the gemstone business at the time and some guy from Guidoval owed him money. One day he decides to collect. Diego picks him up in the car and they drive there together. That's when they find out that this guy is the brother-in-law of Jôjo's other woman. Would you believe? He's got her set up in a house. Supports her and the two girls. The guy said they look just like Diego... At first I didn't buy it, but Zana corroborated the story." João Lúcio of all people... So proper, Catholic... "I know Wellington's no angel," Isinha continues. "He is or was mixed up in all kinds of stuff... But he'd never do something like that. And they say she isn't even pretty. Worse yet, that she's poor like me..." Isinha dries the dishes and stacks them in the steel cupboard. "Of course, she'll be taken care of. Or at least her girls will. 'Cause the law's got their backs, hasn't it?" "So you're saying he has two children outside marriage?" "Two girls! No doubt they'll want a share of Maria Luísa and Maria Fernanda's inheritance... His legitimate daughters..." "This could get ugly," I venture. Isinha dries her hands on her apron and palms the broom. "Now go sit outside," she says. I get up and heft the chair into the backyard. From the annex comes the sound of a fan, either rotating or stationary. Daniel walks out, groggy-eyed. He says, "Ma, I'm heading over to Dími's." Isinha drops the broom and runs to open

the metal gate. "Oh, honey, I've got to call your Tia
Zana... I'm out of minutes..." "Not now, Ma, when I get
back." They round the house. I hear Isinha's voice in the
front yard—"...see about buying a pair of pants, Dâni?"—
as she throws open the wood-slat gate. "C'mon, Ma. You
know we don't wear knockoffs. Please..." Daniel retorts
and accelerates. Daniel has left the fan on. The annex, a
rectangular room with no windows and a corrugated iron
roof, is a furnace. Inside is a bed, a desk with a computer,
countless wires plugged into an extension cord. Two posters,
of the band Sepultura and of a Ninja Z-14 motorcycle, are
tacked up with Scotch tape. "I was just shutting off the
fan... Daniel forgot to..." I explain. "Don't," says a
panicked Isinha. "Otherwise Daniel won't step foot inside...
'Cause of the heat... Then he'll go and pick a fight with us
about it." Hulk emerges, tongue lolling, and sprawls beneath
the table covered in jeans. In the lean-to, Isinha fills a
bucket with water from the tank, then hefts it to the
kitchen along with a rag and the squeegee. She splashes
detergent on the red burnished concrete and begins to mop
vigorously. Around the neighborhood, sertanejo music and
evangelical songs mix with funk carioca in a thundering
duel. The air is stuffy. Zé squats in a corner with his beak
open. "You're retired, right?" Isinha asks, panting. "Yeah."
"Zana told me." "It's next to nothing, though. Hardly
enough to pay for... Hardly enough to survive on." "But
you used to make good money..." "It was a different
time... The pay wasn't great, salary-wise. But I earned on

commission...I have nothing left. I gave Marília the apartment, for Nicolau...I walked out of that marriage empty-handed..." "See, that's why I don't leave. We don't own a thing, but if you put together the little I earn with what Wellington brings in...If I left him—and mind you, he deserves it—I'd feel awful about it. 'Cause how's he going to manage? The man doesn't have a pot to piss in...You know, he doesn't get on with his family. They're all still back in Leopoldina...And he hates it there. He'd end up on the street. Damned if I do, damned if I don't..." She wrings the rag out over the tank, and places the squeegee and the broom in the cupboard. She washes her hands and dries them on her apron, sighs and tidies her hair. "All right, let's iron your clothes!" She fetches a blanket from the house. She folds it in half and drapes it over the table, shoving aside a mound of jeans. She grabs the iron from the lean-to and plugs it in. She fills a milk-white spray bottle with tap water and turns off the faucet. She collects the clothes from the clothesline. "Is the backpack yours?" she asks. "Yeah," I say. "All right. I'll stick the folded shirts in there." Isinha grabs the socks and turns them right side out. She spritzes and irons them, then puts them away. She grabs the underwear. "Are you renting?" I ask, sitting beside her in a chair. "Yeah. We had enough for a down payment, but then Diego decided to start his car business...So we lent it to him. We never saw another penny of it. I mean, the money's there, but it's tied up in the cars, isn't it? At some point, he'll get bored and move on..." "Is the neighborhood decent?" "As decent as any other. Some good neighbors, others that aren't so great…The problem is drugs. The kids haven't got anything to do so they spend all day gadding around…They get mixed up in trouble. There's a lot of theft. You can't leave anything outside. The other day, somebody lifted the cardboard box where we keep the boys' toys. Would you believe it? An empty box! All right, here's your clothes. Nice and clean, and ironed!" "Thanks, Isinha." She turns off the iron and leaves it to cool on the floor of the lean-to. She puts the spray bottle back in the cupboard. Unfolds the blanket and carries it to the house along with my backpack. She sits back down, grabs the scissors, and starts finishing the pants. "Do you ever think about Lígia, Isinha?" I ask. "Lígia?" Isinha's eyes wander, as though rooting around the past. Her hands mechanically snip threads. "She'd be fifty-four years old and seven months today," I say. "She was born August 4… 1960…" Her hands pause. "Goodness…Honest, it's been a while since I've thought about her. All those years of my life…They feel like a dream…" Her body dips into work. "I think about her all the time…There isn't a day I don't remember…" "I pray for her…Now and then…" Isinha offers, by way of apology. The boy with dark hair turns up at the kitchen door, rubbing his eyes. Isinha is startled. "Oh hi, sweetie. Did you wake up?" She leaves the scissors on the table, as if the scissors somehow stood for the unpleasant subject. She holds her grandson in her arms. "You hungry?" she asks. The boy with blond hair emerges, dragging behind him the cloth diaper. "Gramma's gonna make you some porridge. Yum...How does that sound? More coffee, Zézo?" "No, thanks, Isinha." An oblivious rooster crows in the distance, the sound deadened by the chorus of a funk song. "Chacoalha, chacoalha / Chacoalha, chacoalha / Joga a buceta na pica / Doidona de bala." Hulk scampers away. Wellington huffs into the kitchen. "Zinha, have we got five pants ready to go? Diego's on his way. I'll have him give me a ride to Djalma's. He's just called..." Isinha points to the room. "Dresser drawer. They need wrapping, though." She stirs the pot with a wood spoon. "Cornmeal porridge. They love it. Want some?" she asks. "No, thanks...I'm full." "You used to love porridge..." She's right...I did love porridge...And I loved Mom's coconut cheese flan...And taioba...I never had any of it again. "Do you remember Mom's coconut cheese flan?" A car honks. "Diego!" The Júnios rush to the front yard, all of a sudden wide awake. Wellington returns with the plastic-wrapped jeans. "These are the last ones, Zinha." "They're collecting this lot on Monday. I can put another order in then...How many do we need?" "About twenty." "Have we got labels?" "Jadson's delivering them tomorrow." Diego walks into the kitchen with the two boys and Hulk tangled in his legs. He doesn't recognize me. "Diego, say hi to your uncle!" says Isinha. "Uai, Uncle..." "Peninha, your mom's brother," Wellington explains, knocking back a shot of cachaça. Diego hugs me, pats me on the back. "Wow, Uncle Peninha. It's great to see you..." He adds, "Ma, could you grab the paperwork for the Fiesta? I think I've found a buyer." "Have you had anything to eat, hon?" asks Isinha, and Diego sticks a spoon in the bowl of porridge cooling on the table. "Yeah." "Where?" she pries, jealous. "At Nicole's." "Nicole? Who's Nicole?" Isinha seems concerned. "Bagged yourself another, huh?" Wellington pokes, with sarcasm. "Your son's sure got a sugary pecker... Christ Almighty!" He laughs and Isinha heads to the bedroom, embarrassed. "How's it going?" Diego asks as he lights a cigarette. "All right," I say. "Just passing through?" "Just passing through." Wellington butts in, "Peninha's going to get Daniel a job... He's pals with the mayor..." "You're friends with the mayor, Uncle Peninha?" I say nothing, and instead just smile. Isinha comes back with a plastic sleeve and hands it to Diego, who slips it into his pocket. He licks the porridge spoon and drops it in the sink. "Is Uncle Peninha really getting Daniel a job, Ma?" Diego blows smoke through his nose to impress his boys. "It's all talk, Diego." "He does need one," Diego says. "That's what I said," Wellington adds as he horses around with the Júnios. "Pa, let's hit the road, yeah?" "Diego, could I bother you for a ride?" I ask. "But Zézo, it's still early," Isinha objects. "I really should get going. I've been enough of a nuisance already..." "Not nearly," she says, tearful. Wellington grabs the pants. I hug Isinha, then pat the two Júnios on the head. "When will you visit again?" she asks. "I'm not sure," I say as I grab my backpack and put on my hat. We climb into the red Fiesta, Wellington in the front seat and me in the back with the jeans. Tears streak Isinha's wrinkled face. "Women... Always fucking crying," Wellington grumbles. The Júnios start smacking each other, Isinha intervenes, Diego accelerates. "Bye!" I hear her yell. A barking Hulk chases the car for a few meters, then gives up. Diego connects his cell phone to the stereo. "Eu te dei / O ouro do sol / A prata da lua / Te dei as estrelas / Pra desenhar o teu céu." The husky voices of a sertanejo duo celebrate the love they've finally found in each other. The Fiesta speeds down the pitted asphalt road as the air-conditioning chills my clothes. "Where to, Uncle Peninha?" "Anywhere near the center. No need to go out of your way for me." "No problem. Just name a place." "Hotel dos Viajantes, near the station." "All right, that's where I'll drop you," he says, solicitous. "Diego, I've got to take these pants to Vila Minalda," Wellington gripes. "It's all right, Pa. I'll drop Uncle Peninha first then take you to Vila Minalda." "But he's already waiting," Wellington insists. "We've got plenty of time, Pa." Diego glances at the rearview mirror. He asks, "Why didn't you want to stay with us?" Wellington jumps in. "We haven't got anywhere to put him, Diego!" "We'd have figured something out... Wouldn't we, Uncle Peninha?" "Diego thinks everything's easy," Wellington remarks. The car's digital clock reads 16:58. "So who's this Nicole chick? It's Nicole, right?" Wellington asks. "A friend," Diego answers. "For Chrissake, Diego, you're like a fucking rabbit... All these women... And a kid with each of them... But who's stuck bringing them up, huh?" Wellington pats his chest. Diego laughs. "You, Pa? Like you've ever lifted a finger for the boys…" "You ungrateful shit! If it's not me, then who—" "C'mon. You know Ma's the one who looks after the boys. She's got a right to complain. You, on the other hand…Sure, you think of the boys every now and then. Buy them candies, give them hugs…But the person who takes care of them, like really takes care of them—who feeds and washes and nurses them when they're sick, puts them to bed and educates them—that's Mom." "Is that right! And who brings home the bacon?" Wellington cries, in a fluster. "Who? Come on, Pa!" Diego laughs. "Mom does! If we had to rely on you…" Wellington becomes vexed. His face clouds over. He mutters, "I guess that's the way things are…All right…" His eyes settle on a strip of old houses on Avenida Astolfo Dutra. The red Fiesta comes to a sudden stop. "Would you look at this, Uncle Peninha? You'd think we were in São Paulo. There are so many cars, the road never clears up…" I gaze out at the stalled traffic. "Diego, I think I'll walk from here. It'll be faster. That way you and your dad can go deliver the pants." "I don't mind. But if you'd rather…" I say goodbye, sling on my backpack, and climb out. My body shudders from the brutal change in temperature. My glasses fog up. I wipe the lenses with the edge of my shirt. I walk along the sidewalk, skirting tables outside bars. It's Friday, and everyone seems anxious to cast off their dirty work clothes. Rows of cars honk frantically. Clouds of sparrows swoop back into the trees to wait out the long night. Mom used to believe in omens...Sino's disappearance on the evening before Lígia...The day when all of that...happened...The kitchen wall clock smashed on the floor...Four thirty, it read...There wasn't a breath of wind...A pharmacy! I go in. Grab a plastic basket. I scan the display racks and pick out toothpaste, dental floss, shampoo, conditioner, soap, deodorant...I make my way to the cash register, place everything on the glass counter, stuff my hand in my back pocket, pull out my worn leather wallet, take out my last bill, and give it to the woman. She puts everything in a plastic bag and hands me my change. I thank her and walk out. I need to find a barber...Sweat fuses my shirt to my skin. Dad was never the same after Lígia...after her...death. If before he'd have a glass of wine with his meal, a large bottle of Maravilha de São Roque always chilling in the fridge—on Sundays he even went overboard, turning in as soon as lunch was done, stuffed with spaghetti and wine—after, he made it a habit to stop at every boteco on his way back from work, and came home drunk day in and day out, violent and nervy. João Lúcio had already moved to Rodeiro, so we—Mom, Rosana, Isinha, and me—were left to deal with his bouts of aggression. And if before he had never smoked in the house—the pompous ashtray that lived in the hutch was reserved for guests—going so far as to scrub his hands with Pasta Joia and gargle mint tea to stamp out the stench of cigarettes, after, a rank smell marked his passage through the rooms. And if before he'd tended to his looks with almost womanly fussiness—hair and mustache daubed with Glostora, face meticulously shaven, shirt ironed, pants pressed, shoes buffed, in Lancaster cologne—after, he was so slovenly as to be almost unrecognizable. When he was on the verge of losing his job for negligence—he, the man once named "employee of the month" by Industrial—the factory doctor diagnosed him with pulmonary emphysema, cinching his disability pension. By then I'd already moved to São Paulo and Isinha was shackled to Wellington. Mom, exhausted and probably under João Lúcio's influence, kicked out Dad, who, retired, retreated to a shack in Paraíso, a ruin of his former self. Salão Dois Irmãos—Édson and Edinho. The arrow points to the back of the arcade, the paint on the sign peeling. I walk in. One of the brothers immediately folds up an issue of O Globo and leaves it on the sofa. He gets up and says, "Good evening!" His name, Edinho, is stitched in black on the pocket of his light-blue smock. "Good evening!" echoes the other brother—whose name, Édson, is stitched in black on the pocket of his light-blue smock—as he coolly cuts the hair of a man who sits listlessly beneath a large yellowish-white sheet. "What'll it be?" asks Edinho. "A shave," I say. I remove my backpack and hat, leave them on the sofa beside a small plastic bag. He points at an old chair facing a Botafogo pennant, champion of Brazil, 1995. I sit. Aside from the chair, everything in the parlor is old; the tiles, the high ceiling, the counter, the mirrors, the scissors, the trimmer, the combs, the brushes, the stained walls, the cobwebs on the ceiling, the talcum powder, the lotion, even the two men, short, squarish, almost identical, their hair dyed jet black and parted to the side. Edinho removes my glasses, drapes a cloth over my chest, dumps powder into a small, ceramic white bowl, turns on the faucet, adds water, and stirs up some foam with a shaving brush. "Besides, David Luiz wasn't even born here," he says, taking up an earlier conversation. He patiently sharpens a razor on a leather strop. "But his father's from here!" argues Édson, standing opposite the Flamengo pennant, 1981 champion. "If that's the case," Edinho argues, "then it's got to be Friaça, hands down!" "Friaça?! The one who played for the national team in 1950?" asks the man, practically engulfed by the sheet. "The very one! Friaça was from Porciúncula, but he had relatives in Cataguases," Edinho explains, now sharpening the blade on a whetstone. "Our mom's cousin was married to a Friaça. Seu Argemiro," Édson adds. Edinho assiduously rubs an alcohol-soaked tissue on my beard and mustache. I shut my eyes. "If we're only counting players born in Cataguases, then it's easily Rosene!" he says. "Rosene?" echoes Édson, indignant. "Rosene doesn't hold a candle to Dinheiro. Remember him? He used to play for Manufatora." "Rosene played out of state, in Rio de Janeiro," Edinho argues. "Dinheiro didn't want to. Some scouts even came up from São Paulo to try and convince him," Édson explains. The man dwarfed in his seat offers, his voice faltering, "Far as I'm concerned, nobody beats Wilmar, who played for Atlético, for Inter de Limeira, for

Bangu, who even played on the juniors national team, and who..." On the day Mom told us Dad had moved out, João Lúcio drove over from Rodeiro and said, He can go to hell for all I care, then repeated the same thing to each of us. He refused to help, even though he knew Dad was sick, even though he knew his pension barely covered the cost of medication, even though he knew he lived in a leaky, rat-infested hovel. Obstinate, he didn't attend the wake or the funeral mass or the burial or

"that my godfather, God rest his soul, gave me. A French brand, L'Alpin," Edinho explains as he spritzes me with Aqua Velva. "They ran off with it that time they broke into the parlor, when it was still in Vila Domingos Lopes," he continues, fanning my irritated skin with the white cloth. "I don't know why. It's not like they could do anything with it," he laments, softly dabbing my freshly shaven face with a cotton pad. "That's when I found out about Filarmonica, a Spanish brand. Best razor under the sun," he boasts, scouring my face for a microscopic hair. "Second best," Édson contests. "There's nothing quite like Solingen," he says, brandishing his razor. "Everybody knows Germans are the best steel producers in the world." "They make the best steel, I'll give you that, but they don't make the best knives." Edinho rights my chair, satisfied. "There you go! The torture's over!" Satisfied, he hands me my glasses and turns the seat so I am facing the mirror. I get up, a little light-headed, and glance at the price chart. I take money from my pocket, pay, open my backpack, stuff my hat and the small plastic bag inside, and sling it on my back. I say goodbye to Edinho and Édson, and to the man whose face is now slopped in foam and who wishes me a good evening with his eyes. I leave the arcade. Clouds of swarmers gather around the streetlamps. I walk slowly, knocking into sweaty passersby rushing to bus stops. The shops are closed. The heat inflames my swollen, tired legs. In the bars, beer drinkers holler as they try to make themselves heard over the babel of voices, over the music spilling out of the television, over the din of car engines and horns stuck in traffic, over the trilling of sparrows. The last street vendors have taken down their stalls. A cart sells popcorn; another, corn on the cob; yet another, various sweets. Even though she was a good cook, Mom never had time to prepare individual meals every day; she was chained to the basement and to the tireless rat-tat-tat of the sewing machine as she turned out dresses, skirts, blouses, shirts, pants, shorts. On Sundays, though, she used to wake up early and spend the morning making desserts that kept in the fridge for weeks, and always did her best to please every single one of us: coconut cheese flan for Dad and me, rice pudding for João Lúcio, chocolate icebox cake for Rosana, brigadeiro for Lígia, cathedral-window jelly for Isinha. But on the day Lígia...died...Mom declared the end of desserts. As though it were a sin to soften the bitterness of such a loss. Once, when I was in Cataguases for New Year,

João Lúcio showed up without warning at the house in the company of an older woman. He walked in, hugged Mom, and explained he wanted her to teach his housekeeper to make rice pudding. Mom, overwhelmed with sewing commissions, greeted them both and asked, with majestic condescension, if the woman really had no idea how to make something as straightforward as rice pudding. João Lúcio said she did know how to make rice pudding, just not *her* rice pudding. Mom protested, claiming she had too much work on, that she didn't remember the recipe and didn't want to think about it anymore, but at the end of the day, she couldn't say no to João Lúcio, her darling son. She sent him to the center for Piemonte rice, milk, cloves, cinnamon sticks, and lime, and went back to her errands, while the woman sat in the living room, awkward and still. As soon as João Lúcio returned, Mom taught them to make rice pudding with teacherly precision. She tossed the rice, cinnamon stick, cloves, and lime zest into a large pot of water and let it simmer over a low flame. Once the water had evaporated, she poured in milk and sugar and brought it all to a boil. Then, she lowered the heat and waited for the mixture to thicken, stirring occasionally with a wooden spoon. The woman observed everything studiously and without speaking. Then, Mom put the rice pudding in a glass baking dish and left it to cool on the windowsill. She returned to the basement, visibly shaken. João Lúcio went out for some beer and salami, then sat in the living room listening to his favorite old records on the turntable: Ray

Conniff and his Orchestra, Franck Pourcel, "Tales from the Vienna Woods," Paul Mauriat. The woman sat unmoving in a corner of the room. Two hours later, Mom summoned everyone to the kitchen—besides João Lúcio and his housekeeper, Rosana and I were also in the house. She showed us the baking dish, took a teaspoon and plunged it into the rice pudding, then gave the teaspoon to João Lúcio. He tasted it, said, Wow, that's it! Mom asked the woman, Do you know how to make it now? And the woman nodded. Mom dumped the whole thing in the garbage and burst into tears. I cut across Largo da Estação and enter the hotel lobby. Morais greets me with a smile. "Mr. Nunes, room nine, hehehe. Good evening. How are you doing today?" "Good evening," I say, taking the key from him. "What's for dinner?" "Bean soup...Hehehe. There are some à la carte options too..." I heft my suddenly heavy body up the wood staircase, walk down the dark hallway, open the door to my room, flip on the light, drop my backpack on the floor, and sigh. Sweat pours down my forehead, neck, and underarms. I fling open the window. There's no wind to ruffle the leaves. I exit the room and cross the hallway into the bathroom, switch on the light. I unzip my pants, piss. Be quick. Leave the bathroom clean for the next person. That next person might be you. I flush, wash my hands, wipe them on my pants—I forgot my towel...The dark circles under my eyes emphasize my exhaustion. I wipe my glasses with squares of toilet paper. I switch off the lights, close the door, lumber down the hall and the wooden staircase. Morais intercepts me, effusive, "Dinner? Hehehe." I squeeze through the curtain of colorful plastic strips and enter the near-empty dining hall, where a man sits on his own, drinking beer and watching the seven o'clock telenovela. On a table in the corner is a smoking stockpot and a handwritten sign that reads, Please help yourself. I take a ceramic bowl from the stack, then dip the ladle into the soup, filling it. I grab a spoon and napkin and find somewhere to sit, far from the sound of the television. A server approaches me. "Good evening," he says. He requests my room number and wonders whether I'd like to order anything off the menu. I shake my head, so he asks if I'd like anything to drink. "Still water," I say. He turns around and disappears. The TV presenter reels off the news items that will air momentarily on *Jornal Nacional*. I slurp a couple of spoonfuls of bean soup and feel my body leach out from every pore. The server walks in carrying a tray with a tin cover for the lone man, who decides to order another beer. A couple stumble noisily into the dining hall—he, short and potbellied, already a little drunk, in an auburn wig, and she caked in makeup, squeezed into a low-cut dress, trotting in high heels. The server walks in carrying a tray with a plastic bottle of still water and a glass, then places both theatrically on the table. He asks if I'd like anything else, I say no, and he turns his attention to the new arrivals. They must be regular customers because I hear them roaring with laughter, and, though they're nowhere near me, can make out the man in the auburn wig as he says, "…Cuban steak, but hold the apple, 'cause, you know, Jaque's not a fan." "They kicked Adam out of Paradise over an apple," she says, with thundering laughter. In winter, Mom used to make minestrone and leave it sitting on the gas stove. As people came home, they would light the burner, serve themselves a bowl, and dig in. Mom always waited until the last person had had his or her fill. Only then, sometimes in the middle of the night, would she check if there was any left, scrape the bottom of the stockpot, devour the minestrone with relish, then wash, dry, and put away the dishes. The server comes back carrying a tray with a glass of whiskey on the rocks and another glass with a straw submerged in a pale red liquid. I drink the rest of my water, wipe my mouth with the paper napkin, get up. The lone man, his plate clean and beer bottle empty, watches the news program while worrying his teeth with a toothpick. I head through the curtain of colorful plastic strips, and Morais, who'd been sitting on the red sofa, jumps to his feet. "How'd you like the food, Mr. Nunes? Good, isn't it? Hehehe." "Good," I say as I plod up the staircase. I walk down the dark hall and open the door to room nine, switch on the light. I take off my shirt, drape it over the back of the chair. I sit in bed, place my glasses on the nightstand beside the can of Coke, steering clear of the large grease stain. I pull off my shoes and socks, nudge them under the bed, undo the button on my pants. My eyelids are heavy and I feel dizzy. Like I'm on a moving bus. The outside of the house was green. Every year around

Christmastime, Dad would hire Seu Julião to paint another coat and then studiously inspect his work, insisting the color had to be the exact same shade of emerald green. He didn't mind if the inside walls were various hues of blue, so long as they were blue. Yet Seu Julião's trips back and forth from the hardware store—until Dad gave him his blessing to start painting—became legendary. There was a tiny veranda at the entrance, and through the door, its glass window never fully closed, was the living room, which featured the enormous morado-wood cabinet that held the Philips tube turntable and two dozen records. The three-seater sofa in yellow corduroy faced the Colorado RQ TV, which stood on a peroba-wood sideboard. On the wall, an oval sepia portrait of Mom and Dad on the day of their wedding; she in a white dress, he in a suit and tie, both cloaked in the golden cloth of happiness. I pad through the rooms like a thief, in the gloomy night quiet. Under an enormous wooden crucifix, Mom and Dad sleep with their backs to each other—she with her hands nestled between bent knees, he in his striped pajamas, belly-down, snoring softly. One time, while looking for something or other—I was always looking for things to distract myself with—I'd found a box of condoms under the mattress. That was the moment I realized, disappointed and furious, that my parents were man and woman. On the headboard, on Dad's side, a chrome Herweg alarm clock—Mom used to proudly remark that she'd never, not in her whole life, needed anything or anyone to help her wake up. I'm always awake, she boasted. And it must have been true, since we never saw her turn in at night, and the table was always set for breakfast when we rose in the morning, while she was already cooped up in the basement pumping the pedal of the sewing machine. Dad liked to sleep. He found it torture to wake up at five a.m. to clock in at Industrial at six on the dot. On Saturdays, at the end of his work week, he'd take a long bath, shave, spritz himself with cologne, have a bowl of soup, hang a blanket over the window to block out the light, and happily sign off until the following morning, when he'd be woken by the radiant Sunday sun and could busy himself with cleaning his bicycle, listen to his cornball music—as Mom liked to quip—and read the *Jornal do Brasil*, all while looking forward to his postprandial nap, full of spaghetti and wine. I walk into the girls' bedroom. On the single bed, beneath the window facing the street, Rosana lies on her belly. On the dresser are rings, a necklace, a watch, and a wallet. On the bottom bunk, Isinha sleeps facing the wall. Up top, under the light of a small lamp, Lígia avidly reads *Steppenwolf* by Herman Hesse. I enter the bedroom I share with João Lúcio. Two single beds and a closet. He sleeps on his side, head resting between open hands. I'm wide awake, watching the shadows twirl on the ceiling. Why had I shown Lígia the gun? Why

a train whistle nearby in the distance a gun lígia lígia lígia

saturday,
march 7

i wake up, and it feels like a train is chugging right beneath
the window, dun-dun-dun dun-dun-dun dun-dun-dun,
making the building shake under the weight of freight
cars loaded with bauxite. The lamplight stings my eyes.
I take my glasses from the nightstand, get up. Drape the
towel over my shoulders. Outside, the dead of night. I
open my backpack, pull out the plastic bag, grab a pair of
clean underwear and my toothbrush, and head down the
dark hall—whistles, psssts, hisses, purrs, shushes, sighs,
moans—into the bathroom. I flip on the light and lock
the door. Hang the towel off the curtain rod in the shower
and my clean underwear off the ceramic towel hook. I
dump the contents of the bag on the toilet cover. I take
the toothpaste out of the box and place the tube on the
sink beside the dental floss and deodorant. I unwrap the
bar of soap and set it on the windowsill. I put the shampoo
and conditioner on the shower floor. I pull down my pants,
careful not to let my wallet and other small items fall out,

and hang them on the ceramic towel hook. I pull down my
underwear, lift the toilet cover, and sit. I relieve my bladder
and guts. Be quick. Leave the bathroom clean for the next
person. That next person might be you. On the ceiling,
black splotches of mildew and cobwebs. I lower the toilet
cover. Flush. The water, meager, trickles down without
force. I draw the plastic curtain and turn the taps, cold
water spits this way and that. I leave my glasses on the sink.
I flush again. Get under the water. I wet my head, douse it
with shampoo. I lather my body, which is covered in goose
bumps, with unscented soap. I rinse my hair, douse it with
conditioner. It's the dead of night... The water flows slowly
down the clogged drain. I turn the taps in the opposite
direction. Wrap my body in the rough towel, which
scratches my skin. I pull on a pair of clean underwear and
pants. Tear off a square of toilet paper and clear the mist
from my glasses. My face looms in the mirror. I look away.
I floss and brush my teeth. Spray my chest and underarms
with deodorant. I collect the shampoo and conditioner,
dry them with a towel. I collect the bar of soap and slip it
back in its package. I toss everything in the plastic bag—
shampoo, conditioner, soap, toothpaste and toothpaste
box, brush, dental floss, deodorant. I push back the water
with the squeegee. I collect the towel, dirty underwear,
and plastic bag, unlock the door, and turn off the light. I
tread down the dark hall—whistles, psssts, hisses, purrs,
shushes, sighs, moans—into the room. I leave the plastic
bag and dirty underwear on the floor, stretch the towel out

on the windowsill, switch off the light. A faint blue gleam draws an imperfect rectangle on the dusty floor. I take off my pants and glasses, arrange the top sheet, and lie down. In another era, I might have been happy at this time of night. Sometimes I'd wake up only to sigh and roll over to the edge of the bed and sleep a while longer, happy just knowing João Lúcio was there with me, through the wall the sound of Rosana and Lígia and Isinha snoring, in the other room Mom and Dad resting... The past is ruins ruins the pa

i wake up! The day stirs, frantic. I put on my glasses and step into my pants, pull on my socks and slide into my sneakers. I get up. Sweating, I lean out the window. Street vendor stalls occupy the sidewalk. Saturday is ablaze, overrun by the sound of voices. Cars honk, motorcycles honk, buses honk. I grab the towel and drape it over my shoulders. Collect my toothbrush and toothpaste, toss the plastic bag on the unmade bed, and head into the hall. The bathroom's empty. I lock the door, lift the toilet cover, unzip my pants, piss. Flush. I brush my teeth. Wash my hands and face. Dry myself off. The mirror shows a creased face with forehead wrinkles and crow's-feet. Small gray hairs bristle from my dried skin. I cut across the hallway back into my room. Stretch the towel out on the windowsill. Take a deep breath of air that smells of green leaves. I spray deodorant on my chest and underarms. Pull on a clean

shirt. I open the door, plod down the hall and down the
wood staircase, and greet Pereira, who responds, congenial,
"Good morning!" The Roman numerals on the old wall
clock show 9:25. I walk through the curtain of colorful
plastic strips into the dining hall. Sit at a table near the
television. I fill the enormous white ceramic mug with
coffee and milk, pumped from enormous black thermoses. I
grab a small roll and some butter. Sit down. The sound of
chatter and the clinking of dishes and cutlery drown out
the TV presenter's voice. I take slow bites of the buttered
bread between sips of milky coffee. The faces around me
appear relieved at the prospect of the weekend. The sound
of laughter floats over from a raucous group in the back of
the dining hall. My life on the road and in hotels...I
never enjoyed any quiet again...The sense of peace when
you arrive home, close the door, and tune out the world.
The feeling of safety—No, more than that, of...of...
invulnerability! That's right. The sense that nothing and
no one can touch you, that between the four walls of your
refuge, you are safe from harm...Walls of steel; refuge
outside time...Had I ever experienced that tranquility,
that quiet? Gone were the evenings when the only sound
was the rat-tat-tat of Mom's sewing machine...Gone were
our Sunday spaghetti lunches, when Dad would mix wine
with sugar water for us kids to drink...Gone were the
holidays to Rodeiro, where we helped weed the fields,
wielding hoes and racing to finish our chores so that we
could play with our cousins...Lígia...Everything came

crumbling down...I wandered aimlessly and, spendthrift, frittered away my time...Now...I get up and sidestep the guests drifting drowsily around the dining hall, walk through the curtain of colorful plastic strips, lumber up the wood stairs and down the hall, then open the door. The clamor of the street penetrates the room, heavy with the scent of feijoada that wafts in from somewhere—possibly the hotel kitchen. I drop my backpack on the bed. Separate my clothes—clean in one compartment and dirty in the other, along with the plastic bag (shampoo, conditioner, soap, deodorant, dental floss, toothpaste and toothbrush). From the zippered compartment, I take out the Cebion tube, a small packet of Dimorf, and a makeshift brown-paper package held together with Scotch tape. I uncap the tube, pull out the last few bills, and slide them into my wallet. I pop out each of the fifty morphine pills, tip them into the Cebion tube, and return the tube to the zippered compartment along with the brown-paper package. I toss the unopened can of Coke, the crushed toothpaste box, and the empty pill packets and blister packs into the wastebasket. I scan the room to make sure I haven't forgotten anything. I lean out the window over the damp towel and take a deep breath of the muggy morning air. I sling on my backpack, put on my cap, shut the door, walk down the hallway and stairs, and step onto the worm-eaten wood parquet. I stop at the counter and ring the bell—the old black-and-white photograph of Cataguases, already quite faded. Pereira appears, "Leaving already?" he asks, rote. "That's right," I say, as he takes the key and hooks it to the spot on the corkboard reserved for number nine. Pereira opens the black notebook, "In terms of extras, we've got one meal. Is that right?" I say yes, and he tells me what I owe him. I grab my wallet and pull out a bill. Pereira presses a couple of buttons on the cash register and pulls the crank; the drawer shoots open with a ring. He hands me some change, which I slide into my pocket. I shake his hand. "Safe travels! Come again," he says. I turn, hear the ring-ring of the drawer closing, and cut across the lobby, where a man reclines in one of the greasy-looking red napa-leather armchairs with white frieze, smoking as he reads *Jornal Cataguases* with rapt attention. I step onto the sidewalk, teeming with people. True-Blue Ricardo... I remember the advice of the woman on the bus and change the position of my backpack, slinging it over my chest to avoid any issues, even though I have nothing worth stealing. I zigzag, dodging people here and there, the sun stoking the street vendors' cries on my way to the coach terminal. At Mom's funeral, Ricardo, perspiring in a black suit and sunglasses, had held out his fat hand and said, My condolences. We were at the entrance to São Sebastião Church, in Rodeiro, where the wake was held on a stuffy November afternoon. There were no longer monkeys in the trees of the square, which people referred to as the *garden*, and the sloth that had piqued our curiosity when we used to make the trip from the countryside to church—during summer holidays and wearing our Sunday best—was long gone. Mom had died in the middle of the night. I'd been given fair warning and driven to Cataguases the evening before. Don't wait till the weekend, Isinha had said over the phone. In the hospital, we gathered around her eyes, the only part of her body the illness hadn't depleted. She ran her thin, dry hand over each of our faces in farewell, and appeared happy to see us together again—even Dad, who was clean and sober that day, a caricature of the man he'd once been. Somehow, in that moment, we were once again the good, obedient, responsible, and bright-futured children she'd always believed we were as kids. Though I pretended not to notice Ricardo's gesture, he angrily wove his arm through mine and pulled me onto the street in feigned intimacy, as though to discuss the mournful reason we were gathered there that day. I tried to break free from him, but he kept a firm grip. You think you're better than me, don't you? he hissed between gritted teeth, his breath shot through with whiskey. But you're as much of a fuckup as anybody, Peninha. This isn't the time or place for us to hash out our differences, Ricardo, I said. But he pressed on. You go around talking shit about me, spreading lies and painting yourself as a saint...I may not be better than you, Ricardo, but my conscience is clear. That's all, I said. What are you insinuating? I may not have much, but I've worked for every scrap of it. Are you implying I'm crooked? Is that it? You said it, not me. He shoved me off and spat, his voice quivering—by that point we were edging the wall around the Spartano soccer field—You've got nothing because

you're an amateur! Sure, I inherited some stuff from my
father, but none of it was in order. His generation didn't
believe in documentation. I had to sell off some houses to
clear up others. I took out a loan from the bank—and I've
got proof—to put up that building in Vila Teresa. While
you were happy pansying around as a traveling salesman,
Rosana and I worked around the clock to give Tamires a
better life. Tamires, I was about to say, Tamires, that
poor... But I kept mum. Everybody knows you're a loan
shark, Ricardo... Loan shark? I've got good money set aside.
Folks who've been blacklisted, who can't get a credit line at
the bank, who're desperate, they come to me and I scare up
the cash... What harm is there in that? Your criminal
interest rates, I said. Of course my interest rates are higher
than banks. After all, I've got no collateral... Your...
Your... But your henchmen are the collateral, Ricardo. I
said. Already red from the sun, he looked as though he
might burst any second, like a ruby-red balloon. Henchmen?!
That's a low blow—and bigoted too! So, some of my
employees have got rap sheets for theft, drug trafficking.
They're just guys who fell in with the wrong crowd because
they were naive or poor. Men who did their time, but
nobody will hire. I try to help them reenter society, and
what do I get in return? Your judgment? Come on... People
should be lining up to thank me for giving jobs to folks who
might otherwise go back to a life of crime... I was familiar
with True-Blue Ricardo's methods. On the due date, his
employees would show up at the debtor's house, and if the

poor sod couldn't pay off the money he owed, they'd make off with something of value—sometimes even a family member...And woe be to the welcher who tried to rise up against him! The people I work with, Peninha, he continued, aren't allowed to touch illegal substances, and if they get caught drunk, it's sayonara. I've got dozens of godchildren across the city...Folks grateful to me for the loans I give...Rosana and me, we donate food to the needy every month. Do you do anything to help others, Peninha? Do you do anything for the poor? I'm a member of Rotary, and make a monthly donation to both the National Association for Parents of Exceptional Children and São Vicente de Paulo. On Christmas, my henchmen—as you call them—distribute presents to children who live in slums. What about you, Peninha? Have you ever helped anybody, in your whole life? Huh? "Please help," says a vagrant on the sidewalk outside the coach terminal, stinking of sweat and piss as he reaches his filthy hand toward me. I step around him and into the small hall, its ceramic floor dark with grime, where bystanders patiently await their arrival and departure times, eyes glued to the screen. My forehead, feet, and underarms are drenched in sweat. The wall clock reads 10:45. I take a long sip of chilled water from the drinking fountain, then head over to the ticket booth. "Good morning," I say. The clerk's mustache remains still. "When's the next bus to Rodeiro?" His mustache speaks, "11:35." "One, please. A window seat if possible." I take my wallet from my back pocket. "What

time does it get there?" I ask. "Around 12:45," grumbles the
mustache. I ask him what I owe, pay, collect my change,
and slip it into my wallet. I'm running out of money... I
slide my ticket into my shirt pocket, shuffle over to the
wood bench, take off my backpack, and get comfortable.
On the television, cartoon heroes are busy fighting evil.
Dad's health took a turn for the worse in the last few
months of his life. Isinha used to call with news on Sunday
mornings, the only time when she knew she would find me.
He's had a stroke; he's in the hospital. He's back home now,
but he's bedridden and can't talk. He's in diapers, eating
through a straw. You should go see him before it's too late.
He's in the hospital again; he can only breathe with an
oxygen tank. The doctors had disabused him of any hope.
Marília would say to me, I don't get it. We feel sorry for
animals. We take them to the vet and ask for them to be
put down. Why can't we do the same to end the suffering of
our loved ones? That's why I've never wanted a pet. So that
I wouldn't get attached. Sino, whom we had for years,
wasn't so much an animal as the eighth member of our
family. He disappeared the night before the... that...
tragedy... befell us. When Dad came home from the
factory, he was surprised not to see Sino waiting for him
at the street corner like he usually did. He asked Mom,
Where's Sino, and, overwhelmed by all the commissions,
she said, Like I've got time to keep track of a dog! He asked
me, Where's Sino, and I said I'd been out all day running
errands for Mom. He asked Isinha, Where's Sino, but Isinha

never knew anything. Frustrated, Dad scrubbed his hands with Pasta Joia and gargled mint tea. He carefully put away his shoes and headed into the bathroom to shower and shave. He sat at the table in his pajamas, smelling pungently of Aqua Velva, and we all—Dad, Isinha, and me—ate our minestrone dinner in silence. Unnerved, instead of turning in, he changed into clothes and we went around the neighborhood to ask if anyone had seen the dog, to no success. We came home late, he apprehensive and me quiet. He broke with routine and sat on the low veranda wall by the entrance, smoking, when normally he'd have smoked his last cigarette on his walk home from Industrial. He caught Rosana climbing out of Ricardo's car at around eleven p.m. and startled her; João Lúcio was at the barracks fulfilling his military service. I heard his steps coughing through the night. We were still waiting for Sino to come home the next day when I heard the sound... I ran to the kitchen, the wall clock was in pieces on the floor... Mom hurried into the living room, and I rushed after her. She clung to me and tried to cover my eyes, her body trembling, quiet and distraught. That's when I saw the body sprawled on the sofa, blood trickling down the yellow corduroy, eyes wide open. Lígia... Behind us Isinha stood stock-still in the doorway. A woman in a headscarf sweeps the floor. A green-and-yellow bus with the destination sign Cataguases–Ubá pulls into a parking space. I get up, sling my backpack to the side, take my ticket from my shirt pocket, check the seat number—eleven—and wait to board. The fare collector has the same mustache as the man working the booth—they must be related—and stands at the bus door to check our tickets. Before me are an old man with a crackling-new polyester bag, a couple dressed for mass, and a fat woman perched on a pair of high heels. I put my backpack in the overhead bin, take a seat by the window, and study the other travelers. There aren't many of us. I count ten, which, added to the four people who got on before me, makes fourteen passengers—fifteen, including myself—sitting scattered around the bus. It will take an hour and ten minutes to travel forty-five kilometers. We'll make several stops on the way. Dona Eusébia. Astolfo Dutra. Sobral Pinto. Diamante. Rodeiro. I never came back for Dad's funeral. We had driven to Paraná to see the Kempczynskis, Marília's Polish family—parents, siblings, uncles and aunts—for Labor Day weekend. He died on May 1 and was buried on May 3, 1997. Though I'd promised to visit the family plot and pay my respects at the earliest opportunity, I'd put it off and off and then off again until finally it slipped my mind altogether. I'm going to keep my promise. The bus driver, spotless in his uniform, gets on, adjusts the side view mirrors, crosses himself, rearranges the seat, and reverses. Outside, the fare collector helps him maneuver. The woman, with her headscarf, dustpan and broom, sweeps up piles of trash on the curb. The fare collector gets in, the driver shuts the door, honks, rounds the coach terminal, and I catch a quick glimpse of Alcides, Alcides the Beast, lurking in his lair. I throw open the window. Hot air whips my face. I never admitted to anyone that I had told Lígia about the gun. I stopped attending mass, not wanting to confess to the priest the mistake, the misstep, that continues to haunt and suffocate and devastate me. The bus stops at Avenida Astolfo Dutra. The fare collector gets off and tosses a lumpy burlap sack into the luggage compartment. Two passengers get on, a tall man, gaunt, head stuffed in a straw hat, and a young woman holding a baby under a veil. Though at first the gun caused confusion, Dad finally explained he'd bought it a year and a half earlier to protect the family after two strangers broke into the house. A .22-caliber Caramuru. I got it to scare off the burglars, it was just to scare off the burglars, he swore, disconsolate, I never would've dreamed... The bus leaves behind cars parked on cobblestone streets in front of low-slung houses where laid tables anxiously await Saturday lunch, and clatters onto the asphalt road. It was cold on that July afternoon in 1975. The exact date has fallen into oblivion. Mom was working in the basement with Isinha, who was probably playing with Durvalina, the cat. The silence was almost perfect, broken only by the rat-tat-tat of the sewing machine. I was wearing an orange turtleneck, a hand-me-down from João Lúcio. I was bored and had the sudden urge to show off to someone. I strode into the girls' bedroom and sat on Rosana's empty bed. Lígia was lying in the top bunk engrossed in a book, and either didn't notice I was there or else decided to ignore me, which was not unusual for her. After a few minutes of me restlessly shuffling my feet and clearing my throat, I asked, Hey, what're you reading? She patiently moved the book away from her face and marked the page with her index finger. *Steppenwolf*, she said. Is it any good? I pressed, before she could start reading again. What do you want, Zézo? she asked. I've found something amazing, I said. Impassive, she replied, Oh, really? Wow! and opened her book again. It really is amazing, I insisted, trying to pique her curiosity. Is that right? Lígia gave up and closed the book. I went to the door, glanced around, and came back. I boasted under my breath, A gun...A gun?! she exclaimed with excitement as she leapt out of the bunk. A gun, Zézo?! Where? The bus speeds down the steep Barão de Camargo hill, past the abandoned railway station whose train tracks are dusted with residues of yellow earth from bauxite-laden freight cars, then crosses the bridge over Rio Pomba, whose riverbed is shallow from the ore wash, and turns onto the highway toward Dona Eusébia. I was so enthralled by the power of my secret that it wasn't enough to just share it—I needed something in return. What do I get for showing you the gun? I asked. She thought for a second. I'll take you on the ghost train! There was an amusement park set up in the Cataguases stadium, and Lígia knew I was desperate to go. You don't have money, I needled. I do too, she said, then snapped, Are you gonna show it to me or what? I hesitated as I tried to decide which was worth more, my secret or a ride on a ghost train...But Lígia was shrewd. She climbed back on the top bunk, picked up her book, stretched her

legs, and sneered, You're lying, there's no gun. The tall
man, gaunt, head stuffed in a hat, rises, walks up to the
driver and says something. The bus slows down and stops
on the side of the road, in the middle of nowhere. The
man steps off the bus and is swallowed by dust. The fare
collector follows him and opens the luggage compartment,
takes out the lumpy burlap sack, then sets it on the ground.
The sky is perfectly blue, cloudless, the hills green and bare
of trees. The bus clatters back onto the road, which still
flanks Rio Pomba. Heat drenches my clothes. I take off my
hat, wipe my head with my shirt sleeve, and put my hat
back on. The wind that gusts through the cracked-open
window is as warm as the air around a woodstove. Like a
fool, I fell into Lígia's trap. I thought I was being challenged,
so I said, No gun, huh? Come and see for yourself! We crept
into Mom and Dad's bedroom. I slowly hauled over the
nightstand and climbed onto it. Eye-level with the top of
the wardrobe, I shoved the shoebox with Christmas
ornaments out of the way, stretched my arm as far as it
would go, and pulled the other box to the edge. I grabbed
it, got down, laid the box on the bed, opened it, and showed
Lígia the green-felt bundle. Slowly, I unwrapped the felt,
relishing the suspense, and revealed the gun—chrome
body, wood handle, on its side the word Caramuru. Lígia
stared at the revolver, unmoving, her eyes sorrowful. Though
she wanted to hold it, I wouldn't let her, out of fear and a
sense of possessiveness. I felt as if the gun were mine, after
all I'd found it. See? I faltered, hands shaking and breath

uneven. Panting, I wrapped the gun back up in the green felt, climbed on the chair and then onto the nightstand, eye-level with the top of the wardrobe, shoved the box toward the wall, got down, hauled the nightstand back, and put the chair in its place. We left the room in silence, and shut the door gently behind us. Back in the top bunk, before returning to her book, Lígia said, both breathless and dismissive, It's old, probably doesn't even work ... We never spoke of it again—not even about the ride on the ghost train. Frightened by what I'd discovered, I began avoiding Mom and Dad's bedroom. The next time I saw the gun was at four thirty on the afternoon of September 3 ... Fallen on the rug, in a small puddle of blood that was slowly growing ... Along the highway are greenhouses with orange, tangerine, lime, acerola, pitanga, star fruit, and mango saplings, shops selling decorative plants (azaleas, dracaenas, palms, bromeliads) and native trees (golden and pink trumpet trees, ironwood, angico, cedar, and jatoba), and a fruit-juice factory, all of which announce the imminence of Dona Eusébia. The bus lazily draws into the city and pulls up at a stop opposite a bakery. Three people get off—the fat woman perched on a pair of high heels, a scrawny teenager with black curly hair who hangs off her cell phone, and a young man in a screamingly yellow shirt. Five more passengers get on: an old couple with a threadbare travel bag, a man who reeks of cachaça and greets everyone as he walks down the aisle, a young man with enormous headphones that press against his temples, and another who judders uncomfortably in a suit several sizes too large, Bible tucked under his arm. The fare collector makes a show of closing the luggage compartment, grabs a small paper bag from the bakery counter, and gets back on the bus, which sets off. The fare collector takes a cream donut from the paper bag, wraps it in a bouquet of napkins, and hands it to his colleague. He takes out the second cream donut and bites into it with gusto, licking his hands and mouth. The young believer who'd just gotten on the bus has decided to change seats, perhaps bothered by the drunk clowning around in the back, making other passengers laugh, and sits beside me. He nods hello, opens the Bible, and starts reading. The fare collector takes a handkerchief from his pant pocket, and wipes his hands and mouth. The driver grabs a bottle of water and takes a long glug then says something, voice dulled by the rumbling of the bus outside the landscape seems muted by the heat

i wake up! I must have nodded off. Where are we? Outside the window are reams of barbed wire stretched between concrete posts that hem rolling hills the pale green of signal grass, gullies that show their yellowish bowels, a lone seriema in exile, two or three rangy bulls crammed under a solitary tree, the pointless soaring of a seagull, and a small abandoned house. The religious man isn't sitting next to me anymore. Has he gotten off? Or did he change seats again? The passengers are no longer laughing, which means the drunkard must have fallen asleep. The fare collector watches something entertaining on his cell phone. We'd traveled by train a couple of times, back when trains still cut through these mountains. I was a young boy when they were taken down. We'd spend hours swaying on uncomfortable wooden benches...I always threw up...The listlessness of the diesel locomotive as it hauled heavy mixed train cars along the foothills of the Mantiqueira Mountains...The grating of steel wheels against steel train tracks...The air whistles that scattered birds and startled cows at pasture...The long waits at every station—Barão de Camargo, Sinimbu, Dona Eusébia, Astolfo Dutra, Sobral Pinto, Diamante...Aha, we're in Sobral Pinto! The bus pulls up under an almond tree, three passengers get off, and the fare collector opens the luggage compartment to hand out their belongings; no one climbs on. There used to be a fertilizer plant here. We could tell by the smell that we were approaching our destination. The driver honks, accelerates, sets off. On one of our *adventures*, as Mom used to call them, when I was—what was it?—four or maybe five, we were all dressed to the nines, even Dad, who still hadn't fallen out with the *guidos*, which is how he'd later refer to his brothers-in-law with vitriol. The train left Cataguases in the early morning, and by ten thirty we'd reached our stop in Diamante. Blue-eyed Uncle Paulino was already waiting for us at the platform, tall, slender, hat planted on his head, feet planted in his boots, clothes ripe with the smell of

corn-husk cigarettes. We greeted each other awkwardly—
we weren't, we aren't, the sort to hug—and Mom, Isinha,
and Rosana climbed into the buggy he'd brought over from
the fields, taking our knickknacks with them. Dad, João
Lúcio, Lígia, and I went by foot. We walked slowly so that
we'd be sure to manage the four kilometers to Rodeiro; Lígia
and I led the way, picking at the mortadella sandwiches
we'd brought with us, watching the birds chittering in the
trees, and coughing behind every car that rolled by kicking
up a thick curtain of dust that then idled heavily in the
air. Behind us, Dad and João Lúcio walked side by side,
chatting companionably. An hour later, in Rodeiro, we
filed into Zelito Crovato's ice cream parlor and Dad bought
us each a round popsicle. Mine was red (raspberry?), Lígia's
white (coconut?), and João Lúcio had an almond one, and
we ate them on São Sebastião Square, while playing with
the monkeys. Before tackling the remaining half league to
the farm, we stopped at Pivatto's bar, where we stood at the
counter and drank an ice-cold family-sized bottle of Coca-
Cola, and went into Seu Giácomo Paro's bakery for two
trays of coconut cheese flan, because it was a tradition of
ours to bring some for the family, whenever we got together
at Uncle Paulino's house. Uncle Paulino Mom's oldest
brother liked to

i wake up! I dozed off again. A string of enormous furniture
warehouses lines the left side of the highway. Rodeiro! The

bus flanks the roundabout. Shirt drenched in sweat, heart pounding frantically, legs trembling. Several passengers are already standing in the aisle, holding bags and cell phones. The city has spread like wildfire through arid woods, fast and unchecked. Box trucks clutter the narrow streets. Motorcycles and cars adorn low-slung, drab houses with enormous satellite dishes. The bus passes in front of the Spartano soccer field, honks, rounds São Sebastião Square, and parks. I get up, sling on my backpack, adjust my cap, stuff my hand in my shirt pocket, take out my ticket, hand it to the bus driver, and get off. It's been twenty years...I need to eat something. "Excuse me," I say to a man crossing the street. "Yes?" he asks, warily. "I was hoping to get lunch. Could you recommend somewhere?" He scratches his head, thinks, and settles on a place. "Casa Nova. Best restaurant in town. Just walk down that way, far as you can go," he says, pointing at a street that runs crosswise. I thank him and head through the *garden*. Before turning the corner, I glance behind me and spy the man standing in the same place, watching. I head back along the bus route under the blistering sun. I walk down the sidewalk of Rua João Bicalho, squeezed between the curb and the walls of modest houses whose flung-open windows show elderly people enthralled by the television. Uncle Ênio used to love soccer. Whenever he could, he'd take us—me, João Lúcio, his two sons, and two other nephews—to watch Spartano play in their yellow jerseys with blue detailing. We'd head over from the countryside by bicycle and buggy, lugging with us half a sack of oranges to snack on throughout the match. The boys—Amauri and Marino—were still kids when Uncle Ênio moved the family to Rio de Janeiro, where he had more children. He never came back, and is now buried somewhere in those parts. He was a die-hard fan of Botafogo and Mom used to pretend he visited Maracanã stadium every Sunday. There are no Morettos left in Rodeiro, except for João Lúcio. Uncle Ítalo's daughters moved to Brasília one by one—first Cíntia, the youngest, who passed her public service exam and now works, or worked, as a stenographer in the Senate, followed by Verônica, the middle daughter, and Lucília, the eldest, who'd held a candle for João Lúcio, became disillusioned, and never married—along with their mother, Aunt Biquinha. Uncle Paulino had two daughters and two sons. Dequinha wasn't even eleven when he drowned in the reservoir where he'd gone to swim in secret. The daughters moved away after marrying, Nilda to Ubá, and Ana Paula, whom Aunt Alcina apparently still lives with, to Juiz de Fora. Rogério dropped off the map—he enlisted in the army, was sent to join the Jungle Infantry Brigade, and was never heard from again. At the end of Avenida Raul Alves Ferreira, near the roundabout, I enter Casa Nova, a crowded buffet with clinking cutlery and a hubbub of voices. "Good afternoon," a young woman chirps amicably. "Are you familiar with the system?" she asks. She is walking before I can say anything, her voice drowned out by the racket. We dodge patrons, who wind through the restaurant balancing trays, and she shows me to a table, packed between a loud group of friends and a young couple who rock a stroller as they eat, their baby wailing relentlessly, frightened by the commotion and bothered by the heat, which the ceiling fans do nothing to temper. I hang my backpack and hat off the chair and make my way the bathroom. I push open the door, head to the urinal, unzip my pants, pee, zip up my pants, and step over to the sink. I hang my glasses off my shirt collar, wash my face and hands, dry them with a paper towel, and put my glasses back on. I stand in line by the hot food station, pick up a tray and spoon white rice, black beans, a slice of fried polenta, a piece of pork loin, and some greens (maybe chicory) onto my plate, then grab a knife, fork, and napkins. "Anything to drink?" asks the woman as she weighs my food. "Water," I say. She puts the bottle and plastic cup on the tray, then hands me a plastic card with a barcode, which I slip into my pant pocket. I circle back to my table. The mother now toddles the still-screaming baby in her lap, as her husband smiles awkwardly. It's possible we had witnessed the end of an era, in which large-bellied men with grayish hair flaunted their good health and money as the women contemplated their jaded grandchildren with admiration. Rodeiro was a small and quiet town then, a square and four streets down which buggies, bullock carts, bicycles, Dr. Jerônimo Novaes's Volkswagen Beetle, Rubens Giusti's Rural Willys, the town van, and the milk truck slowly rolled. Time, on horseback, with its showy harness, trotted leisurely, hat doffed in gentlemanly greeting at the women leaning out the windows and the men sitting in chairs on the sidewalk, G'morning, G'afternoon, and G'night. On a Saturday like today, Italians would flood country roads, bringing with them sacks of rice for milling, corn for grinding, colts for shoeing, and popcorn, jiló, okra, tomato, oranges, eggs, chickens, and suckling pigs to sell in the market; and with the money they made, they bought sugar, wheat flour, and ant and rat poison, as well as notions for sewing. By that time, though, it would have been empty, evening having quietly withdrawn behind closed doors. The small farms peppered along the mountain range rose and slumbered with the sun. They'd wake up and have piada for breakfast, eat lunch at nine, grits with milk at noon, have dinner at three, and at seven they ate cornbread with milky coffee or else stuffed themselves with popcorn while playing truco; by nine they were sound asleep. On Sundays, there was mass, and the whole family would head back into town. They'd wake up early, dress in their Sunday best—clothes proper for seeing God in—and make their way to São Sebastião Church. Father Jaime, a systematic Dutchman with a fondness for the bottle, who spoke in a language impossible to understand, had a habit of drawing out the end of the ceremony with his sermonizing, to the dismay of his congregants. Then, people caught up with each other—it was a time for seeing relatives and friends, for sharing news and information, for enjoyment. Business was handled, relationships sparked, animosities cemented. It's all come to an end. If, for example, I were to strike up a conversation with the couple now sitting in the place of the young parents with the baby and not speaking to one another, busy fingering their phones every second, if I were to ask these two people who are more or less my age if they remembered the old days, if I were to mention names, or raise incidents that were either humorous or tragic—like when Seu Matias Rinaldo, whose wife had cheated on him, tried to hang himself with a rope he'd fastened to a girder but instead brought the walls and roof of his house down on the few pieces of furniture he owned, and then spent the rest of his life brooking the quiet derision of his compatriots—if I were to ask them if they remembered this episode, I wouldn't even get a sigh. I wonder if all these people stuffing themselves with food and drink realize they walked these streets as children. Because they are the same streets...except different...I wipe my mouth with a paper napkin, get up, shove on my cap, sling on my backpack, pull out the plastic card, weave through the tables, and grab another bottle of water. The woman behind the scale adds it to my tab. I make my way over to the cash register, where the barcode reader shows the price of my meal, take my wallet out of my back pocket, and pay. I fill a small plastic cup with coffee, mix in two drops of sweetener, drink the warm, watery substance, toss it in the bin, and leave. There isn't a breath of wind on this sun-drenched afternoon. Maybe these men and women, young and old, who eat and drink with dispassion, are right... These are the same streets... except... different... You can't bring the past back to life... I walk down the narrow sidewalk, squeezed between the curb and the walls of modest houses whose flung-open windows show elderly people paralyzed by the television, fans humming. A house's rooms don't hold the voices and joys and sorrows of those who lived in it. A house exists only here and now; there is no before or after. You may be able to touch the furniture, the objects, but never the people, much less their stories... These houses will one day also crumble, and not even the memory of them will survive. You're right, Mr. Mendonça, it's the present that matters... But if I were to walk as I am now, anonymously, along the front of the Spartano field, down Rua João Bicalho and through São Sebastião Square, and cross paths with no one, could anyone say I had been in Rodeiro today, when nobody saw me? Steam rises from the cobblestones, turning everything hazy and undefined. I walk through the Rodeiro of my childhood... Zelito Crovato's ice cream parlor was over there... And Bar do Pivatto... And the Turk's store... I head down the street bordering the cemetery, where soon I will see Mom, Dad, and Lígia again... Dad had never paid much attention to me. He may have always been locking horns with João Lúcio and Rosana, but at least he respected them. They're opinionated, he used to say, and pigheaded. But they've got grit! He thought of me as shy and cow-hearted, while the world belonged to people who were daring and audacious, A man's got to be gutsy, the weak get trod on, he would claim. The specter of failure had stuck to my skin. I'd failed as a son, as a husband,

as a father...I'd failed as a brother...As a member of our
family...Maybe Dad's anger had to do with the fact that
out of all his children, I resembled him the most—in face,
body, and manner—and that he had big dreams for me.
Maybe—why not?—a portrait of me in academic dress to
hang on the wall. Even his redneck brother-in-law, Ênio,
who couldn't write his own name on his voter registration
card, had gotten his life on track in Rio. But I had proven
to be changeable, fearful, unworthy...Though he never
accused me of it, deep down I know Dad suspected that I,
his failed son, had been the one to find the gun on top of
the wardrobe and show it to Lígia. His contempt only grew,
and I don't recall us exchanging anything more than
formalities after Lígia...after she...after Lígia died...He
couldn't hide how uneasy he felt around me...I spot the
gate to the cemetery—sweat drenches my shirt and hat—
cross the street, climb the concrete steps—my pulse
bounds—and pant up the steep hill, tombs on either side,
some modest, others ostentatious. It's no use trying to cheat
death. Whether they bear photographs and epitaphs, names
and dates, every tomb—in marble or brick, or even those
shallow graves whose only adornment is a white-painted
wood cross with handwritten names and dates, almost
entirely faded—is the same as those more humble resting
places that lie in a corner by the crumbling wall, small
mounds of dirt with no identifying markers. Death renders
us equal in annihilation. Just as our bodies decompose, so
do the memories of our passage through the world. Here is

the enormous, black-marble Moretto family vault that João Lúcio commissioned to house our history. I open my backpack, grab the bottle of water, now tepid, and take a sip. On the vault, large oval portraits of Anacleto Moretto (07/03/1897–08/22/1962) and Luigia Peron (04/18/1902–12/09/1970) bear no epitaphs as they reign over the dead. Grandpa Anacleto, spindly and blond, his face stern but kind, it was said, died when I was one. Grandma Luigia, hot-tempered—always in a black dress, long hair up in a bun—used to curse around the clock, despondent. Inside the three niches, illustrated by small, round photographs: André Bortoletto Moretto (11/26/1963–07/11/1973), or Dequinha, skinny and quiet, and Paulino Moretto (09/29/1926–12/29/1992), intestinal obstruction; Lígia Moretto Nunes (08/03/1960–09/23/1975), for whose soul Father Jaime refused to pray, and my mother, Stella Moretto (11/06/1933–09/02/1995); Ítalo Moretto (08/17/1929–01/01/1985), bedridden for years, bitter, reeking of shit and piss, covered in sores, and my father, José Nivaldo Nunes (02/27/1931–05/03/1997), who passed away in hardly better circumstances. Now incommunicable, inaccessible, unreachable. Soon I too will be a portrait, a date, a name . . . Body, bones, dust . . . Nothing at all . . . I did everything wrong . . . And time has run out . . . I'm a sack of guilt and remorse . . . Lígia . . . We weren't much for photographs . . . I wonder when this was taken, and who took it. "I'm sorry to bother, but are you family?" asks a man around my age, pointing at the tomb. I nod. Bashful, he says, "Then we must be related...I mean, Zilma, my late wife, may she rest in peace, was the niece and goddaughter of Dona Alcina Bortoletto, who was the wife of Seu Paulino Moretto, who is..." "My uncle," I say, annoyed. "My mother Stella's brother." "Oh, so you must be João Lúcio's brother!" "That's right." He holds out a hand rough with callouses, "Pleasure to meet you." "Sure, a pleasure," I say. "I'm the caretaker here," he boasts, sweeping his eyes over the cemetery's entire, awful expanse. "I've got your brother to thank for it. Great man," he says, "I do my best to live up to the trust he's put in me." I take off my hat, wipe the sweat off my head with the back of my left hand. "Are you passing through?" he asks. I tell him I am as I put on my hat. "Can I interest you in a coffee, or some water? I live just over there, see." He points to a row of houses in the distance. "Third one from the corner." I thank him but explain that I'm in a hurry and just came to pay my respects. He asks where I live. "São Paulo," I answer. He sighs, "Ah, São Paulo!" And adds, "I've got two kids who live there...Quite a ways, isn't it? And big, huge...And what about all that violence, huh? I visited once and was scared so stiff I never went back... The stuff you see on TV...It's the wild, wild west..." He asks again, "Can I really not interest you in some water, or coffee? Vanessa, my current wife...Zilma died several years back, not even the doctors could figure out what she had. So I married again, you know how it is, the kids spread their wings and then you're left to grow old on your own.

And that's no good, is it? Being alone like that...So I got together with Vanessa. She's a good woman, attentive. So if you like we can head down there, she'd be over the moon to meet a brother of João Lúcio's. He's been so helpful, and not just to me, since you could say I'm family and all, but to anybody who needs a hand. He may have gotten rich, but he never forgot where he came from." "No, thank you though, really. Maybe some other time," I insist. He says goodbye and hefts his slender body downhill, skirting ditches gouged by heavy rain, which sweeps pieces of coffin and bits of bone onto the street when it falls. The air is still, the silence only broken by the occasional distant sound. A metallic clanging, someone striking metal with metal. The shrill voice of a child riling up a dog that runs and barks with glee. The engine of a speeding motorcycle. The monotonous dun-dun-dun of an unintelligible song. Before making my way down, I spy, up on the hilltop, the white marble vault where Prazeres lies under the name Barboza Vieira Moretto and family. I heft my slender body downhill, skirting ditches gouged by heavy rain, and reach the street. I seek out the scant shade of the skeletal trees that dot the pitted sidewalk. A cat sits at a window watching the movement outside, drunk on the heat. That's where Maneco Linhares's grocery store used to be...And Giácomo Paro's bakery was over there...And the bocce ball court was right there...Nothing's left...Here is where the warehouse with the rice huller once marked the end of a city that now stretches on for three more blocks, practically all the way

to where the widower Seu Tatão Ribeiro lived in seclusion
with his brood of children in a rickety thatch house made
of cob walls and bamboo stakes, smoke always rising from
its woodstove chimney. The deafening thump of carioca
funk crackles through heavy-duty speakers installed in the
trunk of a black lowered Punto parked in front of a boteco.
"É o caralho do caralho / Do caralho mesmo / Ô recalcado,
não rouba minha brisa / Eu comprei com meu dinheiro /
Então cuida da sua vida." Young men and women drink
beer around a portable metal grill, a green awning
sheltering them from the sun. A few steps later, a small
group of believers gathers in the tiny, single-exit room of
Breath of God Ministries, yelling with Bibles lofted over
their heads, their sounds stifled by the frenzied rhythm of
the music next door. Little by little, the houses thin out.
The cobblestone road morphs into a long tongue of gravelly
sand. There isn't a breath of wind, or a single cloud... I pull
labored gulps of hot air into my lungs. The strong scent of
weed hangs in the still air. I hear laughter but can't tell
where it's coming from... After a curve in the road,
through a grove of eucalyptus trees, I spy Seu Maneco
Linhares's farmhouse perched on a hilltop in the distance. I
cross the small bridge over which Mom had once leaned in
delight as she urged us children to point out the small tetras
and piabas whirling in the stream's clear waters, now
muddied and fetid, plastic clinging to the brush lining the
banks... Lígia lying in her coffin in a white dress, a plastic
bouquet of baby's breath in her gloved hands, veil covering

her face...My heart raced as the afternoon fell away...
Even addled by the Tryptanol Dr. Gilson Machado had
prescribed, I used to wake up in a sweat in the middle of
the night and see Lígia idling in the shadows, quiet, her
eyes sorrowful, trying to say something...A motorcycle
buzzes by and the passenger yells something I can't make
out. A pickup speeds in the opposite direction. The
motorcycle vanishes into the dust. The pickup vanishes
into the dust. I vanish into the dust...I cough and cough
and cough...I wipe my glasses with the edge of my shirt.
Slowly the cloud lifts, revealing a canopy of avocado trees
that were already old when I was a kid, and had marked the
entrance to the land of Seu Orlando Spinelli, murdered
some years ago, they said, by an employee he'd raised as his
own son. Nothing remains of the stone house, not even its
foundation...The termites eat through everything, in a
fury...Lígia used to like stopping here to drink fresh water
from the well. She'd fearlessly climb over the fence,
ignoring the dogs of ragtag coloring that charged toward
her, and cross the path into the garden, where the Spinelli
kids—a bunch of ugly, red-faced bumpkins who were pale
blond and ungainly—used to hide away. There was no
point in telling Lígia off, she always went and did the same
thing every time. Unimpressed, Mom would rush to
apologize to Dona Assunta, who laughed it off and politely
offered us a bucketful of ripe star fruit to eat on our walk.
We used to stop at the crossroads to catch our breath. A
cross wrapped in crepe paper stood lodged in the mud, a

sign that some traveler had been ambushed there...Ahead of us, a long uphill trail led to Bagagem and Serra da Onça, where the Bettios, Finettos, Benevenuttis, Prettis, and Michelettos lived scattered around the hills, people we knew by name...Behind us, a downhill road skirted large grottoes called Angicos, home to the families of Seu Rubens Giusti, Seu Beppo Chiesa, Seu Giacinto Bettio, and to the Spinellis, Seu Federico, and Seu Tarciso. Grandpa Anacleto's farmstead crested another road; the Furlanetos, Visentins, and Bortolettos dwelled in the direction of Três Fazendas; and on the way to Os Gomes, past Seu Raimundo Ferreira's greengrocer, were the rocky lands where the Rinaldis lived in penury and the Scarpas lived in sin. I trudge down the steep slope with the sun at my back. In the past, summer storms would isolate these families. Streams, brooks, and small rivers spilled over, flooding paths, trails, and tracks. The days were gray and wet, and the mud slick. Everything—the grown-ups, the animals, the hours— would become gloomy; that is, except for the plants and for us kids. We used to cook up all kinds of fun and games, whether it was squelching in the mud outside, or playing truco, buraco, burro, brisca, or scopa indoors, for a couple of coins or for nothing at all. We'd leap over gates and cattle guards, dodge mad dogs and furious bulls, run from geese and be startled by snakes. In the farmlands that we passed, the rows of corn and the rice paddies, the fields of tobacco and beans, the corrals of dairy cattle, and the vegetable gardens all doffed their straw hats in greeting,

G'Morning! From the houses edging the road wafted the smell of lard being rendered, and the sound of someone beating laundry on mine rocks. Today the meadows are riddled with weeds, pimpled with termite hills, cut through with gullies, the barbed wire is rusted, and the fence posts have fallen...In the crumbling walls, windows frame gnarled branches...Water trickles from a pipe into a concrete tank green with mud...There is the lazy groaning of bamboos rubbing together...The plopping of a traíra that's snapped a dragonfly from its hidey-hole...Somewhere, a white-tipped dove coos...Mom was the first to move away. She met Dad in Rodeiro during St. John's Eve. He'd been buying something at an auction at the São Sebastião Church kermis organized by Seu Santo Chiesa. Less than two years passed between their first meeting and the day Mom donned a veil and tossed her bouquet. Dad lived near Corgo do Sapo and every Saturday rode to Grandpa Anacleto's farm on horseback. Mom claimed her father had taken a shining to his son-in-law, though the same couldn't be said of Grandma Luigia. She ragged on him till the very end, accusing him of being an *impiastro*, a *bastardo*. As a woman, Mom had no right to an inheritance. It was rumored that Dad was the illegitimate son of Commander Joaquim Santiago Nunes, though all he got from him was his name. Having never met his father or mother, he lived as a ward in Corgo do Sapo, where he did a little bit of everything, until the age of around twenty-five. After they were married, Mom and Dad moved to Cataguases, without a penny to their name. Being naturally gifted, it wasn't long before Mom had fine-tuned her skills and become a consummate seamstress—permanently cooped up in the basement surrounded by patterns and mannequins. Dad got a job at Industrial. He started from the bottom, sweeping the weaving room, and soon won the trust of the foreman and assistant foreman, who promoted him to weaver. Not long after, his smarts and eye for detail landed him in the fabric warehouse, of which he would eventually become the manager. He hated leaving Cataguases, and on the rare occasion he did, sulkily, he steered clear of Corgo do Sapo, perhaps out of fear he might bump into one of his *adopted siblings*. Mom used to carp at Dad about it and accuse him of having an inferiority complex. But Dad insisted he was a man of the present, A guy's got to look ahead, he used to say with pride. I stop in the shade of a silk floss tree, grab the bottle, and have a sip of water. Warm. I take off my hat, wipe sweat from my head with the back of my right hand, and put my hat back on. I wipe my glasses with the edge of my shirt. My legs ache...I wonder what time it is. A smooth-billed ani watches me with interest from its perch on the wire fence. I fill my chest with hot air and continue walking. Uncle Ênio...Married with two small children, he decided to try his luck in Rio de Janeiro, even though he'd never been anywhere bigger than Ubá, where he used to go to visit the Perons, Grandma Luigia's side of the family, who lived around Campo de Aviação. After hearing no word from Uncle Ênio for over a year, everyone expected

the worst. He was her favorite sibling, and Mom was sick
with worry. We were thick as thieves, she'd cry, heartbroken
at his disappearance. One day out of the blue, he showed
up in Rodeiro with a heavy wallet, and treated everyone
to beer and cachaça. It took him all day to get from São
Sebastião Square to the farm, there were so many people
to greet and rounds to buy. In a week, he got rid of the few
pieces of furniture he owned and took his wife and kids
with him to Campo Grande, in practically the clothes
on their backs. Campo Grande, *the important state of
Guanabara*, as he solemnly explained and we repeated
with pride. Whenever Campo Grande played Botafogo
for the Carioca Championship, we thought of Uncle
Ênio...He ended up selling his part of the land he'd
inherited to Uncle Paulino, who vowed to never leave the
place where he'd been born...Uncle Ítalo soon left the
countryside too. At first, he single-handedly ran a sawmill
that he had bought for next to nothing—a bandsaw that
turned logs into planks and a circular saw that turned
planks into boards, laths, rafters, and timbers. This was
around the time when he was financing João Lúcio's bus
fare from Cataguases to Rodeiro, so he could spend
weekends playing ball for Spartano's B team. Dad groused
left and right about how ungrateful his son was, When it's
time to help out around the house, suddenly nobody's
around...Uncle Ítalo didn't last long. After he had a stroke,
his youngest daughter Cíntia moved to Brasília, taking
Verônica with her. Lucília, the eldest, had been promised to

João Lúcio and stayed behind to help Aunt Biquinha nurse
Uncle Ítalo, who could neither walk nor talk, and even
needed assistance when it came to doing his business. By
the time Uncle Ítalo died—of spite, they said—the old
sawmill was already manufacturing wardrobes and beds,
and João Lúcio was engaged to Maria Teresa. So Aunt
Biquinha and Lucília left too. None of them ever stepped
foot in Rodeiro again. Uncle Paulino held out for as long as
he could. He buried Dequinha, and Aunt Alcina spent the
rest of her days in deep mourning. He married Nilda off to
the owner of a fruit store in Ubá. He married off Ana
Paula, who moved to Juiz de Fora and convinced Rogério to
do his basic training there. Her husband was a police
sergeant, and Rogério fell under the spell of his uniform,
joined up, and was dispatched to Humaitá, in Amazonas,
never to be heard from again. Uncle Paulino bought a small
house in Rodeiro up near the road to Ubá, at the insistence
of Aunt Alcina's family. Yet every morning he rode out to
the country, where he kept a handful of rangy, tick-ridden
cows in the meadow, grew beds of puny vegetables, and
fattened up barrows in the mango grove. Mom said it
saddened her to see him wake up before dawn, wolf down a
handful of piada, knock back a cup of coffee, light his
corn-husk cigarette, climb into his buggy, and vanish into
the gloom, whether rain or sunshine, as though making his
escape...As soon as he came into money, João Lúcio
bought Uncle Paulino's parcel, which encompassed Uncle
Ênio's—at his request—so that it wouldn't end up in the

hands of a stranger, as he explained to family. By the time Mom died, there were trucks all across Brazil with the name Pádua Furniture slapped on the side of the trailer. But even though his business had continued to grow, and even though it now occupies the biggest warehouse on the outskirts of the city, he still hasn't managed to incorporate Uncle Ítalo's land. His daughters hate João Lúcio with such passion they'd rather let the whole thing be overrun by wilderness, out of pure obstinacy. Whenever we used to reach this point, at the tip of the scarp, Aunt Biquinha would holler, Praised be, it's Stella! and ask her daughters to meet us while she spruced up for her guests. Uncle Ítalo would wave and immediately drop the hoe to scrub his face and hands. After the bend, having heard Aunt Biquinha's cry, we would find Aunt Lola at the front door to her house, Amauri in her arms and tearful, snot-nosed Marino standing beside her. Uncle Ênio, busy weeding the high fields, would make an appearance later. Bitter-melon vines grow amid shards of tile and chunks of brick. A brindled dog races toward me, barking. I stop. What now? He corners me on the ledge. I take off my backpack and place it between my trembling legs and his sharp, bared teeth. My heart races. I whisper, "Quiet now...Quiet..." and fix my eyes on the dog to show him I am not the enemy, just as my dad had taught me. Then I hear—we both hear—a voice. "Tainha! Tainha!" A bald man in glasses, barefoot, no shirt, and belly jutting out from his shorts rounds the bend, fighting to hold a thick leash pulled taut by a white pit bull.

João Lúcio! "João Lúcio, it's me, Oséias!" I shout. "Cut it
out, Tainha!" He scolds the brindle, who growls in retreat.
João Lúcio wraps the leash around his hand and steps closer
to study me with his nearsighted eyes. "Oséias...?!" he says
with surprise. He turns around and tells me to follow him.
"I've got to tie Chicão up." João Lúcio still wears the gold
chain and cross he got for his First Communion...He tugs
along a placid Chicão, while Tainha pads cagily behind me.
We walk those two hundred meters in silence, enough for
my body to settle down after the fright. There is the scent
of grilled meat...At the next fork, where Uncle Paulino
used to live, stands a tall wall. A black, grimy Triton pickup
truck is parked on the crushed-rock yard, in the shade of
five American pepper trees. We walk through a side gate
into a grassy backyard. To the left, a pool and a seven-a-side
soccer field. In the middle, a house of exposed brick ringed
by a veranda, the roof plated in solar panels. To the right, a
pool house with a grill, whitish smoke curling up to the sky.
João Lúcio locks the pit bull up in a dog pen at the back of
the property, by the orchard. I stand under the weak sun,
which still burns my skin. João Lúcio returns and tells me
to leave my bag inside, gesturing at the kitchen door. I cut
across the veranda into a large room whose walls are
half-laid in white brick. In the early evening light, it
resembles a sultry, yellow grotto. Long rustic wood table,
ten chairs, French-door refrigerator, six-burner gas range,
outsized china cupboard, outsized sink. I place my bag on
the burnished concrete floor, near the hallway. The hands

on the wall clock read 5:10. One sheet of a Coração de Jesus desk calendar shows "Mar 7, 2015. Sat. Sts: Felicitas and Perpetua." I walk out. Tainha, sitting alert at the door, gets up and eyes me. I spot João Lúcio in the pool house and step cautiously past the dog, who follows me in silence. In one hand, João Lúcio holds a can of beer, while with the other he rakes the embers. "Help yourself to a beer," he says. Tainha quiets down and shuts his eyes, stretched out near the grill. I open the fridge, take out a can of beer, open it, and have a sip. "You still living in São Paulo?" João Lúcio asks, pulling up a chair and sitting down. I take a long drink of the beer. "That's right," I say and set the beer down on the table next to a greasy cutting board, a toothpick holder, a napkin holder, a cell phone, and a golden—or is it gold?—wristwatch. "What are you doing here, Zézo?" he asks. I remove my hat and hang it off the back of the chair. "Just passing through . . ." "Passing through?!" he barks with sarcasm. "Did you try to find me in Rodeiro?" he asks. "No." I take another long swill of beer. "You walk?" he asks. "Uh-huh," I mumble. João Lúcio gets up, tosses the empty can into a black trash bag, grabs another beer from the fridge, opens it, and has a sip. He walks to the grill, turns over the sausage rack, and flips the metal skewer. "I came to visit the cemetery," I say. "Then I felt like going for a wander . . . Then . . . I didn't expect to run into you." What little hair João Lúcio has left is now gray. He seems tired. He lifts the skewer from the grill, rests the tip on the cutting board, and carves off bloodied hunks of meat.

Tainha sidles closer, perhaps hoping to be rewarded for his recent show of fearlessness and courage. João Lúcio returns the skewer to the grill. He carries the dripping cutting board to the table and dumps the sliced meat onto a metal tray. I drain the can of beer. Get up, toss it into the black trash bag, and fetch another from the fridge. João Lúcio sits down and has a swig of beer, stuffs a piece of meat into his mouth. "You gonna eat or what?" he asks. "I had lunch in Rodeiro," I explain. "The meat's delicious," he says, pressuring me to try it. I have a sip of beer, grab a piece of meat, stuff it in my mouth, and chew. It really is delicious... We sit in silence. João Lúcio scratches Tainha's head. He has age spots on his hands, just like Mom. "How are you doing?" I ask. He stuffs a piece of meat in his mouth. "All right," he says, and falls quiet. Mosquitoes whir, drawn to the smell of blood. Charcoal crackles in the grill. Canaries warble in the veranda rafters. "I visited Isinha and Rosana in Cataguases," I say. "Oh," he mumbles, uninterested. He has a sip of beer, gets up to rake the embers. "Isinha's still working like crazy... Did you know Rosana's a school principal now? She travels to the U.S. every year..." I continue. I have a sip of beer. Stuff a piece of meat in my mouth. The sun sets slowly. João Lúcio grabs a piece of meat from his plate and flings it at Tainha, who catches it midair. Satisfied with the result, he does it again, flaunting the mutt's dexterity. "So, you quit smoking?" "I did." Bit by bit, birds twitter to the trees in droves. "Is all of this yours now?" I ask, raising a subject I'm sure João Lúcio will be eager to discuss. He takes a long swig of beer. "That's right... I'm trying to piece together Grandpa's farm," he says. "All I'm missing is Uncle Ítalo's parcel... I haven't bought it yet 'cause his moneygrubbing daughters think I'm swimming in cash and insist on asking for more than it's worth," he lies. I can tell he's lying because his eyes sweep the thick concrete floor as he talks. He has another sip of beer, gets up. "I'm in conversation with some folks at a university over in Viçosa... I want to restore the native growth... Like it is over that way." He signals at the lush green blanketing the mountain beyond the dog pen. "That section was preserved because of the mines," he explains. "Do you remember the time we went in there?" I ask. "Galego had chased after some critter, an armadillo, I think it was, and you, me, Uncle Ênio, and Rogério set out to look for him. Except we lost sight of Uncle Ênio. We walked and walked and walked until we could see all those little houses from way up high..." "Rodeiro, wasn't it?" he ventures with a smile. "And then there was the time that pregnant heifer went missing... They searched for her high and low... Thought somebody had lifted her... We only found her much later. One holiday, we happened across her skull in the middle of the forest. A snake probably got her..." João Lúcio polishes off his beer and tosses the can in the black trash bag. He grabs another from the fridge, opens it, and sits back down. "How come you remember all that stuff?" I have a sip of beer. "You had this double album, *Músicas Inesquecíveis*. You'd listen to it, lying on the yellow sofa..."

João Lúcio calls Tainha over and pretends to examine his fur. "You went to the pictures a lot...To watch westerns... Especially spaghetti westerns...Do you still do that?" "Do what?" "Watch movies?" He has a sip of beer. "At home, we've got cable TV with a bunch of channels on it, but I always nod off the second I sit down." Tainha vanishes, bored, into the backyard twilight. "You used to tell anyone who'd listen that you were going to visit Italy someday..." "Is that right?" "Yeah." João Lúcio gets up to flip the skewer and turn over the sausage rack. "Did you?" "Did I what?" "Visit Italy." "I did..." He seems a little flustered as he chops up the sausage. "Twice...But at the invitation of factories that manufacture furniture-making machines..." "Is it beautiful? Italy, I mean." "I don't know...Can't say I saw much of it. Mostly just visited factories..." he answers, short. Then, maybe a little contrite, he has a sip of beer, and, sliding the rounds of sausage onto the metal tray, adds, "I mean, the little I saw was beautiful. But I don't even remember the names of the places I visited...I think one of the cities was near Vicenza...Another near Treviso...Paludi, something like that...The train went through this sort of flat region...Thick fog...I ate a lot of squash-blossom pasta, just like when we were kids... Drank a lot of wine...Funny, I understood practically everything people said...But I couldn't say a word...I'd just start stammering...Both times I bought machinery to expand the factory..." He has a sip of beer. "Did you see the family vault?" he asks, with pride. "I did." "Had the

whole thing redone... Turned out nicely, don't you think?"
"It did," I concede as I have a sip of beer. Night had fallen
without our noticing. João Lúcio's profile shudders in the
flickering light radiating from the grill. "I was thinking of
Sino the other day..." I remark. "One hell of a dog..." he
says with emotion. "As good as a person, he was." "Yeah."
"I've got a picture of him at home," adds João Lúcio. "The
one where Dad, you, Sino, and me are standing in front of
the house?" I drain the last of my beer. "That's right..." he
says. I get up and ask for the restroom. João Lúcio signals at
a pair of doors on the other end of the veranda. "The one
on the right," he says. I wipe my mouth with a paper
napkin. I make my slow way past a small alcove that holds
a picture of St. Anthony of Padua, and through the
bathroom door. I switch on the light, unzip my pants,
empty my bladder. The mirror shows a caved face.
Wrinkles. Gray beard hairs furiously pocking my flaccid
skin. I switch off the light. Gently close the door. Wash my
hands in the sink, wipe them with a towel. I make my slow
way back, glancing sidelong at St. Anthony of Padua's
now-illuminated alcove. I wonder if the picture had been
brought from Italy. João Lúcio has switched on the lights in
the pool house, now crowded with clouds of swarmers.
Thousands of stars gleam on the horizon. The full moon
washes everything in a soft blue light. João Lúcio sits with
Tainha at his feet. I grab a round of sausage, stuff it in my
mouth, and chew. I toss the empty beer can in the black
trash bag, take another from the fridge. I open it and have

a sip. "And how are the wife and kids?" I ask. "All right,"
he says, and falls quiet. I sit at the table. A chill breath
swathes the gloom. "You spend Saturdays here on your
own?" I ask. "It's how I wind down," he says. "It's nice up
here. There's not even cell service…" João Lúcio has a sip
of beer and stuffs a piece of sausage in his mouth. A
cricket strikes up its tinny song. "Things will be a bit
livelier tomorrow, you'll see. The factory hands start
trickling in around ten o'clock… They grill meat, play
ball, fish in the reservoir… Do you remember the
reservoir? I've cleaned it up. It's teeming with fish now.
Tilapia, tetra, carp… At the end of the day, they head
home. All of it, on my dime. Except for the meat and
drink, which is BYO. It's worth the expense. They leave
here feeling happy… Start the week in high spirits…" he
concludes. "You're really well liked, aren't you?" I say. He
gets up to flip a batch of sausages he must have set on the
grill in the short time I was away. "I met the caretaker…
Used to be married to Aunt Biquinha's goddaughter," I
explain. "Afonsinho?" "He didn't say. The man was
determined to have me over for coffee." "Did you take him
up on it?" he asks, sipping anxiously at his beer. "No." "So
you haven't met his… his new wife?" he asks. "No." João
Lúcio sighs in apparent relief. He checks his wristwatch,
abandoned on the table. "The road's in good shape up this
way. Gravel and everything." "Yeah… Leozim, the current
mayor, is a former employee of mine," he says. He drains
the last of his beer and tosses the can into the black trash

bag. Bored, Tainha rolls around in the grass. "Look, Zézo, I've got to get going soon." João Lúcio fixes his eyes on the thick concrete floor. "I...uh... I've got...I've got some stuff...to sort out...in Guidoval... So...Come with me." I get up and follow João Lúcio as he walks into the kitchen and flips on the light. I collect my backpack from a corner. He flips on the light in the hallway and opens a door to the left, flips on the light in one of the bedrooms and says, "You can sleep here." The queen-sized bed is meticulously made. "If you get cold—the temperature always drops because we're so close the woods—there are blankets in here." He opens the wardrobe, revealing two colorful duvets. I set my backpack on the floor. He walks out into the hallway and opens another door. Flips on the light. "Bathroom," he says. "There are clean towels in the closet," he explains. "Make yourself at home." He steps into another room and shuts the door. I flip off the bathroom light, flip off the bedroom light, and make my way back to the pool house. The fire gives its last gasp. I stoke the embers with the rake. I grab the skewer, steady the tip on the cutting board, and carve the meat with a knife. I return the skewer to the grill, carry the board to the table, and slide the hunks of meat onto the metal tray. I decide to play nice with Tainha and toss him a piece of meat. He sniffs it, bolts it down, cheerfully wags his tail. I shake the can. Though there's still some beer left, it's probably warm by now. I tip the liquid into the grill—the embers sizzle—and toss the can in the black trash bag. I take another beer from the fridge, have a sip. I sit down,

stuff a piece of meat in my mouth. Chew. João Lúcio
pitched these walls along the exact floor plans of Uncle
Paulino's house, which Grandpa Anacleto had built. To do
so, he'd had to knock the whole thing down... Thick wood
logs set on a stone foundation had held up adobe walls and
a colonial-style roof. Through the front door, which once
led to an enormous courtyard—now a parking lot—where
beans were threshed and coffee set out to dry, was the
living room, up a set of six wood steps reserved for the most
illustrious guests. On the wall, an austere black-and-white
portrait of Grandma and Grandpa. Three stools and a
small table covered in a lace tablecloth. On the right side, a
guest room with a queen-sized bed and chest. On the left
side, the living room: a floor-to-ceiling cabinet with small
glass doors that showed stacks of thick ceramic plates,
heavy iron skillets, and spare cutlery, and a pair of solid
locked doors that hid glass jars of compote and tins of meat
preserved in lard, drawers brimming with documents,
notions, medicine, and wood bins for storing rice, beans,
corn, and coffee; a table with eight chairs; and a corner for
stocking the harvest—burlap sacks of unhulled rice, corn
kernels and coffee beans, braids of tobacco. To the left, the
bedrooms. First, Grandma and Grandpa's—large, tall bed,
mosquito net, and chest. A passage to the boys' room—two
large, low beds and a chest. And a passage to Mom's
room—low, narrow bed—the only one with no window.
All of them sporting a feather mattress and comforter.
Beneath the pitted floor, a basement used to shelter a

rooster, hens, cockerels, and pullets. To the right of the living room stood the kitchen, which on an average day doubled as the main entrance, with a pantry and a woodstove that was always burning. A door led to a small chamber that opened onto the fields and had a half wall into the living room; in winter, this space served as a stable, harboring calves that in turn warmed the house with their bodies. This was also where the broody chickens nested. The dog pen is now over what was once the granary, filled with corn stover kept as animal feed for when the pastures failed. Where the pool now stands was once the barn for the buggy, the bullock cart, and the horses' saddlery. Hanging from the eaves in the living room there used to be a gray, long-abandoned wasp's nest. Scattered around the rooms were cats—Grandma Luigia's *little treasures*—in all colors, shapes and sizes... If I had any cigarettes, I'd probably smoke one now... Here comes João Lúcio... Freshly showered in khaki shorts, black moccasins, and a black polo shirt. In his hands is a plastic container and a roll of tinfoil, which he sets on the table. I have a sip of beer. He grabs the sausage rack and opens it onto the cutting board. He tears off a piece of tinfoil and wraps the sausages, then places them in the plastic container. He puts the rack in the sink. He circles back to the grill for the skewer, carves off a large hunk of meat, and drops it on the cutting board. He wraps the meat in tinfoil and sticks it in the plastic container, which he then closes. He returns the skewer to the grill and carries the tinfoil back to the

kitchen. Tainha watches him come and go. I have a sip of
beer. João Lúcio takes his time in the house and lumbers
out smelling heavily of cologne. He grabs his gold-tinted
watch from the table, fastens it on his wrist, and slips his
cell phone into the pocket of his shorts. "See you tomorrow
then," he says. "Oh, I'll be long gone by the time your
guests start arriving," I explain. "Uai, how come?" he asks,
taken aback. "I'm...uh...leaving, early in the morning..."
I say. "Well...then...then I guess I better send a car to
collect you." "No, no, don't bother...I'd rather walk...
enjoy the fresh morning air..." "If that's what you want..."
he says, obliging. João Lúcio takes the plastic container,
turns toward the gate, and vanishes into the night gloom,
with Tainha trotting ahead of him. I hear the car unlock
with a beep. João Lúcio circles back and says, "Follow me."
We leave the pool house and cut across the veranda, past
the illuminated alcove of St. Anthony of Padua and the
bathroom. "When you leave, lock the kitchen door behind
you and leave the key right here." He points at a space
between the wall and the rafter. "The gate will lock on its
own. They've all got keys..." We walk back without
speaking. I think of asking if the picture of St. Anthony of
Padua had come from Italy, but I am cowed by our silence.
João Lúcio marches straight to the dog pen. I linger in the
pool house. I hear João Lúcio call tenderly for Chicão, then
see both of them emerge—thick leash clipped around the
pit bull's neck—and make their way to the parking lot. I
walk beside them on the lawn, at a distance. I don't want to

get Chicão riled up. João Lúcio picks up the dog and puts him in the truck bed, fastening the leash to the latch. "Someone tried to kidnap me," he says. "They wanted me to get a security guard...Can you picture me going around with a security guard? Chicão commands respect..." He rounds the car and opens the passenger door. Tainha bounds into the front seat. "Tainha's my alarm," he says, slipping his hand into the glove compartment and pulling out a gun. "This is my life insurance." João Lúcio steps back around the car and opens the driver's door. He slides the gun under his seat. Looks up at the blue night sky, now studded with wisps of clouds. "Is everything all right with you, Zézo?" "Yeah. Don't worry about me." We shake hands. "Come by again, when you've got more time..." he says. He climbs into the car, turns on the headlights, starts the engine, accelerates, honks, and turns onto the road. I stand in the dark and watch as the lights of the pickup truck disappear behind a cloud of dust. My body is swathed in cold and quiet. I walk back over crushed rocks that warp the soles of my shoes. I shut the gate and cross the lawn. Swarmers whirl madly around the lights of the pool house. I cut through the kitchen, down the hall, and into the room. Flip on the light. Grab the plastic bottle from my backpack. I open the zippered compartment, take out the Cebion tube and the brown-paper package held together with Scotch tape. I flip off the light and leave the bedroom. Walk down the hall, through the kitchen, and back to the pool house. I place the plastic bottle, Cebion tube, and brown-paper package on the table. Stoke the embers with the rake. I have a sip of beer, spit it out. It's warm. I unwrap the package, which holds a small wood mortar and pestle. I feed the brown paper to the fire. Uncap the Cebion tube. I tip the pills into the mortar and crush them into a powder. The palms of my hands are raw and sore. I fill the plastic bottle halfway with tap water. Riffle through the drawers for a small spoon. I transfer the powder into the water bottle, cap it, shake it, and stare at the milky liquid. I wash the spoon and return it to the drawer. I look around for a hammer. On a shelf, I find a hatchet and a bottle of ethanol. I break up the mortar with the hatchet, douse the wood pieces in ethanol, and feed them to the fire blazing in the grill. I try to chop up the pestle, to no success. I douse it in ethanol, toss it in the grill, and bury it under a mound of red embers. I grab my wallet from my back pocket, pull out my ID and driver's license, and feed both to the fire. I put away my wallet. Place the hatchet and the ethanol back on the shelf. I pick up the Cebion tube and the plastic bottle and head into the kitchen, gently shutting the door. I step down the hall and into the bedroom, flip on the light. I place the bottle on the nightstand. Slip the empty Cebion tube into the zippered compartment. I take out some clean clothes—shirt, underwear, and socks—and lay them out on the table. I sit on the bed, slip off my shoes, socks, and shirt. I pull the plastic bag (shampoo, conditioner, soap, deodorant, dental floss, toothpaste, and toothbrush) from my backpack. I pad barefoot down the hall and switch on the bathroom light. I pull down my pants and underwear. Hang them off a hook on the door along with the plastic bag. I sit on the toilet. Grandma Luigia used to love showing her cats off to guests, angering Grandpa, who thought their sole purpose was to kill mice. In the evenings, she'd sit on a stool hauled into the garden, and brush her long hair in the company of her *little treasures*. I empty my guts. Flush. Place my glasses on the sink. I open the closet, grab a towel. Put the shampoo and conditioner on the shower floor. Unwrap the bar of soap and set it in the soap dish. In the drain are strands of a woman's long black hair. I turn on the shower, and warm water runs down my body. Grandma used to christen the cats with patrician names like Prince, Duke, Marquis, Count, Viscount, Baron, and their female equivalents... When one died, another would immediately inherit his or her title. I rinse my hair. Mom used to claim Grandma loved her *little treasures* more than her own children... I close the tap. Dry myself on a wooly towel that smells of softener. I put on my glasses, collect my pants and underwear, step out of the bathroom with the towel wrapped around my waist. In the bedroom, I pull on a pair of clean underwear, fold my dirty laundry, and stuff it in my backpack. I tread back to the bathroom, hang the wet towel on the curtain rod in the shower. Squeeze some toothpaste onto my toothbrush. Carefully brush my teeth. I rinse my mouth. Pat my face dry with a hand towel. Take a square of toilet paper and wipe my glasses. I collect the shampoo and conditioner and dry

both with a towel, toss them into the plastic bag. I grab the
bar of soap and slip it back into its package, toss it into the
plastic bag. I flip off the light, walk down the hall and into
the bedroom, tuck the plastic bag in my backpack. I open
the wardrobe and pull out a duvet. Take off my glasses and
set them on the nightstand beside the plastic water bottle. I
extend the duvet over the top sheet and lie down. Frogs
croak. Birds trill. The ceiling seems to press down on my
body... A mosquito buzzes crickets chirr frogs

sunday,
      march 8

i wake up! I wonder what the time is. I wriggle free of the duvet, get up, put my glasses on. I open the window. It's the dead of night. A little chilly. My head aches. I shove my feet into some socks. Pull on a pair of pants and sneakers. Step down the hall and turn on the bathroom light. I squeeze some toothpaste onto my toothbrush, and brush my teeth. I rinse my mouth. Remove my glasses. Wash my face. Pat it dry. Put my glasses back on. I lift the toilet cover, pee. Flush. I catch my reflection in the mirror. Switch off the light and shut the door. I put on a shirt. Look around to make sure I haven't forgotten anything. I slip on my backpack. Flip off the bedroom light. I head down the hallway and turn the light off. Lock the door with the key. I cut across the veranda toward the bathroom, past the alcove with the picture of St. Anthony of Padua and slip the key into the space between the rafter and the wall. I circle back, keeping my eyes averted from St. Anthony of Padua's illuminated alcove. The fire in the grill has died out. I use the rake to check for remnants of the mortar and pestle. Nothing. Just charcoal. I look out at the dog pen, at the seven-a-side soccer field, at the pool, the orchard, the house...I open the gate, slam it shut. I hear the lock click. Clouds cluster just outside Rodeiro. I round the wall, treading the bluish dark. I scramble up the steep incline and skirt the forest on my way up the hill. I take careful steps, making sure to avoid holes hidden by clumps of crabgrass. One morning, I'd snuck into the forest on my own. All night a calf had lowed, leaving me unsettled and unable to sleep. Lying on the dewy forest floor, I tried to parse the wind whispering through the branches, the birds chattering, and the babel of animals I imagined stealing around me, watchful. So I closed my eyes and pretended I was dead, and that the peace and quiet all around me were Paradise, the same Paradise Father Jaime would speak of in his garbled accent at mandatory Sunday mass, as the farmers watched dumbly from the uncomfortable pews of São Sebastião Church. I must have fallen asleep, because when I woke up, heart pounding, the sun was bright in the sky. I ran from the forest and down the hill, assuming everyone was anxiously searching for me. For a brief moment, I savored the sensation that I mattered, that I was somebody, and that my absence had been felt. When I arrived at Uncle Paulino's house, I explained my adventure excitedly. My mother listened, then tore off her flip-flop, grabbed me by the arm, spanked me and forced me to spend the rest of the day in the darkly lit room that had once been her own. I reach the hilltop. Stop and gaze down. I forgot to turn off the light in the pool house. The building is like a ship bobbing in the night sea. I turn and wade into the forest. My feet crunch as they tread over tangles of dried branches, litterfall, underbrush, lianas. I knock into trees, skin pricked by thorns. I choose a place in the dark. Set down my backpack. Grope around for the plastic bottle and shake it so that the powder completely dissolves in the water. I unscrew the cap. Take a long swig. My stomach turns. I sit. Breathe deeply. Take another long swig. The bitter liquid slips down my throat, my chest. I stretch out on the ground with my backpack as a pillow. I wait. Damn it! I left my hat on the back of the chair...Grandma Luigia's *little treasures*...Prince...Duke...Possible rain tomorrow...Mom used to sing Isinha to sleep, her cradle next to the sewing machine, Come down little kitty, off the rooftop, to watch little baby, gently nod off

Song Credits

Lyrics on page 77 from "Just My Imagination" by The Cranberries, 1999. Written by Dolores O'Riordan and Noel Hogan.

Lyrics on page 78 from "Time Is Ticking Out" by The Cranberries, 2002. Written by Dolores O'Riordan and Noel Hogan.

Lyrics on page 203 from "Fudendo o Psicológico" by MC Brisola, 2016.

Lyrics on page 205 from "Na Linha do Tempo," composed by Sérgio Porto and Marcelo Martins, 2013.

Lyrics on page 250 from "Tchuplin Tchuplin" by MC Bin Laden, 2014.